killingyousoftly

Books by Lucy Carver

Young, Gifted & Dead
Killing You Softly

killingyousoftly

LUCY CARVER

MACMILLAN

First published 2014 by Macmillan Children's Books
a division of Macmillan Publishers Limited
20 New Wharf Road, London N1 9RR
Basingstoke and Oxford
Associated companies throughout the world
www.panmacmillan.com

ISBN 978-1-4472-4298-7

1 3 5 7 9 8 6 4 2

A CIP catalogue record for this book is available from
the British Library.

Printed and bound by CPI Group (UK) Ltd, Croydon CR0 4YY

chapter one

It's happened again – they found another body.

Unlike last time, when we lost my best friends and fellow students, Lily and Paige, this recent killing has nothing to do with St Jude's, thank God.

They found another body – not in the lake, but it was a watery end like Lily's and it was a teenage girl. So some things were the same – enough to make me shake and tremble and feel like life on this cold January morning was playing dirty tricks.

I found out about the murder even before I got back to school for the start of term. It was when I stepped off the train from Paddington on to the platform at Ainslee Westgate and I ran into Tom Walsingham. Tom, you remember, is the kid who lives in the Old Vicarage in Chartsey Bottom. He doesn't go to my school, but I clicked with him as soon as we met last September and I've got to know him pretty well.

'Hey, Alyssa.'

'Hey, Tom.' We'd travelled on the same train but hadn't known it – me with my heavy suitcase crammed with clothes from the Oxford Street sales (shopping therapy to help deal with the trauma of losing Lily and Paige), him with his small backpack stuffed with footie boots and computer games. 'Good Christmas?'

'Nope.'

'Me neither.' I'd stayed with my Aunt Olivia in Richmond, we'd done the turkey roast and Queen's speech without enthusiasm. Same old, same old. 'Why were you in London?'

'Catching up with mates, getting the hell out of Chartsey for New Year.' Tom wore a black knitted beanie pulled low over his forehead and a black ski jacket. He offered me a lift out to Chartsey Bottom in the car he'd parked down a side street near the station. 'What's in the case?' he asked as I heaved my luggage into the boot of his car. 'A dismembered corpse?'

'Ha ha, Tom.' Not funny, given last term's body-in-the-lake events.

We finally got the case into the boot and ourselves into the car. 'Talking of corpses – did you see this?' He thrust a rolled-up *Metro* into my hand.

'Nope.' I unfurled the newspaper and read the front-page headline. *Body Found in Frozen Canal*.

Tom choked the car engine into life.

My heart faltered as the image of my roommate Lily Earle forced itself to the front of my mind. Lily, fizzing with energy, throwing her stuff around the room we'd shared with Paige Kelly in the girls' dorm at St Jude's. Lily the brilliant painter, Lily the rich-kid rebel, my beautiful, thin-skinned, up-and-down, bipolar friend whose body had ended up at the bottom of the lake.

Pulling myself together, I read the article. '*Police divers*

2

discovered the body of Scarlett Hartley, seventeen, late yesterday.
Scarlett, a sixth-form pupil at Ainslee Comprehensive School in
Oxfordshire, had been missing for two days.

'Few details have emerged about how she died though
residents in houses overlooking the canal report hearing a
disturbance during the night of thirty-first December. The stretch
of canal where the body was found has been cordoned off and is
being treated as a crime scene.'

I read the report once, twice, three times. I looked at
the picture of a blonde girl, elfin-pretty. She was wearing
school uniform, smiling straight at the camera. Retina
registers image, brain processes information and stores it
in prefrontal cortex and parietal lobe. That's how memory
works. With me it stays there forever whereas with you it
fades. I'm not showing off – it's just to remind you that I'm
freakish that way.

'You knew her?' I asked Tom.

'She went to my school,' he said. 'But, no, I didn't really
know her.'

My heart faltered over thoughts of Lily then kicked back
into life as I rode with Tom out of town, down Cotswold
country lanes. I pulled out my phone and read a text from
Zara, a girl in my year – Guess what – we're roommates ☺

And one from my lovely Jack – Snow in Denver. Plane
cancelled ☹

☹ ☹ When will I see you? I texted back.

Tuesday pm at earliest. Love you x

Love you too. x Hurry back x x

3

Today was Saturday. I counted the hours between now and Tuesday afternoon. It came out as way, way too many.

Then I forced myself to stop thinking about Jack and replied to Zara instead.

Is it just you and me sharing? I texted.

No – you and me plus new girl, Galina, Zara texted.

Galina who?

Dunno. But she's mega rich and Russian.

Have you met her?

Not yet. Where are you?

Bottoms with Tom. Will call taxi from here.

'No need for a cab, stupid – I'll drive you all the way to St Jude's,' Tom offered when I asked him for the number of a taxi service. He passed his house in the village and carried on until we reached St Jude's, which was fifteen minutes out of his way – bless. We chugged through the broad wrought-iron gates in his tiny white Peugeot, up the drive to the main entrance.

And here I was at St Jude's Academy – a school for exceptional students, ready to begin my second term.

It was the same and different. The same ancient stone building steeped in history, looking out over lawns and a lake to oak woodland, but different because we were minus Lily and Paige after the tragedy of last year.

'Thanks, Tom,' I said as he drove under the archway with the *Nihil sed optimus* crest carved in local honey-coloured stone. *Nihil sed optimus* – nothing but the best. A school motto like this weighs heavily with someone like me. I mean, I'm not the world's most confident person and genuinely struggle to see myself in the *'optimus'* category.

We stopped in the quad and I hauled my case out of Tom's boot.

'*I* didn't really know Scarlett, but Alex definitely did,' he said, *a propos* the dead girl in the canal.

'They were – what – an item?'

Tom nodded. 'Pretty full on.'

'Alex Driffield?' I was finding it hard to picture the football-mad kid whose dad ran the car-repair place in Chartsey Bottom being full on with any girl, let alone a blonde, smiley-eyed, dead one.

'How many Alexes do we know?' Tom muttered.

'Right. That must have happened since the end of last term.'

'In the run up to Christmas, yeah.'

'Tell him I'm sorry,' I said. I was, but I was also glad that it still had nothing to do with St Jude's, nothing directly to do with me, so I set my case on its little wheels, said goodbye to Tom and rolled my luggage across the empty, stone-flagged quad. 'Thanks,' I called again as he turned his car and set off back down the drive.

Zara intercepted me before I reached the door leading up to the first floor dormitories. 'Alyssa!'

I was pleased to see her, although I have to say I hadn't hit it off with her straight away, not like I had with Lily and Paige. She'd seemed too girlie and flirty for my taste and I would guess I'd been too shy and uptight for her. But those deaths last term changed things and we'd grown close. She sashayed towards me in a cloud of Chanel Mademoiselle.

'Ditch the bag, come and say hi to Connie.'

So I did – I ditched the bag at the bottom of the stairs because when Zara issues a command you obey. I'd learned that during my first term at St Jude's.

You need to be able to picture her. Tall, curvy, blonde. Think of a young Kate Winslet – yeah, sickening. Plus an intellect the size of a planet. Today she was dressed in skinny jeans and a short chestnut-coloured, bomber-style jacket with a fur collar, brown leather boots to match. Her to-die-for hair was scrunched up on top of her head, ready to be shaken out in a cascade of golden curls.

'Who's Connie?' I asked as I trotted dutifully after her.

She led me out of the quad towards the new technology building tucked away behind a stand of copper beech trees. An icy wind blew. 'Connie – Connie Coetzee,' she said in a tone that made me feel two centimetres tall.

'Connie Coetzee?' Catching up with Zara as we approached the entrance lobby to the steel-clad building, I repeated the name with an upward, questioning intonation.

Zara pursed her luscious lips. That's all she needs to do to express the fact that she thinks you're an ignorant, ill-informed bimbo with zero IQ, so what are you doing here at St Jude's, school for weirdly gifted kids? How come I didn't know Connie Coetzee? She paused then relented. 'Oh yeah, I forgot – you've only been at the school since September. Connie went home to Johannesburg last term – family stuff. Her dad divorced her mum and stopped paying the school fees. Anyway the courts forced him to pay again so she's back.'

'Is that good?'

'That depends,' Zara countered. We went into the technology centre, down the wide central aisle with banks of computers on either side. 'If you're Luke Pearson, it's good. If you're Jack Hooper, not so good.'

'Hooper doesn't like her?'

'No. Connie scares the crap out of him.'

'Ah.' Hooper was quiet and kind. I admired his sensitive, artistic soul so if he didn't like Connie Coetzee I was tempted along that road with him before I'd even met her. 'But Luke thinks she's cool?'

'Yeah. Actually Luke was out there in Johannesburg over Christmas – getting over . . . y'know.'

I knew exactly. Luke's family had obviously taken him on a trip to sunny South Africa to help him recover from what happened with Paige. I expect you think I'm dwelling too much on past horror, but the way Paige died in the hospital with stents draining fluid from her injured brain will stick with me and Jack for the rest of our lives. And Luke had been going out with her at the time, so it must have been twice as bad for him.

'Alyssa, Zara – hi!' Dr Bryony Phillips waved at us from the raised platform at the far end of the room. She was laying out papers on a table, getting ready for a staff meeting. Bryony teaches English. I get on better with her than with any other member of staff. 'Welcome back to the rhubarb farm,' she said.

'Rhubarb farm?' I queried.

'Yeah, where we force rare, tender intellects into precocious fruition,' she called. 'Like rhubarb shoots under terracotta cloches – Temperley Early, Stockbridge Arrow, Cawood Delight.'

'What are you talking about?'

'Varieties of rhubarb, obviously.' Zara wasn't interested in the chit-chat and cut it short. 'Have you seen Connie?' she asked.

Bryony pointed to a bay set back from the main aisle where we spotted an unfamiliar figure sitting behind a computer screen. The figure didn't stop what she was doing even when we went right up to her.

'Connie – hey!' Zara didn't care that she was interrupting, naturally.

'Wait just a second,' came the reply.

Which gave me time to decide whether I would have the crap scared out of me like Hooper or join Luke and Zara in the Connie Coetzee Appreciation Society.

You too can make up your minds.

Connie Coetzee speaks down her nose with clipped vowels and consonants. She was sitting down but it was obvious she was tall – I mean if I'd had to guess right then and there I would have put her at over six feet. Tall and sporting a boy's haircut – short at the back and sides with a longer sweep on top and down over her forehead. Her hair was dark, her eyes pale grey. She had a small blue star tattooed high on her neck, just under her left ear, and she was wearing a black, chunky jumper, androgynous in its effect, but her wrists were slim and feminine and her fingers tapered with long fingernails painted dark blue as she tapped at the keyboard.

OK, like Hooper, we were one sentence into a conversation with her and I was shit-scared.

Zara gave Connie ten seconds to finish what she was doing. 'Bad news,' she pouted. 'They moved me out of Twenty-two. We're not roommates any more.'

'They can't do that,' was Connie's calm response.

'They did. I'm in Twenty-seven with Alyssa and a Russian kid called Galina. By the way, this is Alyssa.'

Connie flicked a glance in my direction and said hi. 'Don't worry, I'll fix it,' she told Zara.

'But not with D'Arblay. There's a new bursar – Molly Wilson. She organized the room switches.'

'Why – what happened to D'Arblay?'

'He's in jail. Don't ask.'

Connie didn't but I'll explain anyway. A quick resumé – D'Arblay was the previous bursar at St Jude's and, as I discovered, a dirty little fascist. I was the one who found out that he was a member of the group who put pressure on Lily Earle's media-baron father to stop him exposing their racist activities. The pressure involved threatening to harm Lily, which indirectly is how she ended up in the lake and he landed in prison, awaiting trial. That's it in a nutshell.

So now we have a new bursar called Molly Wilson working for Saint Sam. Dr Sam Webb, school principal – he steers our elite group of gifted, hothouse Temperley Earlies towards future glory. From St Jude's we all go on to Oxbridge or Harvard and any high-flying career you care to think of – financiers, top civil servants, traders in utilities, stuffers of dead cows and sharks suspended in formaldehyde tanks, in other words zillionaire concept artists. You name it – the worlds of science, finance, politics and the arts – St Jude's alumni are there at the heart of things.

'OK, I'll fix it with this Molly woman. You do want to share a room with me again?' Connie checked with Zara.

'Doh – what do you think?' Zara didn't care that she was simultaneously hurting my feelings and abandoning me to the mercies of a Russian oligarch's daughter. 'Cool tattoo,' she told Connie.

I was busy studying Luke and Connie later that day when they sat together at lunch.

Hooper came and sat next to me. 'Jeez,' he muttered, following the direction of my gaze.

'I know. Luke moved on from Paige pretty damn quick,' I agreed.

'To the Black Widow – I mean, jeez!'

I asked, 'Why the nickname?' and it turned out that Black Widow Spider was Hooper's nickname for Connie. BWS for short.

From what I learned in a biology class when I was twelve, the Latin name is *Latrodectus hesperus*. The female spider eats the male after mating. Nature's weird. And so's my eidetic memory. I have total recall and I never forget. This too must have some Darwinian advantage, though like the black widow's sexual cannibalism I have yet to work it out.

I mean, I can be slow to make friends sometimes – I think it's because people find me and my memory too weird.

'So, Hooper, how was your vacation?' I asked.

He shrugged and ate.

'What did Father Christmas bring you?'

'We don't do Christmas at our house,' he told me through a mouthful of honey-roasted ham. 'My mother's a pagan and my dad's a mean bastard.'

'Hah! Well, I got money from Aunty O and in a fit of extravagance I blew it all on January-sale bargains. Is your mum really a pagan? I thought she was a photographer.' I knew from Paige that Hooper's mother took society portraits of the Earl of this and the Marchioness of that, plus the occasional superannuated supermodel. And everyone knows without having to be told that his tight-fisted novelist dad, Martyn Hooper, has won the Man-Booker Prize *twice*.

'She's both. She worships the natural world so she asks famous people to dress in green robes and wear flowers in their hair. Then she takes pictures of them in forests and up mountains.'

'What we'd both give for normal parents, hey?' Or, in my case, for any parents at all. I sighed as I watched Luke offer Connie a spoonful of the Eton mess he was eating. Yummy crushed meringue, whipped cream and fresh raspberries, so why did I flick back to thinking of sexual cannibalism?

Here's an explanation about my parents. They died in a plane crash when I was three, which is how come I sit with Aunt Olivia watching the Queen's speech every Christmas

Day, closely followed by a DVD of *The King's Speech* starring Colin Firth.

'They put me back in Room Twenty-seven,' I confided in Hooper.

'The one you shared with Lily and Paige?'

'Yeah, but I guess the new bursar doesn't know that.'

'You could ask to change.'

'I could.' Connie ate the mess hungrily, I noticed, and Luke fed her another spoonful. I pulled a sad face. 'Jack can't get back before Tuesday. He's stuck in Denver.'

'How will you go on living without him?'

'I have no clue.'

'Maybe I could stand in for him for seventy-two hours,' Hooper offered with a hopeful look.

I laughed. Hooper's cool – we joke along and say all kinds of stupid things.

'No?' he asked.

I shook my head. Hooper's amazing but he's not my type. Jack is. End of.

Talking of types, there's a new kid on the block.

All Saturday afternoon people arrived with designer luggage. I knew most of them even if I haven't mentioned them before.

Eugenie Clifford, Charlie Hudson, Will Harrison – don't bother to remember all these names right now since they'll come up again soon enough.

Will was the one without the Louis Vuitton bags. This is explained by the fact that Will is a scholarship pupil, like me. We're the only two out of an intake of sixty in Year Twelve, which makes us classic outsiders, though I felt it more than him at first. He used to go to the local comp with Tom Walsingham, Alex Driffield, Micky Cooke and the rest (likewise with the names), until his French teacher realized he was a linguistic genius and persuaded his parents to put him in for the St Jude's entrance exam. His family still lives in nearby Ainslee.

'Hey, Alyssa,' he said. He'd had his hair cut shorter over the holiday, I noticed, and it had been dyed a couple of shades lighter. He'd also acquired a bruise under his right eye and put on a few pounds of solid muscle, both thanks to working out in the gym he later told me.

'Hey. Did you hear about the Ainslee girl in the canal?' was my opening gambit. Obsessed with dead girls – *moi*?

'Well, yeah,' he drawled. Meaning, how could anyone who lived in Ainslee not have heard?

'You knew her?'

'Yeah,' he said again.

'Did she fall or was she pushed?'

'They're not sure yet. Why?'

'Just wondering.'

'Quit that, Sherlock, while you're ahead,' he advised. 'You worked things out for Lily, but you should leave this one alone.'

'So I'm going to take your advice?' I quipped with arched eyebrows, surprised that he'd taken this line with me.

'No?'

'Correct.'

'Just make sure it doesn't mess up your head,' Will said as he went off to find his room in the boys' dormitory wing.

I like Will, but, like I said about Hooper, he's not my type.

'Hi, Alyssa!' Eugenie hardly paused as she noticed me out of the corner of her eye and got her driver to wheel her cases across the quad. Eugenie Clifford – daughter of Sir Roger and Lady Mary Clifford, musical prodigy, wannabe opera diva with masses of amazing red hair against a porcelain-white complexion. People say I look like her, but I disagree. Her hair's darker and mine's wavier for a start.

Charlie Hudson showed up next and gave me a little bit more of her precious time than Eugenie did. 'Who is that?' she exclaimed, looking over her shoulder. Each short syllable contained a world of wonder, like Miranda in *The Tempest* – 'Oh, brave new world that has such creatures in it!' – '*Who . . . is . . . that!*'

I followed her lust-struck gaze. 'I have no idea.'

OK, at last the new kid. Starting with the eyes – very large, very brown with thick black lashes. Then the lips – wide and full. The bod – six-three, sporty and perfectly proportioned. The car he parked in the car park reserved for staff – metallic silver Aston Martin. Do I even need to mention the custom-made bags or that he's more my type because he's built exactly like Jack?

'Marco Conti,' Zara informed us as we stood open-mouthed. She was busy carrying her stuff from her car to Room 22, knocking into me with her pile of party frocks and pairs of Manolos stacked high on top.

Again, we were obviously meant to know the name. Since Charlie and I didn't have a clue, Zara spelled it out for us. 'Son of Paolo Conti, Azzurri centre back from 1994 to 2001, most capped player since Luigi Riva in the 1960s, now a casino owner in Monaco and director of a big online gambling company.'

'Azzurri?' Charlie echoed. She can be forgiven for not knowing because she holds dual American–British citizenship. Her family lives in Dallas (English mother, Texan father) and so she does American football, not our football.

'The Italian national team,' I explained as Marco clunked his car door shut and strolled into the quad, hands in pockets, jacket collar turned up, a glimpse of something gold hanging round his neck.

'What's he doing here?' Charlie breathed.

'Studying for his baccalaureate?' Zara suggested smugly as she walked on and deliberately dropped a strappy Laboutin right in Marco's path.

The gallant Italian picked it up for her. She smiled; he smiled. There was immediate chemistry.

Charlie narrowed her eyes and bit her lip. 'Hmm,' she said.

I was trying to look forward not back as I sat in my room after dinner.

I searched on my phone app for the temperature in Denver – still minus ten degrees centigrade so I texted Jack.

How are you dealing with the weather?

15

Freezing bollocks off. Miss you.

Me too :x

He'd promised Tuesday at the earliest for our reunion. I thought of the old saying – absence makes the heart grow fonder – and realized there wasn't space in my heart for even the tiniest scrap of extra fondness for Jack without making it pop like a balloon.

Who are you sharing room with? :x he texted.

New girl, Galina Radkin. Am back in Room 27 :x :x

What's she like? :x

Don't know. Haven't met her yet. :x :x :x

Change rooms if you don't like her he suggested, forgetting the kisses this time. Then he added: Change anyway?

Maybe I replied. He knew Room 27 was full of painful memories and I loved him for realizing. Sounds of new girl arriving – gotta go :x

Galina didn't so much arrive as enter with a fanfare of trumpets. More Shakespeare here – this time from *Antony and Cleopatra*. Not quite purple sails and decks of beaten gold, but still Galina was impressive in every respect as she entered the room.

She was tall with long, lustrous dark hair and a symmetrical oval face. She was slender and graceful, regal, happy in the knowledge that everyone who saw her would fall under her spell. No, it's no good – I give up. Words can't do it justice. The impact of Galina Radkin is impossible to convey. Here comes the actual Cleopatra reference – she beggars all description.

'Put the bags on the bed,' she told the two male assistants who accompanied her or, rather, trailed with the luggage three steps behind.

The silent, muscle-bound lackeys were about to lift bags on to my bed by the window until I pointed across the room at two empty ones. They hesitated and looked at Galina.

'Change with me?' she asked in a heavily accented voice. 'I hate small rooms. I think of gulags back home. I choose bed next to window so I can see sky.'

'Course – that's cool.' Her playing the gulag card meant that I gave up my view of lawns, lake and oak trees without a whimper. 'I'm Alyssa. Alyssa Stephens.'

'Galina Radkin,' she told me as she turned to bag carrier number one. 'Raisa unpacks bags. You two can go.'

I swear they backed out like gangsters from a Tarantino film – men in black with unsmiling, stubble-shadowed faces.

'Mikhail and Sergei – they speak English not so good,' she told me before the door was closed and she'd started to look around the room with the professional curiosity of an anthropologist discovering a lost tribe in the South American rain forest. 'They follow me everywhere – my father pays them.' Then she changed the subject to what was really fascinating her. 'We live here – in a room so . . . small?'

The rooms in St Jude's dormitory block are tiny – I admit. The buildings are three hundred and fifty years old, built in the Jacobean style, which means long corridors and galleries, wood-panelled walls, oil paintings in gold frames and low, arched doorways. I believe people were shorter then and there's firm evidence for it in the size of exhumed seventeenth-century coffins and the measurement of the bones inside. That's not macabre – it's just fact.

'*Three* people stay here?' she said, counting the beds and looking aghast.

'No – just two.' I explained that Zara had moved out into Connie's room.

'You and me?' She paced the three-metre-square bedroom from the window to the door, sighed, paced again from the wash basin to Lily's old bed. 'At home my bathroom is bigger.'

I nodded and went back to texting Jack on my phone. **Russian roommate moved in. Delusions of grandeur. Nightmare.** ☹

There was no doubt in my mind that the first thing Galina Radkin would do either tonight or tomorrow morning at the latest was to call her oligarch dad and demand to be taken away, back to their Knightsbridge mansion or to their holiday house in the Bahamas, say – anywhere but St Jude's.

Which would leave me alone in Room 27 – an idea that had left me feeling shaky.

Raisa, Galina's maid, expert in remaining invisible as she went about her work, arrived to unpack Galina's bags while Galina meticulously laid out her make-up on the deep stone windowsill of our shared room. It ended up looking like the most expensive cosmetics counter in the world.

Jumpers, shirts and dresses soon spilled out of the wardrobe we were meant to share. Lacy, racy balcony bras were left on the spare bed because the chest of drawers was full to overflowing with silk nightdresses, thongs and bikinis.

'How do I live like this?' Galina sighed.

Raisa didn't volunteer an answer. A round-faced, dark-haired, middle-aged woman in a high-necked grey jumper, black trousers and flat shoes, she went on silently hanging and folding until Galina said 'Enough!' and Raisa gave a resigned, obedient smile then quietly withdrew.

'How do you do this?' my new roommate asked me in total disbelief.

'You get used to it, I guess.'

Galina pouted then sat heavily on the edge of her bed. 'My father – I hate him,' she said.

From this I guessed it wasn't Galina's choice to be a pupil at St Jude's so I sympathized and tried to be nice. 'I know it's hard. This is only my second term and for the first few weeks I felt totally out of the loop. The others – Zara, Connie and Eugenie – have come through main school together.'

'Eugenie – yes. My father knows the Cliffords.'

'In London?'

'No, in Monaco.'

I worked it out – I'm thinking it was last autumn and Sir Roger and Lady Mary went to cocktail parties with the Radkins. They rubbed shoulders, standing in a balmy breeze and looking out from penthouse balconies at the yachts bobbing in the bay. 'Our daughter goes to a school for exceptional pupils,' Lady Mary tells Mrs R. 'It's way out in the country, in the Cotswolds, with no distractions. Eugenie is studying to be an opera singer under Bruno Cabrini. He's her private tutor.'

Mrs R says she likes the sound of a quiet, out-of-the-way boarding school for exceptional pupils. She thinks it's time that Galina stopped acting the spoilt princess and learned how to develop her own talents, whatever they turned out to be. Mrs R is Mr R's second or third wife, Galina's young-looking stepmother, and Galina presents far too much competition when the paparazzi train their long distance lenses on the mega-wealthy Russian family aboard their super-yacht. It's really the wicked stepmother's idea to send her to St Jude's, not Daddy's.

Lady Mary tells Mrs R that her husband will put in a quiet word with Dr Webb – he and Sir Roger were at school together – and she's sure there will be a place at St Jude's for Galina, whatever her academic talents may be.

'She won't like it,' Mrs R predicts, 'but it will do her good.'

I'm surmising all this, of course, but I'd say I'd got this at least seventy per cent correct. 'Give it a chance – you might get used to it,' I told Galina, who was still pouting, but now skimming through contacts on her phone and starting to text.

'Never!' she vowed. 'And why? Why does anyone who is not crazy want to stay here?'

*

It's difficult to get to sleep while your new roommate fumes and frets. Galina didn't even do it silently. 'Shit! . . . Stupid phone – what do you mean *failed to send*? Why doesn't anyone text me back?'

Maybe because it's gone midnight, I thought, tossing and turning in my narrow bed. I turned out my light, hoping that she'd get the message. But no – she went from texting to making actual calls.

'Papa – it's me . . . Yes, I know what time it is . . . Yes, don't worry. Mikhail and Sergei are with me. Listen, Papa, it's horrible here – kids live in Dark Ages. I have to share room.'

I turned my light back on, looked for something to read to send me off to sleep, found only the rolled-up copy of the *Metro* that Tom had given me. '*Body Found in Frozen Canal*,' I read again. I studied the school photo of the smiling blonde girl who luckily at that point had no idea that her life was to be so short or would end so tragically.

Her name was Scarlett Hartley. I knew hardly anything about her, only that she was seventeen like me, was a pupil at Ainslee Comp and she was Alex Driffield's short-term girlfriend. I read that neighbours overlooking the canal had heard a disturbance on New Year's Eve. A 'disturbance'. Why the hell didn't someone go out to investigate and possibly save Scarlett's life?

'Everyone is stupid,' Galina complained to her dad. 'Even Eugenie – all she likes is Rossini and Verdi. There's nothing to do. I kill myself if I stay.'

Why didn't a neighbour open their back door on to the

canal when they heard people yelling? What was so good on TV that they ignored a girl fighting for her life practically on their doorstep?

'You can't make me be student here – I run away,' Galina threatened over the phone. 'Mikhail and Sergei, they can't stop me.'

Didn't they hear the screams and the splash when Scarlett Hartley went into the water? How did they feel now that they knew what had happened? Did they look out at plastic tape currently surrounding the crime scene and feel cut to the quick with guilt?

Having recently learned a little bit about the darker side of human nature, I decided probably not.

'Papa?'

He'd cut her off.

'Papa!' Galina got no reply so she threw her phone across the room. It skidded under the spare bed, the one that Lily used to sleep in, while Galina buried her beautiful head under the pillow and started to cry.

I put down the newspaper and pretended to fall asleep.

Galina stopped crying and I drifted. I pictured Jack stuck in Denver International Airport and trucks sent out on to runways to de-ice the planes. Tuesday seemed so far away.

My special eidetic memory brought back to mind the images of Lily in the lake, and of Paige slipping in the stable yard and falling under Mistral's hooves. I saw them clear as day and I heard their voices.

'You'd think,' Paige mutters as she chucks a stinky pair of Lily's jeans out of the window where Galina's cosmetics are

22

currently displayed, 'you'd think just once in her life that Lily would have cleared away her dirty laundry before she left.'

It was the last time we saw Lily – packing her bag and rushing out without explanation, leaving stinky, paint-spattered jeans on her bed.

Four days later she was dragged out of the lake.

I saw and heard Lily before that, at the start of last term, at Tom's party.

'There you are!' she cries, slipping an arm round Tom's waist and standing on tiptoe for a full-on lip kiss. Her eyes are staring, pupils dilated. 'It's ages since I saw you – at least ten whole minutes. Tell me you missed me.'

Ex-boyfriend Jayden is across the room talking to Jack, my Jack – not Hooper. Lily totters to join them but collapses in a heap before she gets there.

It's the first I knew of Lily's 'issues', before I learned about feral Jayden's link with her, before I knew anything, in fact.

My old, lost roommates came alive in my thoughts as I floated off to sleep.

Then I dreamed a recurring dream I have of a cold, black river with a strong undertow, of abbey ruins under a starlit sky. I jerked awake, turned over and took an age to get back to sleep. But the nightmare returned – I felt the water close over my head and I woke in terror at 2.30 a.m. Afraid to go back to sleep, I listened to the silence.

But even in the countryside, in the dead of night, silence is never complete.

I heard the beep of Galina's phone from under the spare bed as it received a message. I heard owls *whoo-whoo* in the copper beech trees that screen the technology centre.

It's no good – I'm never going to get back to sleep, I thought.

There was the click of a door closing along the corridor – some other insomniac going walkabout? Then there was what sounded like a light tree branch rattling against the leaded window – 'Let me in! Let me in!' – totally *Wuthering Heights*, only I knew there were no trees that close to the building. What could it be, then? Was it worth getting up to find out?

No, it was too cold. I decided to stay under my duvet.

Guess what – Russian Princess Galina was a snorer. Who'd have thought it?

Four o'clock came and went. Floorboards creaked in the corridor, there were other things in the ancient building that shifted and groaned and still the strange rattling at the window.

OK, that was it – I had to get up and see.

Yeah, very cold. I shivered as I tiptoed across the room and squeezed past Galina's bed. I cupped both hands round my face to cut out the reflection and pressed them against the glass. Pitch black out there. Nothing moving. As I stepped back, my shaking hand brushed against a bottle of Clarins moisturiser on the windowsill. It toppled and fell on to Galina's bed without waking her. I put it back in its place.

And since I was up and wide awake now, I thought I might as well check the corridor. There was more creaking, squeaking and clicking as I opened the door and peered out. A safety light was on and I could see doors to either side of the corridor plus the gilt-framed portrait of Lady Anne Moore at the far end, complete with lace ruff and pearl necklace, plus lapdog.

I tiptoed towards her until I came to the landing at the top of the stairs. It's corny but the face in the painting has the kind of staring eyes that seem to follow you wherever you go. Lady Anne has hardly any eyebrows and a high forehead, which gives her a permanently surprised, almost scared look.

'You and me both,' I told her.

But there was nothing on the landing and nothing, no one, on the stairs. Whoever was making the floorboards creak had moved off before I'd got there and by this time I was getting serious hypothermia.

I turned and headed back to my room. At Number 22, the door was flung open and Connie Coetzee appeared in her knickers and a baggy black T-shirt.

'What the hell?' she hissed.

'S-s-sorry!' I stammered.

'How long have you been creeping around, keeping everyone awake?'

'Not long. Two minutes.'

She looked as if she didn't believe me – a default mode with her, as it turned out. I guess she was born with an overdeveloped hostile gene.

'Go to bed,' she ordered as she clicked the door shut.

Nice! I sighed, shivered and shook my way back to Room 27.

Galina snored on. Her phone beeped again. The window rattled as I slid my whole body, head included, under the duvet and waited for my core temperature to rise back to normal.

'Let me in!' the voice in my head pleaded.

I imagined a girl's fingers tapping at the glass, a desperate voice – so frantic that she broke a small pane and reached her hand through the jagged gap, cutting her wrist and making it drip with blood. 'Let me in!'

It was Cathy from *Wuthering Heights*, Scarlett Hartley running from her attacker on New Year's Eve, the ghost of Lily rising from the bottom of the lake – a combination of all three muddled together inside my restless brain.

It was someone begging me to let her in, to give her space, to rescue her from a situation too lonely and terrible to describe.

chapter two

Galina woke up with a tear-stained face and panda eyes, thanks to the mascara she'd left on overnight. I was already up and showered, recovering from the bad dreams of the night before.

'Where's my phone?' she wailed.

I retrieved it from under Lily's bed and handed it to her.

'Where are my jeans?'

'Bottom drawer?' I suggested.

'And my socks?'

What was I, her stand-in ladies' maid? I headed off to breakfast before she could ask me any more questions. Along the corridor Lady Anne seemed to raise her faint eyebrows at me and her blank gaze followed me down the stone stairs, where I bumped into Raisa on her way up to help Galina get dressed. I gave her a quick, sympathetic smile. Out in the quad Sergei and Mikhail lurked. They looked cold and bored.

'Hi,' I said, not expecting an answer. Then it occurred to me that maybe they were the ones patrolling the corridor during the night, making the creaks and squeaks. But no, surely not, because the rule was that after eight o'clock the girls' dorm was a female-only zone. I hadn't solved the mystery.

'Good morning, how are you?' Sergei replied.

I hadn't expected him to speak English because of what Galina had said so I took another look – Sergei was the younger of the two security guys, quite small, thin and agile-looking, with prominent, bony features and a brutally short haircut. I wouldn't have put it past him to scale the outer wall of the dormitory building in the dead of night to install a secret camera for spying-on-Galina purposes – hence the scratching noises. Walking on towards the dining hall, I laughed at myself for watching too many Bond movies.

It turned out I wasn't the first one down to breakfast. Hooper was already there, sitting by himself in a corner with his iPad. Connie and Zara were at the counter, choosing between yogurt and fruit or full English, taking ages to decide because Marco Conti was there too.

'So, Marco, how do you like St Jude's?' Zara asked, words being less important for her than body language. I mean, what kind of boring, banal opening question was that?

Marco didn't seem to mind. 'So far I like it. What is this?' he asked, pointing to a dark, congealed mess in the metal container next to the bacon.

'Black pudding.' Zara's expression of disgust involved wrinkling her cute nose. 'Pigs' offal and blobs of fat mixed with blood. I wouldn't if I were you.'

Marco quickly opted for a croissant and some cheese.

Zara grabbed some fruit and went with him to an empty table by the window. 'So how do you like to spend your time?' I heard her ask as she bestowed her special smile that makes guys melt. 'Are you into sport? Football, tennis, rugby? I imagine you're excellent at everything like that.'

Still at the counter, I exchanged glances with Connie. When did Zara ever have a conversation about whacking or kicking a ball? She was exercise-phobic, unless high-octane flirting falls into that category.

'You look knackered,' Connie told me in her no-holds-barred way.

'I am.'

'Less prowling up and down corridors,' she recommended as she went across the room to bother Hooper.

I followed her with my cereal and yogurt, and saw the grateful look on his face when I joined them.

'Why so bleary eyed?' he asked.

'Am I? Sorry.'

'It's not because you regret these pics by any chance?' Hooper turned his iPad towards me and gave me time to study an image of a girl in a tiny red and gold bikini, posing provocatively by the edge of a swimming pool. I say 'girl' because it took me a while to realize that this was a picture of me.

'Whoa!' I gasped.

'Let me see.' The Black Widow grabbed the iPad. 'Jeez, Alyssa, you're not leaving much to the imagination!'

'But . . . !'

'Where did you find this?' she asked Hooper.

'It's on Alyssa's Facebook page.'

'I didn't put that there. It's not even—!' I whimpered.

'Oh yeah. Here's more of the same. Wow, Alyssa.' Connie stood up and called for Zara to come and look.

'It's not . . . I didn't . . . oh my God!'

Zara ignored Connie. Hooper looked embarrassed. 'Sorry,' he mumbled.

I grabbed the iPad back from Connie and skimmed through the pictures. 'It's not even me!'

'It is – look!' Connie leaned over my shoulder. 'You by the side of the pool, you lathered in sun cream, slithering up and down a sun umbrella pole, you spread-eagled on a sun lounger. It says they were taken in the Maldives on Christmas Day.'

'Everyone knows I wasn't in the Maldives. I was in Richmond upon Thames. I don't have a red bikini – it's not me!' It would have been funny except that it wasn't.

'Maybe someone stole your username and password and Photoshopped your face on to existing pictures of a glamour model.' Hooper suggested what he thought was a helpful solution.

'Jeez, Hooper!'

He shrugged and apologized again, while Connie physically dragged Zara across to our table.

'Wow!' Zara said when she saw what she thought was me oiled and spread-eagled. 'Damn, Alyssa, you look hot!'

'It's not . . . I don't . . .' Stupidly my face went bright red and I felt the hot prickle of tears in my eyes.

'It's a joke,' Connie told Zara sardonically. 'Alyssa says she wasn't in the Maldives – she was in Richmond.'

'With my aunt,' I bleated. I didn't care how stupid I sounded.

'Look – she's freaking out,' Connie said as if I wasn't

there. 'I have no idea why. It's not as if they stuck her face on to an ugly body.'

'Whoever did it must have a weird sense of humour,' Hooper commented. 'To me it looks suspiciously like revenge porn.'

Connie considered this. 'Oh yeah, where an ex-partner posts intimate stuff online so the world can see images that were meant to be private. Count yourself lucky, Alyssa – at least you're not fully naked.'

'Only an idiot would think you'd really pose like that,' Zara sympathized. 'Still, you'd better hope that Jack doesn't see it – he'll go crazy.'

'God, yes,' I gasped, punching buttons to delete the photos. 'It's the middle of the night in Colorado so let's hope he's asleep.'

'Text him, just in case,' Hooper advised as I fled.

I wasn't listening. I had to get out of the dining room, away from the Black Widow's smirking face, across the courtyard and out past the main school towards the bike shed, away from St Jude's.

Against my better judgement I cycled shakily along the lanes towards the Bottoms. It was Sunday morning – one of those bleak winter days that never seem to get light. There was no colour in the monochrome landscape, just shades of black and grey.

It was the same monochrome inside my head – grey and shadowy – and would be until Jack finally got out of Denver and was on the plane to Heathrow, until I could look into his honey-brown eyes and hear him tell me that he loved me. Meanwhile, in an effort to take my mind off the fake bikini pictures, I focused on Scarlett Hartley and decided on the spur of the moment to go and see Alex Driffield.

Passing the Old Mill on the outskirts of Chartsey Bottom, I was overtaken by Tom in his white Peugeot. He waved at me as he zipped by. I wobbled and waved back.

Should've worn a thicker jacket, I thought to myself as I reached Main Street. And gloves and a big scarf. I had chosen the wrong clothes, as usual.

I reached the church opposite Tom's place – the church with the lych gate and the churchyard with the leaning gravestones, the inscriptions of which had been worn away by centuries of rain and frost. Worshippers were huddled in the church porch. I cycled on, a girl on a mission, but it was only when I reached the faded sign outside JD Car Repairs that I fully realized what that mission was.

I was being drawn in to the murder case despite myself, making emotional connections between the fates of Lily and Scarlett, on the road to becoming a one-girl crusader to discover the truth.

Anyway, the workshop was closed. I stopped and peered in through the grimy window, saw a rusty blue car on a ramp over a mechanic's pit, a small office at the far end with the usual calendar pictures on the wall. I shuddered again at the memory of the bikini photos on my Facebook page – who, why, when?

'Looking for someone?' a voice asked, and I turned

round to see Jayden striding towards me with Bolt, his bandy-legged dog.

Jayden the gatecrasher at Tom's party, Lily's ex. Jayden who had saved my life when Harry Embsay planned to drown me that night, out by the ruined abbey.

Harry shines his torch beam in my eyes. 'What's wrong, Alyssa?' he asks after he's described how my murder will be explained away and he's dragged me through the reeds into the freezing river. 'Can you spot a loophole?'

I retch and pull away, thinking, if this is it, if this is really what's going to happen, just do it.

The sky is black. The river rushes on.

Just do it!

It's so dark we don't know anyone is there until a dog hurtles out of the cloisters and down the hill towards us. I don't see it but I hear it snarling as it comes. Harry just has time to swing his torch towards Bolt as the Staffie leaps chest-high and sinks his fangs into Harry's shoulder. The torch drops to the ground. I dive down, grab it and swing it along the bank towards the stepping stones. Jayden walks in our direction – strolls actually, with both hands in his jacket pocket, shoulders hunched against the cold. I half run, half stagger to meet him with the chorus of Bolt's snarls and growls playing in the background.

Jayden doesn't say anything. He takes the torch from me and aims it at Harry and Bolt. The guy is still standing, but by now the dog is chewing his face, and blood gushes from the shoulder wound. I groan and retch again.

Reliving every last second of the scariest moment of my life as only someone with my perfect recall can, I came face to face with my knight in shining armour.

'Looking for someone?' Jayden said again.

'Yeah – Alex. Do you know where he is?' I ignored Bolt, who had padded up and was sniffing at my boot. I didn't bend down to pat him – best not to risk it in case he took my hand off. 'Did you hear about the body in the canal?'

Jayden swore, turned and strode away. 'Yeah, don't go near this one,' he muttered over his shoulder in a weird echo of Will Harrison's advice.

I cycled after him with Bolt trotting alongside. 'Why not? Did you know Scarlett Hartley? Why won't anyone talk about it?'

Jayden does silence better than anyone I know. He loped on past the Bridge Inn, hands in the same jacket pockets, shoulders hunched, with that untamed look in his eyes.

'You know something you're not telling me,' I insisted.

'Back off and, while you're about it, leave Alex out of it,' he warned without breaking his stride.

'Look, I understand – it's all very well for you to want to protect your buddy . . .'

This brought Jayden to a halt on the crest of the stone bridge that crossed the stream running parallel with Main Street. His breath emerged as clouds of steam in the damp, cold air. 'You don't understand the first sodding thing, Alyssa.'

That was all I was going to get – a warning to back off and an angry rebuff through narrowed eyes.

'Yeah, well, thanks for nothing,' I muttered as I watched him go.

Alex Driffield lives with his parents in a converted cottage in Upper Chartsey. I found this out by asking the first person to come out of St Michael's and All Angels Church after morning service.

It happened to be an old, bald, beer-gutted guy with a limp and a walking stick, who coughed as he came through the lych gate then leaned against the stone wall of the churchyard.

'Up the hill at Millstones,' he told me through a globule of phlegm. 'I don't think he'll want to talk to you, though.'

'Why not?' I shot back.

The old man looked me up and down. 'Alex just lost his girlfriend – pretty little thing.'

Call me thin-skinned, but I took this as a negative comment about my own appearance (not pretty and definitely not little) and I cleared my throat awkwardly.

'No offence,' Phlegm Man cackled with more perspicacity than I'd expected. 'You're nice-looking enough in your own way. But Alex won't want to fill the vacancy – not any time soon.'

'How would you know?' I challenged. A combination of croaking and spitting hadn't done anything to improve first impressions.

'Because I'm his granddad,' the old man said with a rheumy tear in his eye. 'Our whole family is gutted, along with hers. Pretty girl, and clever with it. Vicar just asked us to pray for her – not that it'll do any good now, of course.'

*

If someone tells me I can't do something, my stubborn streak comes out.

It was the same when I was little. When Aunt Olivia said no to me joining the junior-school football team because it took me away from my studies, I ignored her. I'd stay after school and be busy scoring goals when officially I was in extra maths. Or there'd be a programme on TV she said I couldn't watch – it was too gory, too trashy, too adult, whatever. So what did I do? I would secretly press RECORD and watch it the next day while she was at work. OK, it's not big and it's not clever, but I did it anyway.

So when Jayden told me to back off and Alex's granddad said Alex wouldn't be interested in talking to me I just grew more determined. I got on my bike, cycled up the hill to Millstones Cottage and knocked on the door.

'Alex isn't in,' his dad told me. Alex's dad was a younger version of croaking, gobbing man. That is, he had hair and no limp, but the double chin and beer gut were developing and there were the same sags and wrinkles around his eyes.

'Do you know where he is?' I asked.

Alex's dad shrugged and closed the door.

I knocked again. 'I'm Alyssa Stephens,' I reminded Mr Driffield.

'I know who you are – you're from St Jude's. I saw your face splashed all over the front pages of the papers. You were involved in the Lily Earle business.'

'Lily was my roommate.'

'I know that too. You got yourself involved in the whole

nasty mess instead of leaving it to the police. Too bloody clever by half.'

The force behind what he said made me take a step back. I remembered how strict he was with Alex, how Alex didn't raise his head above the parapet if his dad was on the warpath. Crouch down, tow the line, don't speak until you're spoken to – this was Neanderthal parenting with a vengeance. And I could read that now in Mr Driffield's square stance, which blocked the doorway, and in his small, mistrustful eyes.

'So please tell Alex I called,' I said, realizing that I was getting nowhere.

He made no promises as he shrugged again and closed the door a second time.

Head down and lost in thought, I picked up my bike at the gate and wheeled it towards Upwood House, the National Trust property overlooking the valley. If nothing else, I could make my way past the Georgian mansion on to Hereward Ridge then cycle the scenic route along the bridle path back towards St Jude's.

I'd only got as far as the entrance to Upwood House, however, when I bumped into another familiar figure, and felt that an already bad day was about to get much worse.

'Watch where you're going,' Ursula growled, sidestepping me and my bike.

To be fair, I had almost walked into her. Ursula was Jayden's current girlfriend, following on from Lily and her exact opposite. 'Hostile' doesn't cover the impact her presence makes in any given situation. She's tall, blonde and hard faced – an impression enhanced by nose piercings and rows of studs along the rims of both ears.

'Sorry,' I told her, hurrying on.

She followed me for four or five steps. 'So where *are* you going?'

'Back home,' I muttered.

'How come? I thought you wanted to see Alex.'

I stopped and turned. 'How did you know – did Jayden tell you?'

Ursula nodded. 'He texted just before I finished work at the big house. Yeah, I work there and don't look so gobsmacked.'

'I'm not. No.' It was none of my business where school dropout Ursula worked and I was caught off guard by the fact that she wanted to have this conversation. In the bad old days before Christmas, when I was involved with the whole 'nasty mess' of Lily and Paige, I hadn't been able to get more than a stare and a grunt out of her. I'd even had Jayden's door slammed in my face by her, which is why it felt weird to be standing in the cold, halfway up a steep hill, talking like this.

'I'm a cleaner,' she explained. 'Five mornings a week. It's a lousy job, but I left home over Christmas and this pays the rent. Jayden was no help to you, was he?'

'He didn't know where Alex was, if that's what you mean.'

'Sure he did,' she contradicted. 'I expect he told you to back off, didn't he? That's Jayden for you, trying to protect his mate.'

This was getting more interesting by the second. 'Why does he have to protect him?'

'Why do you think? Alex is in bits – his girlfriend just died. Jayden knows you'd go in like a bull in a china shop.'

'Well, thanks.'

'No, Jayden likes you – don't get me wrong. And I know you're only trying to help. But the bottom line is that Jayden thinks you're trouble. And you are, Alyssa – you and your photographic memory – you're a pain.'

So why was she bothering to talk to me with the wind whipping strands of straw-blonde hair across her cheeks? She was even worse prepared for the weather than me in a lightweight black sweater, thin denim jacket, ballet pumps and leggings. 'You're right,' I agreed. 'It's not my business. I don't know why I'm bothering.'

'It's the drowning thing, isn't it?'

Now I was really hooked into the conversation. I leaned my bike against a street lamp, folded my arms and listened.

'First Lily and now Scarlett. And, yeah, I know they got the right guys for the Lily murder – D'Arblay, Harry Embsay, Guy Simons – little fascist shits. So this new one doesn't look like it's connected. It's just that it got under your skin and wormed its way into your gut – the fact that Scarlett and Lily both drowned.'

I nodded, said nothing and didn't mention the ghostly hand scratching at my bedroom window, begging to be allowed in.

'I get where you're coming from and I'd feel the same if I was you. I knew Scarlett from Ainslee Comp – not as well as you knew Lily, probably, and it's a while since we hung out together – but well enough to want the bastard caught and for them to throw away the keys.'

'I hear you.'

'Personally, I'm hoping that's where you might come in, Alyssa – you and your freaky memory.'

I took this as a rare compliment and gave Ursula a thin smile. 'You say you knew Scarlett at school?'

'Yeah, before they kicked me out. I did half a term in the Lower Sixth until they caught me in media studies with a pocket full of uppers – my gran's happy pills that I'd picked up from the chemist's though no way did they believe me. I was already on a written warning. That was it – they showed me the door.'

'OK. So anyway – Scarlett?'

'Yeah. Really clever but not geeky. Everyone liked her, especially the boys. Alex practically stalked her for a whole term before he found the balls to ask her out. Then, within a week – look what happened.'

'What did happen?'

'You're the super-sleuth, you tell me.'

'I only know what I read in the *Metro* and what Tom told me. But you actually knew her. What was she like? Was there an old boyfriend who got jealous when she chucked him and started going out with Alex?' As I really got into the subject, questions poured out of me. 'Where'd she been on New Year's Eve? Was she at a party? Who with? Did she try to walk home alone?'

Ursula let me run dry before she answered. 'Scarlett didn't

go out with many guys. There were a couple in our year at school – Sammy Beckett and Matt Brookes were the ones I knew about – then there was one with a foreign name that I can't remember. She met him on holiday last summer but he lives in Italy so I guess he doesn't count. And, yes, she was at a New Year's party in Ainslee, but not with Alex because Alex's dad made him go to a boring family party instead.'

'You definitely know that?'

'I was there with Jayden, Micky Cooke, Matt and a couple of other mates. Tom would've been there except he was in London.'

'So Scarlett was by herself?'

'No – we were all together, a big gang of us getting pissed. I was out of it before midnight, so were most of the rest. We staggered out about one o'clock and called a taxi. It took us bloody ages to find one.'

'What about Scarlett? When did she leave?'

'Yeah, right, that's the big question.' Pushing a stray strand of hair behind her heavily pierced ear, Ursula shook her head. 'I've tried to think – when was the last time I saw her and I honestly don't know the answer. It might have been before twelve . . . but then . . . no . . . I've got a definite memory of Scarlett kissing Jayden at midnight and me getting crazy jealous and having a go at her . . . But then again maybe that was later. And she definitely wasn't with us in the cab so she must have left before one o'clock – unless she was still in a dark corner somewhere, snogging a stranger . . . But then no again – Scarlett wouldn't do that.'

'It's all a blur really?'

41

'Yeah. I'm sorry I'm not like you – I haven't got the perfect memory thing going on.'

'It's pretty rare,' I conceded, 'and most people wouldn't want it, believe me.'

She looked at me as if she wasn't sure about making the next revelation then decided to go ahead. 'Actually Scarlett had it. That's weird – right?'

This rocked me back on my heels. I even thought I'd imagined what she'd said. 'Say that again.'

'Scarlett was the same as you – she had total recall. I know – it's a big coincidence.'

'Scarlett Hartley had an eidetic memory?' I whispered. As the news sank in, it did more than rock me back on my heels – it hit me hard between the ribs, right in my solar plexus. Now I was connected directly with Scarlett's death and not just through Lily and the drowning link. Scarlett and I were similar in a totally unexpected way. 'That can't be right.'

'OK, don't believe me,' Ursula sniped back, and her face took on the usual hard expression as she turned and set off back down the hill. 'I was only trying to help.'

'No, I believe you . . .'

Too late, she was gone. And now I saw why. Loping up the hill with that forward hunch and wild-boy glare was Jayden, coming to meet his girlfriend after work, with Bolt trotting obediently behind.

'Translate from English into French,' Justine Renoir instructed her select little group of students next morning.

She asked us to go online to study copies of the morning papers. 'Work in pairs and choose any article you like. You have thirty minutes to complete the task.'

It was the first day of term and to be honest I was glad to be back in a classroom overlooking the lake across the hallway from Saint Sam's office, doing something normal like translating a passage from a newspaper. Since my accidental meeting with Ursula and the revelations about Scarlett, I'd spent more time than I wanted to mopping up after Princess Galina and trying to explain away those fake Facebook photos.

'I cannot stay here!' Galina had told me a hundred times. 'St Jude's is a prison. Why don't they listen?'

'Maybe "they" want you to spend time studying, out of the media spotlight,' I'd suggested. 'I suppose you mean your dad and the rest of your family?'

'My stepmother,' she'd told me, confirming one of my earlier theories. 'But it's not fair! I have business interests – who will take my bags to big fashion shows? I'm face of Radkin Luxury Leather. Without me, it is nothing.'

'You design handbags?' I'd asked.

'Since I was fifteen,' she'd confirmed. 'I give Papa my business plan and he gives me ten thousand pounds for start-up. Small money for him, but enough for me to begin. Now bags are in Paris, Milan, New York . . .'

She'd shown me a website with pictures and I'd been impressed.

'For six months last year they make me do Slavic Studies in California, but I already know more than the teachers.

43

I tell them, I don't want to do this any more. I only want to be designer. So they take me out of class and send me to Monaco, which I love and I have fun with friends. But now they change their minds and make me do this!'

'So did your dad give you an actual reason for sending you to St Jude's?' I'd enquired.

Galina had sighed and her beautiful, cushiony bottom lip had trembled. 'He thinks that here it is safe.'

'But not in Monaco?'

'No. There's accident in boat, which they say is not accident. Someone died.'

'Oh!' That explained Mikhail and Sergei. Security was obviously top priority for the Radkins.

But Galina had shrugged and insisted it was nothing, an accident for sure, then she'd gone on to weep and wail some more. I'd tried to sympathize about her possibly being in danger from God-knows-what Russian mafia gangs, but I'd found it difficult. She wasn't a person you felt sorry for easily and I still had other things on my mind.

Call me paranoid, but I'd waited for Galina to leave then carried out a quick search of our room. Russian mafia might mean hidden cameras and other high-tech bugging devices; it might mean a man in a black balaclava shinning up the drainpipe in the middle of the night. Yeah, like I said earlier, a little too 007, but still a possibility.

'Work with me?' Hooper suggested as Justine set us our translation task for the morning.

I agreed and we began looking for interesting headlines together. Over the weekend the pound had taken another beating on the stock exchange, and a famous footballer worth sixty million on the transfer market had been banned for six matches for punching a linesman in the face.

'Did you text Jack about those photos?' Hooper reminded me as I scrolled through various articles.

'I did mention it – yeah.'

Took nasty pics off my Facebook page I'd texted in one of the gaps between Galina-minding.

Jack had texted back after a few minutes. Why – what's going on?

Someone hacked into my account or else they stole password and posted fake photos.

Fake?

Yeah – of me in the Maldives, and you know I've never even been there.

Wow, weird. Were they really bad?

Sleazy, I'd texted. Felt really embarrassed.

Poor baby, Jack had written. He sent me lots of smiley faces and kisses.

But, anyway, the photos were gone and Tuesday was almost here.

I looked at the photograph of Scarlett on our screen and read that a police inspector in charge of the investigation had called a press conference for later that day. 'Let's translate this piece about the girl in the canal,' I told Hooper, hoping of course that I'd learn more details about Scarlett's death.

'Maybe something more cheerful?' Hooper queried. But then he looked at my expression and saw that it wasn't up for debate.

So we started with the headline – *Police Appeal for Help*.

'*Appel de la Police a l'Aide,*' Hooper wrote.

'*Oxfordshire police are to ask the public for information relating to the death of seventeen-year-old Scarlett Hartley.*'

'Wait – slow down!' he begged. '*La police Oxfordshire demandera au public d'informations relatives a la mort de Scarlett Hartley, dix-sept ans.* How does that sound?'

'Yes, good.' I read on: '*The schoolgirl's body was recently recovered from the Oxford-to-Stratford canal close to West Ainslee lock, and early forensic evidence suggests that she had been killed by a blow to the head.*'

'Slow down! Who do you think I am, Will Harrison?' Hooper said again.

Across the room, Will was working with Eugenie on their chosen piece of text. At the mention of his name, he glanced across at Hooper and me.

Hooper sighed and went on with the task. '*Le corps de l'ecoliere a ete recemment pris de . . .*'

My heart rate accelerated as I finished reading the article. 'It says here that so far no witnesses have come forward. The police are hoping that an appeal for information on national TV will jog people's memories. There's an Inspector June Ripley leading the investigation. She says the murder was particularly brutal and there are worries that the killer may strike again.'

'Impossible – I can't translate unless you slow down,' Hooper complained as Justine stopped by our desk.

She saw my hand quiver over the mouse. '*C'est trop*

horrible, Alyssa. Il fault choisir un autre sujet.' It's too horrible, Alyssa. You must choose another topic.

It was sound advice. I did know that thinking too much about Scarlett Hartley wasn't good for me. Still, I couldn't help it as I drifted through afternoon lessons then took a stroll in the school grounds, past the lake and into the oak woods beyond.

Scarlett had been going out with Alex Driffield and ended up dead in a canal. She had perfect recall of everything that had ever happened to her. The killer was brutal and might 'strike again'. Certain facts hammered away inside my head so I was too preoccupied to notice a mountain biker speeding towards me along the rough track.

Whoa! I only noticed him when his bike hit a tree root on the crest of a small hill, and bike and rider parted company in mid-air then crashed to the ground. I'd run to help the guy up before I recognized him.

'Alex, are you OK? What are you doing here?'

'It's a free country,' he mumbled as he brushed skeletal autumn leaves and dirt from the sleeve and shoulder of his neon-yellow cycling jacket. 'I can ride where I want.'

'Not in private grounds,' I reminded him, picking up his bike and handing it back to him. 'You're trespassing. Anyway, be honest. You didn't just happen to be here – you came looking for me.'

'What if I did?'

'Jesus, Alex, we can go round and round in circles for as long as you like.' I noticed there were streaks of mud down his cheek and caked in his short, dark hair, but I didn't feel I knew him well enough to point it out.

'OK, now that I've run into you . . .'

'Literally!'

'Don't worry – I would've braked.'

'So, now that you've run into me?'

'I guess we could have a conversation,' he mumbled.

I nodded. 'Go ahead.'

'First – I heard you were in the village, sticking your oar in as usual.'

'Who told you – your granddad?'

'No – Jayden.'

'Typical. Anyway, I wasn't sticking my oar in. I care about what's happened. I thought maybe it would help to talk.'

' "Care"?' he mocked. 'Like the journalists who showed up on our doorstep? Or like the cops – "Where were you on the night of the thirty-first of January, between the hours of midnight and three a.m.?" '

'Neither.'

'And why would it help me to talk to you, Alyssa?' Alex grew more hostile as the conversation developed, as if he couldn't help blaming me for something, and I couldn't work out what. 'Are we back to the same old stuff – teenaged super-sleuth with the amazing memory is on the case; she'll have it solved before the end of the week?'

I dropped my gaze and stared at the tyre marks in the mud. Whatever the reason, if Alex Driffield didn't want to talk, that was up to him. 'You're right. I'll back off.'

'Cool.'

'Is that it?'

'Yeah. Well, no. Second of all, it wasn't me – I didn't have anything to do with it.'

'Who said you did? You'd only been going out with Scarlett for about a week. You weren't even at the party, according to Ursula.'

'Anyway, Scarlett?' I remembered asking.

'Yeah. Really clever but not geeky.' Ursula is ready with the low-down on Scarlett, much more open and friendly than I expect. She takes me by surprise. 'Everyone liked her, especially the boys. Alex practically stalked her for a whole term before he found the balls to ask her out.

'Exactly,' Alex snapped. 'I wasn't even there.'

'But you'd had a thing for Scarlett for ages before you started going out?'

'What if I had? What difference does it make?'

I sighed and tried to take the tension out of the situation. 'You've got mud on your cheek.'

Savagely he rubbed the wrong cheek with the back of his hand.

'Other one.'

He rubbed again.

'You actually knew her,' I say to Ursula. 'What was she like? Was there an old boyfriend who got jealous when she chucked him and started going out with Alex? Where'd she been on New Year's Eve? Was she at the party? Did she try to walk home alone?'

'I'm telling everyone I wasn't there, but no one will

49

listen!' Alex repeated, and his voice bounced off the grey oak trunks and fell to the cold, black earth. 'The first I knew about it was the cops coming knocking at my door, not telling me what it was about, asking when did I last see Scarlett? I say, in Starbucks in the shopping centre at one o'clock on New Year's Eve – why? They asked me loads more questions and I felt sick to my stomach because I was guessing now what this might be about – Scarlett had gone missing, or she'd had an accident and she was in hospital. But they still didn't tell me. They asked did we have a fight, how long had we been together, why didn't I go with her to the party?'

'That must have been really hard to deal with,' I murmured, knowing that my pathetic comment would bounce right back at me because the words that were pouring out of Alex were like a dam bursting, sweeping everything before them.

'I'm saying, what's wrong, what's wrong? And my dad is in the hallway behind me, dragging me back and telling the cops I was only a kid and they couldn't throw their weight around like this and why the hell were they asking all these questions? And then they said they were sorry to inform us that Scarlett was dead and it was like I walked off the edge of a cliff and just fell and kept on falling.'

We stood in silence, listening to the wind in the trees until Alex got hold of his runaway emotions and reined them in. 'How could she be dead? I'd only talked to her three days before. We had coffee. We went shopping. She was fine.'

'I'm so sorry.'

'You're sorry; everyone's sorry. And you know what, Alyssa? I'm sorry too. I should've been there and it wouldn't have ended up like it did. I should've gone with Scarlett to the party.' This last thought brought him to another halt – as if his mind had hit one final bump and gone up in the air like the bike had done. He came crashing down into permanent silence.

And I couldn't think of anything to say in the dark wood. Instead, I brushed his dirty cheek with my fingertips, swept the mud from his jacket and let him cry.

Detective Inspector June Ripley was impressive in her press conference. There was the usual desk with its row of microphones, and she was flanked by fellow officers on both sides.

In her dark suit with shiny buttons, with her glossy black hair neatly bobbed and her small, even features maintaining a steely, unemotional focus, it seemed she'd been destined to join the police force since birth. You would have found no Cinderella tiaras or Tinkerbell wings in five-year-old June's dressing-up box. No, she would have been a caped crusader with a light-sabre, putting right all the wrongs of her tiny world.

I was alone in my room, lying in bed watching the press conference on my laptop. The scarily professional inspector gave us the facts all over again – Scarlett's body had been found in the canal close to the lock. A murder investigation was underway and evidence removed from the scene. An intensive search of the surrounding area was continuing in an attempt to discover the murder weapons, believed to be a ligature plus a heavy, blunt instrument. Inspector Ripley spoke quickly but matter-of-factly. She appealed for witnesses to come forward.

'We know that Scarlett attended a New Year's Eve party at a nearby address and that she left alone at around one in the morning. There is evidence from CCTV footage that she stopped outside The Fleece pub near to Ainslee Westgate train station to talk to a man judged to be in his late teens – Caucasian, over six feet tall, dressed in a dark jacket, knitted hat, jeans and trainers. CCTV also tells us that Scarlett, alone again, approached a taxi rank outside the station, but was unable to find a cab. She then walked off in the direction of the canal towards a path that would have been a shortcut to her home.'

I listened to the detective's every word – learned that the police were satisfied that no one had left the party with Scarlett, which fitted Ursula's account, but who was the guy she'd talked to outside the pub? Had the camera caught him from in front or behind? Had anybody there actually seen her with him?

Then my personal line of enquiry was rudely interrupted.

'Go away! I don't want you! I hate you!' Galina screeched from below the window. She lapsed into furious Russian and didn't let up – so much so that I got out of bed and went to look.

There she was, out on the front lawn, caught in a pool of yellow light cast by the lamp over the stone archway leading into the quad, waving her arms at Mikhail. 'Leave me alone, stupid, stinky idiot!' she yelled in childish English after she'd run out of insults in her native tongue.

The bodyguard remained inscrutable throughout, hands behind his back, soaking up the abuse.

'You hear me? Why don't you and Sergei leave me alone?'

Because they're paid not to, was my thought. I leaned over the array of expensive cosmetics for a better view and it was only then that I noticed that two of the small, diamond-shaped panes in the leaded window were broken and a cold wind was whistling in.

'What are you – peeping Toms?' Galina screamed at Mikhail. 'Do you watch me use lavatory? Are you there when I take shower? I bet. Yes, I tell Papa he has perverts working for him. You and Sergei are finished, Mikhail – wait and see!'

The wind whistled in and I remembered the sinister rattling at my window, the small voice pleading, 'Let me in!'

A girl's fingers tap at the glass, her desperate voice sighs inside my head. Frantically she breaks a small pane and reaches through the jagged gap. 'Let me in!'

A tube of moisturiser was leaking on to the windowsill. Galina was still yelling at Mikhail as I screwed the top back on to the tube then recoiled.

There was a small bird lodged between two aerosol cans, its wings spread wide, its neck limp and broken.

'Let me in! Rescue me!'

The bird's breast was red, its eyes glassy.

I gasped and backed away, heard the shouting stop and Galina's footsteps enter the quad.

Poor robin dead on the windowsill, oozing blood on to the stone. A small bird lying in a crimson pool. Not imagined, but stone-cold and real.

chapter three

'No big deal,' Galina told me. 'It is dead bird – so what?'

She'd stalked in out of the cold and then immediately blocked the broken panes with a copy of *Vanity Fair* and chucked the feathered corpse into the metal waste bin.

The robin landed with a light thud.

'Poor thing,' I murmured, wondering whether it had been a bird's wings fluttering against the window that had been the real ghost-child of my dream.

'*Stupid* thing,' Galina insisted. 'It flies at glass and breaks neck. Glass is old and cracked. Anyway, how long does it lie there dead if I don't share a room with you?'

She'd found me cowering in a corner, admitting that I daren't touch it, that it creeped me out.

'You're weird, Alyssa. They tell me, oh she's so clever and so brave, she finds killers of roommate. But no. You run away from tiny dead bird – what do you call it?'

'Robin,' I muttered, and shuddered at the memory of almost putting my hand on the cold, feathered corpse. 'Why were you yelling at Mikhail?' I asked, quickly changing the subject.

'He's so stupid – that's why.'

Everything, everyone for Galina was 'stupid', pronounced with an explosive 'p'.

55

'You want to talk about it?' I asked.

Slumping on to her bed fully dressed and with her boots still on, Galina glowered at her fibreglass fingernails. 'These two men – Mikhail and Sergei – they follow me everywhere like shadows. I'm not free.'

'Yeah, I wouldn't like it,' I agreed. 'And they don't exactly blend in here at St Jude's.'

'I tell my father they're mafia, not nice men. He replies nice men cannot be bodyguards. Bodyguards need to shoot people; they must have cold hearts.'

Realizing that the magazine wasn't doing its job of keeping out the wind, I decided to pile some books against the gap instead. 'What does Saint Sam think about your security?' I wondered. 'Saint Sam – the head teacher, Dr Webb. That's his nickname.'

Galina shrugged. 'He knows Papa doesn't let me stay alone since accident in Monaco. He pays extra money for Mikhail and Sergei to be here. Dr Webb agrees.'

'But they don't actually live here in the grounds?'

'No. They have hotel in Ainslee, I think. In the day they work together, guarding school gates, buildings. At night, one goes to hotel to sleep, other stays here. But don't ask me – I know nothing about their stupid lives.'

'So the accident on the boat – it must have been serious for your dad to need these guys around 24/7?'

'Scary, yes. We're in harbour and another boat drives fast towards us and doesn't stop. It hits us – bang! Our boat tips over. Me, my friend Isabella and her boyfriend, Carlos, we all fall into water. Engine of our boat doesn't stop like it should and now there is no one to steer it so it goes crazy in water while other boat goes away. No one helps.'

'So then you have to swim to the shore?'

'Yes, but our boat is going very fast in circles. Carlos can't escape. The boat crashes into him and he is killed.' Galina shuddered at the memory.

'And they never found out who was in the other boat?'

'No. The police in Monaco – they say that maybe it was accident, that boat engine was faulty to make it go round and round that way and Papa should blame guy he bought it from. Isabella says no because other boat, it drove straight at us – bang! And then it went away. Papa agrees. After this, he tells Mikhail and Sergei, never let Galina out of your sight. And that's what happens – I'm in prison in this horrible place, never alone.'

'Were you very scared?' I pictured a blue bay lined with palatial villas, a hot sun, a speedboat cutting through the water.

'Very,' Galina admitted, her eyes clouding. 'But I don't show this fear and you must not tell anyone. Promise.'

'OK,' I agreed, rearranging things on my bedside cabinet – mobile phone, hairbrush, iPad, small framed picture of Jack, all in order. That's the OCD me coming out. 'Time to turn out the lights?'

'Tell Molly Wilson that someone dumped a dead bird in your room,' Eugenie suggested before breakfast next morning.

Galina had drifted off down the girls' corridor to

57

scrounge some chewing gum. She'd gone into Eugenie and Charlie's room and told them about the robin. They'd all gasped then laughed about it and come back to Galina's and my room. Charlie, still in her PJs, sat down on the spare bed while Eugenie examined the remains of the dried patch of blood on the sill.

'What's the point? Galina thinks it flew into the window and killed itself,' I explained.

'You'll still have to tell the bursar, though. She'll need to get a guy to come and fix the panes of glass.' Charlie came through with the same advice as Eugenie.

'Good point,' I conceded.

'Anyway, if it was a suicide robin, why would there be two panes broken and not just one?' Eugenie said as she checked the damage.

'Yeah, another good point.'

Energetically Charlie took up the argument again. 'I agree with Eugenie – it can't have been a kamikaze robin. I think somebody climbed up and broke the window, reached through and dumped it there.'

'Yeah, poor you.' Eugenie had turned her attention to the waste bin and was poking around amongst the screwed up paper. 'It's another practical joke, like those fake pictures.'

'You heard about that?' I groaned.

'The whole school heard. Lots of people went on Facebook to look before you had a chance to take them off. All the boys drooled over them.'

There was more groaning from me and a Slavic toss of the head from Galina. 'Big deal,' she muttered.

'No, hold it, Galina. If someone's using Alyssa's password and faking pictures and now dumping dead birds on her windowsill, it kind of suggests she's being targeted.' As she spoke, Charlie gathered her fair hair into a knot at the nape of her neck. 'Can I borrow some cleanser, please?'

Galina nodded. 'Help yourself. Maybe I get Mikhail to check it out, find bully,' she told me with a stage wink.

'Funny!' Really, actually. So we all laughed at the idea that macho Mikhail should investigate the case of the expired robin and then we borrowed Galina's expensive lotions, rubbed them over our faces and legs and went on gossiping.

Galina developed the picture for us. 'My bodyguards find bird killer and get confession. He leaves school in disgrace.'

'Or she,' Eugenie pointed out. 'Maybe a girl set up the whole thing. She climbs up the drainpipe in the dark and breaks the glass, deposits the dead robin. Why the hell not?'

'You have enemies here in school, Alyssa?' Galina wanted to know. The idea seemed to perk her up no end.

'Not that I know of.'

'So maybe it's someone with a secret grudge.' Eugenie developed her conspiracy theory. 'Who's left over from last term and the whole Lily and Paige thing? Who besides Harry Embsay and that lot might still have it in for you, Alyssa?'

'No one.' Please God, no one. The right people were in jail, Saint Sam had glossed over the whole thing and St Jude's was sailing on into a future perched at the very top of the independent-school league tables. Students would get the usual brilliant baccalaureate results and go on to Oxbridge, fees would go up again, the school would continue its tradition of taking nothing but the best.

'Who's got it in for Alyssa?' Zara burst into the room, squeezed on to the spare bed and sat cross legged next to Charlie. 'Come on – what am I missing? Tell, tell!'

'Whoever thinks spooking her out by putting a dead bird on her windowsill is a fun idea,' Eugenie replied. 'It turns out she has a phobia.'

'It's not a phobia,' I protested. This whole thing was getting out of hand. 'Look, it's nothing. I'll let the bursar know about the broken window. End of.'

But Zara refused to let it drop and went off on a new tack. 'Maybe it wasn't Alyssa who the jokester was targeting. Maybe it was Galina.'

'And he thinks this scares me?' Galina's voice with loaded with scorn but I knew now that this was a cover for the fear she'd shared with me. 'A bird is dead. It's nothing.'

'Yeah but it could be a metaphor for something, or a kind of warning.' Eugenie had performed in too many melodramatic operas. Her mind was full of gothic events. 'Dead bird sings no more. It represents the fall of something beautiful, the ending of a brief life. Soaring in the sky one moment then dead and cold the next.'

'Thanks for that,' I told her, trying not to shiver and glancing at Galina who by now wasn't smiling.

'Come on, let's go.' Charlie was the first out of the room. 'I have to work with my fitness trainer for a half hour before breakfast, and, Eugenie, you have to practise your scales or whatever it is opera singers do.'

I haven't forgotten that it's Tuesday.

As soon as the others left and Galina had begun another angry conversation with her dad about the pervert bodyguards he'd employed, I went off to take a shower. I washed my hair and rubbed in Moroccan oil, shaved and exfoliated, moisturised and tweezered. Then I went back to my room and set out the clothes I would wear later in the day.

Jack is on a plane out of Denver and I'm getting ready for our reunion at Ainslee Westgate. Focus on that, Alyssa.

First though, I put on my uniform – white shirt (top button undone), red tartan skirt and matching tie. I customized the tie by making the knot big and the ends short then dropped by Molly Wilson's office on my way to breakfast.

I'm glad to report that the new bursar's room had been totally refurbed. Gone was D'Arblay's glass cabinet with its Second World War books and trophies – the medals, the small silver box containing his macabre collection of teeth taken from victims of the Holocaust. The big leather-topped desk was gone too and the walls had been repainted in fresh, cooking-apple green. There were white flowers on the new glass-and-steel desk and Molly herself sat behind it wearing a welcoming smile.

'Alyssa, isn't it?' she asked.

I nodded. Impressive – the woman had done her homework, studying students' photographs attached to our files and learning names off by heart.

'Have a seat. How can I help?'

'Our window's broken,' I replied, sitting on the edge of the seat, not planning to stay. 'Room Twenty-seven.'

Molly made a note. 'Room Twenty-seven – yes. In fact, Alyssa, I've been reading your file and wondering if you might want to change rooms, considering what happened last term. Make a fresh start, maybe?'

'Thanks, but it's OK.'

'You're not reminded too much of Lily and Paige?'

'Yeah, but I don't mind. We had fun together in Twenty-seven. I like to relive it.' On balance I decided that it lifted my mood to give my crazy memory free rein to roam through the happy times – Paige polishing horse tack, smelling of saddle-soap, Lily energetically slapping paint on to her canvases and abandoning clothes in a heap on the floor.

Molly sat for a while without speaking, pen poised over her pad. She looks like the type of person who springs out of bed and into her clothes without a crinkle or a crease, whose short dark hair never suffers from bed head and whose lip gloss lasts the whole day without smudging or fading. I admire that even though I'm never going to be that way – my hair's too wavy and wayward and my clothes don't make much contact with an iron.

'I was a student here once,' Molly said at last. 'A scholarship girl.'

'Like me.' I said. OK, I decided I liked the new bursar – we had things in common.

'Yes. I saw that you scored top marks in our entrance exam in summer of last year – one point above Will Harrison. Anyway, I'm a local girl and my family still lives in Ainslee. I went away, though – first to King's College, Cambridge, then I threw it all up to do voluntary work in Tanzania, which was a good move on my part. I never really felt I fitted in, either at St Jude's or at Cambridge – I was always a bit of an outsider.'

We were deep in conversation and I was relaxing back into the chair, identifying with Molly in a big way – except for the hair and clothes, of course.

'You didn't mention how the window was broken, by the way.'

I thought about it then chose the easiest answer. 'It was a bird – a robin. It flew straight at the glass.'

Molly nodded. 'Leave it with me,' she said. 'I'll see that it gets fixed.'

'Here comes Justine – whoo, check out the shoes!' Zara hissed across the breakfast table, and Connie, Eugenie, Galina and I clocked the red-soled Laboutins.

Our French teacher was seriously stylish, we agreed.

Justine sat down across the room from us, next to Shirley Welford, head of maths. Shirley was over fifty and not stylish, but what she didn't know about non-right-angled-triangle trigonometry and the unit circle and radian measure wasn't worth knowing.

'Forget Justine's killer heels, here comes Marco,' Eugenie sighed.

'With Charlie,' Connie noted, which made Zara sit up and pay attention.

While Marco and Charlie chose their food from the breakfast bar and selected a quiet corner to sit, Connie went off to join Luke.

'I bet Charlie and Marco aren't talking about football,' Eugenie said over the clatter of cutlery and the hum of conversation, while our American friend dazzled the playboy newcomer with her perfect teeth and a quick flick of her big, hot-rollered blonde hair.

Zara frowned and rethought her Marco strategy.

Anyway, I wasn't really listening or contributing to any of this. I was looking at my phone to check the time, thinking, Only seven more hours to go.

'When does Jack get here?' Hooper seemed to read my mind as he passed by with his muesli and milk.

'Two o'clock into Ainslee on the Paddington train,' I answered. At this moment he was 36,000 feet above the Atlantic, inching towards me on the airline map that showed miles per hour, distance travelled and distance to destination.

'Are you going to meet him?' Eugenie asked.

'Is the Pope a Catholic?' Zara must have noticed my clock-watching and lack of participation in the serious bout of Marco worship going on around our table.

'Who is Jack?' Galina wanted to know, while Zara went on plotting how best to break up the budding romance between Marco and Charlie.

Only five more hours to go, then four then three. I drifted through my English literature class with Bryony Phillips, not getting involved in Irish playwrights of the early twentieth century.

'Are you doing OK, Alyssa?' Bryony asked. Normally I would have been deep in discussion about the political situation behind J. M. Synge's *Playboy of the Western World* when it opened at the Abbey Theatre in 1911.

'She's due to meet Jack in Ainslee,' Hooper butted in before I had time to gather my thoughts.

'Ah.' Bryony was steeped in medieval romance and Shakespeare's sonnets so she cut me some slack. She knew that for once I wouldn't care one way or the other about poor Christy Mahon's tragi-comic 'murder' of his drunken old da'.

With two hours to go I was free of classes and up in my room, slipping out of my uniform into my skinniest pair of jeans and Jack's favourite top – an emerald green one that matched my eyes, he said. I looked in the mirror, frontways, sideways and the view from the rear. I tried my hair up then down then up again, changed from flat boots to heels.

'This Jack is special,' Galina observed with a touch of what felt like envy. But she did offer style advice. 'Hair down is best.'

'Thanks,' I said as I shook my hair free and hurried off.

Jack's text came through as I arrived at Ainslee Westgate. **Meet me under the station clock.**

Scarlett Murder Weapon Found I read on the newspaper hoarding at the kiosk outside the main entrance. I didn't stop to pick up the *Metro* but my stomach churned when I read the headline. I walked on and saw someone I recognized as I crossed the station forecourt – Galina's Sergei staring up at the Arrivals screen. Why isn't he patrolling the grounds of St Jude's? I asked myself.

Then, when I took my place under the big Victorian clock at the ticket office, I bumped into Sammy Beckett from Ainslee Comp.

'Did you see this?' he asked, showing me a copy of the *Metro*.

'No. Anyway, why does everyone assume I'm interested?'

'Because you are,' Sammy quipped. 'Everyone knows you're into solving murders.'

I didn't know Sammy well – in fact, I'd only ever seen him playing five-a-side football alongside Jayden, Alex and Micky, and to be honest he wasn't someone who made much impact – just a kid in a soccer team. 'Why aren't you in school?' I asked.

'I'm conducting a survey on station footfall for an economics project, looking at peak times and off-peak times and working out how the station manager could redeploy his staff to maximize profits.'

'OK, too much information,' I sighed. I sometimes forget how geeky and literal-minded guys like Sammy can be.

'Sorry, but you did ask,' he sulked as he chucked

the newspaper into a nearby bin.

I dived in and grabbed it back. There was a front-page picture of the murdered girl beside a photo of a heavy metal tool, a wrench that you find in workshops. The caption read: *DNA evidence links object found on canal bank with murder victim.*

'Actually, I'm turning up some very interesting facts,' Sammy droned on. 'People assume that a train station gets maximum footfall during the traditional morning and evening rush hours, but what they don't realize is that these days people work flexi-time and the journeys to work begin earlier and finish later—'

'Sammy!' I protested.

'OK, sorry.' He cleared his throat then pointed again at the headline. 'I was a mate of Scarlett's,' he boasted. Then added as an afterthought, 'You know she was dating Alex Driffield?'

'Yeah, I spoke to him.'

'What do you think – was he involved in, y'know, the murder?'

'What makes you think that?'

'Alex wouldn't have any trouble getting hold of a wrench from his dad's workshop, would he?'

'No, he's not involved.' I shook my head more forcefully than I'd expected.

'I wasn't there!' Alex's voice echoes in my brain. We're surrounded by oak trees, standing on cold, black earth. 'The first I knew about it was the cops coming knocking at my door, not telling me what it was about, asking when did I last see Scarlett.'

I hear his voice rise to a thin wail as he tells me he feels sick to his stomach.

'They still didn't tell me. They asked did we have a fight, how long had we been together, why didn't I go with her to the party?'

They tell him and he feels as if he's walked off the edge of a cliff and he keeps on falling.

I brush mud from his cheek and I see him cry.

'Not unless he's a bloody good actor,' I told Sammy.

'No, you're right. Alex is cool,' he said. 'It's probably the guy they got on CCTV. All the cops have to do is put his picture out there and wait for someone to identify him.'

'Agreed,' I said, folding the *Metro* and shoving it into my bag. I did have one niggle about Alex, though, which I tested out on Sammy. Alex had met up with Scarlett at lunchtime on New Year's Eve and then there'd been a three-day gap before the news broke about the body in the canal. 'I am wondering why Alex didn't call Scarlett at midnight to wish her Happy New Year, or why he didn't try to contact her any time during New Year's Day.'

'You're sure he didn't?' Sammy asked.

'Yes. He told me the cops came to his house to give him the news and at that point he didn't even know she'd gone missing.'

'So I heard they had a fight.'

This was the first thing Sammy had said that I really registered. 'Over him not going to the New Year's Eve party?'

'Yeah. Scarlett wouldn't have been happy. She'd have told him sod your dad and come with me. That's how she was.'

'That's not how she looks in the picture in the paper.' There she was a smiley, well-groomed girl, not the moody kind who kicked off if she didn't get her own way.

Sammy backed off. 'It was just a thought. Maybe I'm wrong.'

'Let me think about it.' Right now I was determined to distance myself from the Scarlett tragedy and focus on Jack instead. 'Go ahead, Sammy, get busy with your survey.'

The minute hand on the station clock jerked forward and there was a woman's voice telling us that the next train to arrive on Platform 3 was the 13.00 hours from Paddington, the one that was carrying Jack straight into my arms.

The train drew in; doors slid open. People stepped out with luggage and pushchairs.

I stood beneath the clock under the vast glass canopy, searching in vain.

He's not here, I told myself. He must have missed the train.

Passengers streamed by. I saw Sergei meet a slim blonde woman off the train then disappear into Costa. Sammy began to video people at the ticket barrier.

Jack definitely wasn't here – by this time I was convinced.

Then he walked up to me.

I saw him when he was about four metres away. At six foot three, he stood out from the crowd – tanned, wearing a dark blue ski jacket and travelling light with only a battered black rucksack over one shoulder. His arms were wide open and he smiled at me. Then those arms were round me, wrapping me in his strength and scent, breath and warmth. He kissed me; I kissed him back. I breathed him in through every pore.

'I was scared you weren't coming,' I murmured after I'd caught my breath. I still held him tight as if I was afraid that he might disappear.

'You knew I'd be here.'

'I thought of a thousand reasons you might not make it – you got held up in Passport Control, the tube from Heathrow broke down, you missed the train out of Paddington . . .'

'I'd have texted.'

'I know, but . . .' Someone tell me, why was I crying?

Jack held me close as the crowd thinned and the clock above our head ticked on. 'Sixteen days without you,' he sighed. 'That's a long time.'

'It felt like forever,' I told him. Aunt Olivia was a technology Luddite. She didn't have Skype and anyway the satellite signal high in the mountains to the west of Denver was crap. It had been hard to keep in contact, though we'd managed to stagger through phone conversations most days. 'Hi, I love you . . . Sorry, what did you say? I missed that . . . You're breaking up . . . Hi, are you still there? Yes, I love you too.'

Jack had spent his days swooping down the ski slopes in Colorado with a bunch of tennis-pro mates while I vegged out in Richmond with my aunt.

'Next time you have to come with me,' he whispered as finally we stopped hugging and stood back to stare into each other's eyes. 'At Easter, when I go to the tennis academy in Spain, you have to be there with me, Alyssa. We'll be together.'

'Cool,' I murmured.

'Very,' he agreed, leaning in for one more kiss.

chapter four

Jack and I decided to catch a bus from Ainslee into the Bottoms then walk to St Jude's from there.

'We can just about make it back before it gets dark,' I predicted as we stood waiting for a bus outside the train station. 'And before it snows. That's the forecast.'

'I'm used to snow,' he reminded me. 'They had twenty inches of it in Aspen on the day before I left, and twelve inches in Denver. The temperature was minus three for seven days running.'

'Centigrade or Fahrenheit?' Can you believe it? Jack and I were discussing the weather when all I really wanted to do was get lost in his kisses.

'Fahrenheit.' He held my hand and we stood in line for the bus. The streets and the exterior of The Fleece were still festooned with lights, but the decorations felt jaded now.

The bus came and we climbed on, and rode through the grey streets of Ainslee while Jack told me about the guys he'd met in Aspen – two young ski instructors who worked summers at dude guest ranches, a Swedish girl training for the next Winter Olympics' cross-country skiing event. 'And what about you – how was Christmas, really?'

'Lousy,' I admitted, then I kicked myself. Try not to sound

needy – I read in an agony-aunt column that it makes alpha guys like Jack run a mile. So I decided to lighten the mood. 'You met Aunt Olivia at the end of last term – she's not exactly a barrel of laughs. Anyway, I escaped into the West End as often as I could, went shopping, visited galleries and everything.'

'Cool.' Jack rested his arm round my shoulder and leaned across to wipe the steamed-up window. I felt the warmth coming off his body, saw the smoothness of his tanned face. 'Anyway, what else has been happening while I was away?'

'Nothing.'

Jack looked me in the eyes – this is the point when my knees wobble and my heart melts. 'Yeah, right,' he argued, 'you've got something on your mind. Is it the Facebook pics?'

'No, they're history,' I fibbed, but I couldn't quite brush it off. 'If you really want to know, Hooper's theory is that it was a version of revenge porn – I mean, "I" wasn't naked or anything. And when you took a close look they were obviously fake.'

'But then you'd have to have a jealous ex boyfriend that you haven't told me about,' Jack pointed out. 'That's what revenge porn is all about.'

I reached out to take his spare hand and rest it on my knee as the bus trundled over potholes along country lanes. 'No jealous exes,' I promised. Anyway, he knew that my sex life had been practically non-existent before I'd come to St Jude's.

'What – were the guys at your last school blind?' he joked.

I smiled back. It was so good to be sitting next to him as the bus rattled along, swaying against him, holding his hand.

'So how's Gina?'

'Who?'

'Your new roommate.'

'Galina.' It had only been four days since I'd got back to St Jude's yet there was so much to catch up on. 'Her daddy's filthy rich and she designs and sells bags to international fashion houses. What else do you need to know?'

'Do you like her?'

I thought for a while. 'Actually, yes,' I decided. 'After a car-crash start, yeah, I do.'

'I like it when you do that thing with your nose,' he told me.

'What thing?'

'You kind of wrinkle it when you're thinking.'

'You make me sound like a rabbit.'

'Sexy bunny,' he murmured as he leaned in to kiss me.

Some questions for the agony aunt – how do you go on with your own, independent life when you love someone as much as I love Jack? And, secondly, does every girl in the entire world struggle with this?

You want to be with your guy all the time, every minute of every day. But your head tells you to keep some parts of yourself separate, not to smother each other, not to make

74

too many demands. You have to plan for a career, keep a circle of friends, follow your own interests, develop your own talents. I know this in my head, but the reality is – my heart leads me astray.

When we reached Chartsey Bottom and got off the bus outside JD Repairs, it was four o'clock and already dark and beginning to snow.

Jack slung his bag over his shoulder and took a look around. 'You expect the place to change but it never does.'

Always the same Main Street with its church and graveyard, its upmarket greengrocer's shop called Five-a-Day, its cafe and pub. Whatever the season, whether the trees lining the street are full of pink blossom or sparkling with Christmas lights, the Bottoms always looks like a scene from a greetings card.

'Hey, Jack, are you ready to lose our next match big time?' Micky Cooke taunted as he came out of Driffield senior's workshop and spotted him.

'Why – when is it?' Jack asked. They were talking football, acting like I wasn't there. Even Jack has this laddish streak.

'Friday afternoon.'

Jack made a mental note. 'See you then.'

'Yeah, see you.' Micky sauntered off towards the Squinting Cat cafe, talking, looking over his shoulder and grinning.

Jesus – he saw the Facebook pics! was my instant overreaction. It was the lechy way he was grinning and looking.

But I stayed quiet and Jack ignored him as we turned in

the opposite direction, ready to head out of the village. The snow fell more thickly, quickly covering the pavements and glinting white and sparkly under the street lamps.

'The other two things that happened while you were in Denver are, one, a girl from Ainslee Comp got killed early on New Year's Day and, two, I found a dead robin on my windowsill,' I told him as a sleek silver car pulled up at the kerb and Marco Conti stepped out.

'A dead what?' Jack frowned.

'Robin. Never mind, I'll explain later. Hi, Marco – meet Jack Cavendish. Jack, this is Marco Conti.'

They nodded cautiously, taking time to size each other up. Jack saw a guy in an Aston Martin with dark curly hair and Adonis physique. Marco saw a tall, tanned blonde athlete who, alone amongst the students at St Jude's, could match his amazing looks inch for inch. I stood between them feeling edgy.

'Marco's dad played football for Italy,' I told Jack.

'Paoli Conti,' he realized straight away. 'Yeah, I see the resemblance. He was a great player, by the way.'

There was an awkward pause and I saw it as my job to edge the creaking conversation forward. 'Jack likes to ski but his main sport is tennis. He's just got a place in the British junior squad.'

Marco nodded. He didn't seem in a hurry to get where he was going. 'You want to get on to the pro circuit full time?' he asked Jack.

'Yeah, maybe. Listen, Marco, how would you like to join our football team? It's just five-a-side on an indoor pitch, but the St Jude's team needs a striker. You do play football, don't you?'

'No,' Marco contradicted. 'I made a rule when I was a little kid – never do anything my father wants me to do.'

'So how come you're out here in the sticks?' Jack shot back.

'My mother. She chose this place because of Bruno Cabrini. I said OK, I'll come for two terms.'

'You sing?' Surprise showed on my face and in my voice. It came out as *'Y'sing?'* and reminded me of the trouble I had with my pronunciation when I first talked to Jack. I lose vowels and run words together so I sound pissed – totally nerves related.

'Yes. Bruno teaches me guitar and singing.'

I snuck a look at Marco's hands – his fingers were long, definitely a guitar player's hands. 'Oh. Eug'nie h's s'nging l'ssons w'th h'm too.' Stop, stop before you make even more of a fool of yourself!

'So, anyway, the football team,' Jack broke in to save me more embarrassment.

Marco ignored him and carried on holding a private conversation with me. 'Yeah, I know Eugenie and Galina. We spent the summer together in Monte Carlo. Actually, I ran into Eugenie at Christmas.'

'She didn't say.'

'At a party. I was in London, staying at my cousin's house. Then I came here to check out the school for myself. I thought, yeah, I can live here for a while, why not?'

'And h're y'are!' I burbled.

This could have gone on for ages – Marco chatting, me slurring, Jack impatient – if we hadn't been rudely interrupted by Galina.

She burst out of the Squinting Cat, leaving the door open and shouting over her shoulder.

'My new roommate,' I warned Jack. 'Prepare for blast off.'

'Leave me!' Galina yelled at Mikhail, who was in hot pursuit. 'I tell my father what you do!' The rest was in Russian as she sprinted towards us.

The bodyguard started off in a hurry, but he slowed down when he saw us, his eyes still trained on Galina when she veered off across the road towards the churchyard. It was dark, remember, but the street lamps were on, casting pools of light on the snowy pavements.

Something about the situation – beautiful girl running away from thickset man in suit and tie – kicked us into action. Even though the guy was employed by Galina's dad, we felt we couldn't stand by and let it happen.

'Back off, buddy.' Jack stood in Mikhail's way as Galina's minder tried to cross the road.

Mikhail sidestepped Jack and followed Galina.

I quickly followed her under the lych gate. 'Hold on,' I said. 'Tell me what's happening.'

Marco meanwhile took direct action. He ran right at Mikhail, intercepting him outside the churchyard and barring his way.

'Galina, come back!' I shouted.

Either she didn't hear me or she did and chose to ignore

me. She went on running, stumbling and staggering up the path towards the church porch. I followed and found her sobbing, sitting on a stone bench, hiding her face in her hands.

Out on the road, Marco took a swing at Mikhail who sidestepped again and blundered into Jack, the whole thing happening almost in slow motion in a pool of orange light.

'Galina, look at me!' I knelt beside her and eased her hands down. Then I gasped. There was a cut on her bottom lip and a trickle of blood down her chin. 'How did that happen?'

'He did it,' she sobbed. 'Mikhail, he did this.'

'In the cafe?'

'No. Outside the village, on small road. I run away.'

'And he came after you? OK, I get it. He caught up with you and tried to stop you – that's his job. You stumbled, you got this cut, right?'

Back on the street, Jack and Marco grappled with Mikhail. Eventually Jack wrestled him to the ground and Marco put a foot firmly on his chest.

Galina shook her head. 'Not an accident. He punches me.' She touched the bleeding cut with trembling fingertips. 'He tries to kidnap me.'

'No, hang on, that can't be right. What do you mean, he tried to kidnap you?'

'I tell truth. I take walk in school grounds, by lake into woods and he follows me. He wants to snatch me and take me away.'

'Are you sure?' Was this drama queen Galina hatching a

plot to get rid of her bodyguards, or was it for real?

'I am scared, but I escape. I run to village and hide in cafe.'

'But he followed you?' Whether or not he was a kidnapper after a big ransom from the Radkins, it was clear that punching his boss's daughter in the mouth wasn't part of Mikhail's job description.

'I am very, very scared,' she insisted. 'I phone Papa and tell him what Mikhail has done – in cafe I have time to make call, but it is Salomea who answers. She doesn't listen. She tells me I make up story. She goes off phone.'

'But seriously – Mikhail did this on purpose?' I checked as Jack and Marco rolled the bodyguard on to his stomach and pinned him down.

Galina nodded. 'What do I do?' she whimpered. 'Who will believe me?'

'Me,' I decided. 'I believe you, Galina. Don't worry, we'll call the police.'

'They arrested Mikhail.' Once we got back to St Jude's, I told the whole story to Hooper, Will, Luke and Connie.

Marco had waited with Jack for the cops to get there. I'd asked for paramedics to check out Galina's cut and they'd arrived at the same time as the police. The paramedics decided that the cut needed a couple of stitches and they drove Galina to Queen Elizabeth Hospital in Ainslee. I went with her. We had to wait two hours in A and E and it was 8.30 p.m. by the time we got back to St Jude's.

'You know what this reminds me of,' Connie decided as

we sat around a table in the recreational area overlooking the vast sports hall. 'It's a gamekeeper-turned-poacher situation. The guy is hired to protect Galina and instead he tries to kidnap her.'

'If we believe her story,' Luke said, feet up on one of the coffee tables.

Hooper agreed. 'Remember, she hates the guy. Maybe she made this up to get rid of him.'

'She wouldn't exactly sock herself in the jaw,' BWS pointed out. 'She's way too vain for that.'

Touche!

'So where is she now?' Will wanted to know.

'Asleep in our room. She was knackered, poor thing.'

'And where's Jack?'

'With Marco in the head's office. The police are taking statements.'

'Saint Sam won't like that,' Will tutted. 'A visit from the cops is the last thing he needs.'

'You know him – he'll play it down.' I pictured Saint Sam's reaction – cool, calm and beige, assuring the police that security at the school was excellent and if there was another attempt at kidnap and it took place within the school grounds evidence would be captured on CCTV.

'Let's hope he does play it down,' Luke added. 'Galina probably did make the whole thing up as an excuse to go to her dad and get him to take her out of school.'

You can see how this was going – the girls tending to side with Galina, the guys not. Except for Jack, who said he'd picked up bad vibes from Mikhail when the cops arrested him ('Like he wanted to mow me down with a repeat-action rifle the first chance he got.'). I wasn't sure about Marco – I didn't have a clear picture of whose version he believed.

Anyway, it was late so we left the sports centre to head back to our rooms and the jury was out until tomorrow.

I trudged through the snow back to the dorms with Will and we happened to run into lean and hungry Sergei outside the entrance to the quad. 'Lean and hungry' as in Shakespeare again. Cassius in *Julius Caesar* – 'he thinks too much – such men are dangerous'. I'm full of these quotes and I know they might annoy the hell out of you, but they spring into my magpie mind and make the point way better than ever I could.

So, lean and hungry Sergei talked on the phone and watched us go by. I caught two names amidst the torrent of Russian – 'Galina' and 'Salomea'.

'What's that about?' I wondered.

'You really want to know?' Will asked as we walked on across the quad, our footprints the first to spoil the virgin snow.

I stopped in the middle of the lawn. 'You speak Russian?'

'Russian, Italian, French, a smattering of Mandarin.'

'OK, my multi-lingual friend, what did Sergei say?'

'He said things didn't work out. He wasn't happy.'

'I could tell that from his tone of voice. Who was he talking to, do you know?'

'Someone called Salomea.'

'Really! What else?'

'He said Galina had to go to the hospital but not to worry, they fixed her lip and now she was back at St Jude's.'

'You know that Salomea is Galina's stepmother? Sergei definitely told her that things didn't work out?'

'Yeah, but what does that give us? He could have been talking about a plan to go to the movies, an appointment at the dentist's – anything.' Will carried on with the guy thing of backing off from the day's drama and I gave up trying to involve him.

I stared at him – at his guarded expression and the bruise fading from under his eye. 'How did you get that bruise?' I asked.

'Hey, Alyssa,' I hear him say again last Saturday afternoon. His hair is shorter, lighter. He looks in good shape.

'Hey, did you hear about the Ainslee girl in the canal?'

'Well, yeah,' he drawls. Everyone in Ainslee had heard about that.

'You knew her?'

'Yeah,' he says again.

'Did she fall or was she pushed?'

'They're not sure yet. Why?'

'Just wondering.'

'Quit that, Sherlock, while you're ahead. You worked things out for Lily but you should leave this one alone.'

'It was in the gym. I was lifting weights, training for a half marathon at the end of March,' Will told me. End of translation, end of conversation. Goodbye.

For some reason he stayed in my mind and I replayed

83

our short Saturday conversation all the way up to my room. *Quit that, Sherlock, while you're ahead. You worked things out for Lily, but you should leave this one alone.*

Galina's bed was empty. The duvet was thrown back and a pillow with small spots of blood on it was tipped on to the floor.

My stomach flipped – where the hell was she?

Then I saw a scrawled note on my own neat bed.

CAN'T SLEEP. AM IN CONNIE AND ZARA'S ROOM. DON'T WAIT UP – GALINA X

OK, Alyssa – chill. Take off your top, hang it in the wardrobe, do normal stuff to keep yourself calm.

I'd finished with my clothes and was checking to see whether or not Molly had got the guy in to fix the window when I came across another note, printed out in red ink on a sheet of A4, not scribbled in felt-tip pen like the one from Galina. It was on the windowsill where the robin had been, folded then slotted between two bottles of my roommate's miracle moisturiser. This one was in verse and it was really weird.

Who killed Cock Robin?
'I,' said the Sparrow,
'With my bow and arrow,
I killed Cock Robin.'

I read the first verse of the old nursery rhyme then the first two lines of the handwritten message beneath.

84

Come on, Alyssa – they said you were smart! Why so slow to pick up clues?

My hand shook as I read the lines again, turned the paper over, saw that the back was blank, turned it over again and reread the verse. Then my freaky eidetic memory kicked in and I remembered exactly how the rhyme went on.

Who saw him die?
'I,' said the Fly,
'With my little eye,
I saw him die.'

There was a knock at the door and I jumped a mile, screwed up the paper and stuffed it into my jacket pocket.

'I saw him die.'

Jack poked his head round the door. 'Can I come in?'

'I caught his blood.'

'You're not meant to be here!' I cried. The screwed-up paper fell out as I ran to the door. 'It's after eight o'clock!'

He kicked snow off his boots then pointed to the paper on the floor. 'You dropped that.'

I stooped to pick it up, but he was there first. Straightening it out, he laid it flat on my bedside table and read the rhyme out loud.

'Stop!' I pleaded.

'Who'll make the shroud? . . . Who'll dig his grave?'

Jack came to the message underneath the verse. *'Come on, Alyssa – they said you were smart! Why so slow . . .'*

'Stop!' I said again. I knew there was more handwritten stuff – I just hadn't had chance to read it.

'Who'll be the parson? . . . Who'll be the clerk?'

'Why so slow to pick up the clues?' Jack read on. *'Bad things are happening under your nose, Alyssa. It's up to you to work them out, which I'm sure you can do if you're as good as they say.* Who the hell wrote this?'

Who'll carry the coffin?
Who'll bear the pall?

'Don't ask me. I just found the note here on the window-sill.'

'The killer is in plain sight – right under your nose. Love and kisses . . . Why is this guy sending you love and kisses, Alyssa? What's this about?'

All the birds of the air
Fell a-sighing and a-sobbing
When they heard of the death
Of poor Cock Robin.

My head spun. It was hard to get a coherent sentence out as Jack thrust the paper towards me.

'Whose killer?' he demanded.

My head spun, but in my heart I knew. 'Scarlett Hartley's,'

I answered. 'I think the murderer left this note to challenge me. That's what this is about.'

'It takes a seriously sick mind,' Connie decided.

Jack and I had gone along the corridors of the boys' and girls' dorms and called a late-night meeting in the coffee bar overlooking the sports hall. People had thrown on some clothes and braved the snow to cross the quad and hear what Jack and I had to say.

'Tell me again – what's the link between Scarlett Hartley and Alyssa?' Charlie asked. She sat down strategically between Marco and Zara, across from me, Hooper and Jack. Eugenie, Galina, Luke and Will were there too, along with the Black Widow.

'We're not sure,' Jack answered. 'We know that Scarlett had perfect recall, a photographic memory – whatever you want to call it – the same as Alyssa. That's the one link we've made so far.'

In the thirty minutes since he'd read the verse and the message, I'd shared with Jack all the details of the past few days. He'd dragged them out of me, every last one.

'We're together on this,' he'd promised me, holding me so tight I could hardly breathe. 'You don't have to do this alone.'

Zara turned straight to Will. 'OK, scholarship boy – you went to school with Scarlett before you reached the dizzying heights of St Jude's. So is that true – did she have total recall?'

Will looked as if he'd already been in bed when Jack had

knocked at his door. His hair was messed up and he was wearing his sweater inside out.

'Yeah,' he acknowledged. 'She came top in every exam she ever sat, right from the start of secondary school. We all hated her for it.'

'Really?' Charlie looked puzzled. 'Jeez, I don't get you Brits.'

'I'll explain some other time,' Zara said. 'The point is, somebody killed Scarlett and threw the body in the canal and it's bringing up memories of what happened to Lily last term. And now bad things have started to happen to Alyssa and this sick person is setting up a challenge – catch me if you can, signing off with love and kisses.'

'Kiss-catch,' Eugenie murmured, shuddering and pulling her jacket tighter across her chest.

Connie stuck to the practical. 'You need to find out if the sick bastard did the same thing to Scarlett – taunting her and drawing her in with his psycho games to the point when she got too close to the truth, then he had to kill her.'

My heart hammered against my ribs when she put it all out there, but I tried not to show the fear. 'Let's take this more slowly. It's still possible that there's no connection between what happened to Scarlett and the stuff that's going on here. It could just be someone with a warped sense of humour.'

'Yeah, funny,' Hooper commented. He'd hung back from the main group, but was listening intently to every word that was said.

'He won't be laughing when I get my hands on him,' Jack muttered.

I loved it that he sprang to my defence, though that small, independent part of me said, No, let me do this, let me work it out for myself. 'OK, so say it's a pathetic joke by some loser with nothing better to do.'

Connie and Charlie nodded.

'Would that make it a student here at St Jude's?' Charlie asked. 'Or is there someone out there who knows enough about you to hack into your Facebook account and leave dead birds and messages in your room?'

'One message, dead bird – singular,' I said firmly.

'Someone here in the college,' Connie decided, and she looked around the circle of faces in the room. 'Girl or guy? Maybe even a teacher.'

'We're not getting any answers staring at each other,' Luke told her. 'It's not going to be anyone in this room, is it?'

'And say it's not a joke.' Zara broke the uneasy silence. 'Say it's serious.'

'That's why we wanted everyone to be here,' Jack explained. 'We all need to be looking out for Alyssa.'

'Definitely,' Zara and Eugenie agreed. Others nodded – all except Galina who sat quietly in a corner with a hand over her injured mouth.

'We don't want it to be like last time, with Lily and Paige, when Alyssa dealt with it alone.'

'Right.' Luke threw a lot of force into one short word. I guess he still felt that he'd let Paige down by not being there for her, either before her so-called accident or after, when she was seriously ill in hospital.

'Yeah, we know you better now,' Zara conceded. 'Last term you were new to the place. We weren't sure where you fitted in.'

'I'm still not certain,' I admitted. 'It's hard to be the new girl at St Jude's.'

'Yes.' Galina let her hand drop to her lap and we all saw the bright red scar, the stitches and swelling on her lip. 'Very hard to be new girl.'

Saying goodbye to Jack that night was hard too, and we would have stood longer in the quad where the snow was twenty centimetres deep, hugging and keeping each other warm and safe, if Shirley Welford, the member of staff who was on late duty that night, hadn't walked by.

'Further maths, private tuition, midday tomorrow,' she reminded Jack, who quickly stepped away from me.

'I hadn't forgotten,' he told Shirley.

'We'll be doing more work on Newton-Raphson's use of iterative methods to solve equations.'

It was clear that Jack's straight-laced maths teacher was making a point and that she wasn't going to leave the quad before I did.

'Night, Jack,' I murmured as I slipped away.

Up in my room, I was glad that Galina was already asleep. I checked my phone and found two junk emails plus a text message from a number I didn't recognize – no words, just a row of emoticon red hearts.

Forget it – it's a mistake, I told myself. But, as you know, that's the problem with me – it's a physical impossibility for me to forget – so I spent the whole night wondering who had sent the hearts and listening for more creaks in the corridor and more fingers scratching at the window. I lay with my eyes open, my ear attuned to every sound.

And I was still wide awake when another message came though at 7.00 a.m.

They arrested Alex, Jayden wrote. **Meet me.**

When? Where? I texted back.

Today at twelve, Ainslee, Lock-keeper's Cottage.

chapter five

Life was full of surprises – wild boy Jayden, with his hunched, feral look and his warning for me not to go near the Scarlett Hartley murder, had changed his mind.

'Don't worry – I'll be careful,' I told Jack over breakfast.

'I'd come with you but . . .'

'. . . But you've got a class with Shirley. I know.' I was still feeling the afterglow of our train-station reunion so I reached out and took his hand. 'It'll be OK. Jayden is the hero who rescued me from Harry Embsay, remember, and I promise not to get dragged into anything I can't handle.'

Jack was still edgy. 'It's not Jayden who bothers me. It's the nutter who's sneaking into your room and leaving weird notes.'

'Yeah, it freaks me out too. But everyone knows what's happening now and sooner or later the guy is going to make a mistake – someone will spot him or we'll be able to track him down.'

'Why not wait until I'm through with maths? Then we could both meet Jayden.'

'It's not dangerous,' I insisted. 'I can deal with it on my own.'

'So let me write down the number of the text with the hearts,' Jack decided. 'I'll run through my list of contacts, and if it's not there I'll ask around to see if anyone recognizes it.'

'OK, and I'll meet Jayden, find out why they arrested Alex.'

We agreed on a plan and went to our morning classes – Jack to physics with Dr Alex King, and me to English literature with Bryony and Synge's *Playboy of the Western World*.

I got to the classroom five minutes early to find Hooper and Eugenie already there.

'Did you notice that Mikki the gorilla's back?' Hooper mentioned as he lifted his bag from an empty seat and invited me to sit next to him.

'Mikhail? How come? Did they charge him then release him on bail?'

Hooper gave a quick shrug. 'You share a room with Galina – I thought you'd know the answer to that.'

'No, she didn't mention anything.' Actually, I hadn't talked to her at all that morning since she'd still been asleep when I left the room. 'She definitely won't be happy that Mikhail's back on the scene and I don't blame her.'

'Anyway, he's here. I saw him outside Saint Sam's room on my way to class.'

After that, Bryony arrived and plunged us into an analysis of the romance between Christy Mahon and Pegeen Mike – is it more comic than tragic or the other way round? Etcetera, etcetera.

Back in my room at eleven, I found Galina crying on her bed. Her glorious mane of dark hair was tousled, her stitched lip swollen and sore.

'Here,' I said, offering tissues from the box I kept in my top drawer. I sat beside her and waited for her to dry her eyes.

She blew her nose and grimaced when her hand brushed against the scar. 'The police, they let him go,' she murmured.

'Mikhail? Yes, Hooper told me. Did they charge him?'

'No. They do nothing. He tells them it's his job – he must protect me. He says sometimes I am wild and do stupid things. Like yesterday, I yell at him and run away. I fall over in forest and cut my lip. What can he do? The police believe what he says.'

I handed Galina more tissues. 'I suppose they don't have any witnesses or evidence – it's your word against his. And you couldn't make your dad understand what actually happened?'

'I can't talk to him. He is in New York at meetings. Salomea takes his calls.'

'And she said it was OK for Mikhail to carry on doing his job?'

She nodded and blinked back more tears. 'Before Salomea, me and Papa, we have good life. We travel; we have fun. Then he sees her dance in St Petersburg – he loves women like this – my mother too, she dances in Bolshoi Ballet when she is young. Salomea is beautiful as Mayerling in story of lovers who die. She is out of this world. Papa goes backstage to meet her; he falls in love.'

As Galina's voice fell away, I understood for the first time how tough it must have been for her. An image flitted through my head of a beautiful glossy blackbird trapped inside a golden cage. 'How old were you?'

'Thirteen. In this year Papa marries Salomea and runs from Putin's Russia. Putin says Papa is corrupt, that he steals oil and gas from people of Russia. They will put him in prison for rest of life.'

'So he can't go back? But you can, I guess.'

Galina dabbed at her eyes and shook her head. 'There are too many bad people there. They hate Papa so they promise to hurt me. I cannot go back, even to visit my mother.'

'That's really tough,' I sighed. And I remembered her vivid account of the accident that wasn't an accident in Monte Carlo. 'The bad people you're talking about – were they involved in the thing with the boat, where one of your friends died?'

'At first I think no but now I think maybe. These men, they follow us everywhere but you never catch them. They hide, they wait for next chance.'

'You poor thing, that must be awful,' I said. I almost told her about the conversation I'd overheard the day before – Sergei talking to Salomea on the phone, saying that things hadn't worked out – but I held it back for later, after Galina had had time to get herself back together. 'Right now, can I do anything to help?'

She looked at me with moist, puppy-dog eyes. 'Yes, Alyssa. You can be my friend.'

At that point Raisa had come into the room and clucked around Galina like a mother hen. She spoke in short, gentle sentences that ended in an endearment that sounded like *lyublmaya moy*. Then she took up a brush and drew it through Galina's tangled hair.

Relaxing now that my roommate had someone with her, I'd hurried off on one of the school bikes, cycling down the cleared drive between banks of snow and out between the wrought-iron gates, along the lane to the Bottoms, where I managed to catch the 11.30 bus into town. From the bus station I walked on towards the canal and Lock-keeper's Cottage.

Jayden was already there and, though he'd set up this meeting, my heroic rescuer didn't look pleased to see me. Mind you, he never looks cheerful (he has the wrong set of facial muscles, I guess) and there can't be many reasons to smile when a student in your school gets killed and one of your best mates lands in police custody.

Hands thrust deep in his pockets, with biscuit-coloured Bolt sniffing busily at a couple of crushed cans that had recently been dumped on the steps down to the canal, Jayden scowled a greeting. 'You're late.'

'Five minutes. Sorry – the snow was bad. I had a lot to do . . .'

'Oh, I know, Alyssa – you're always so busy, running around picking up clues, chasing killers . . .'

'. . . Dealing with your sarcasm,' I added. 'And, you're right, I am busy so go ahead and tell me what we're doing here.'

'I wanted you to take a look at where it happened to see if you notice anything. It's a hundred metres in that direction.' He pointed along the cycle path, past a high brick wall bordering a supermarket car park. Beyond that I could make out police tape, a square white tent erected by a forensic team and a *'Closed to pedestrians'* notice half obscured by snow.

'I'm not sure what you think I'll see that the cops haven't already spotted,' I told Jayden who was trailing a couple of steps behind.

'Look anyway,' he insisted.

'OK, you lead the way.' I stood to one side then followed him down the steps, noticing a thin film of ice on the surface of the canal and taking care not to slip on the path. Close to the spot where Scarlett's body had been recovered, I saw that the ice had been shattered and transparent shards floated on the black water – possibly where police divers had gone in to search for clues.

Turning to Jayden, I thought one more warning might be in order. 'You have to understand that I might not be able to help this time round. Memory is my thing. I can rerun events that have happened to me – what I saw, what I heard, even smells and how things felt – but I can't conjure stuff up out of thin air.'

'OK, I know you weren't around when Scarlett died. But you did talk to Ursula then Alex, so now you're involved.'

'Even though you didn't want me to be,' I reminded him. 'What changed?'

'They got Alex, remember!'

'So your buddy gets arrested and now you expect me to come riding in on my white charger?'

'You got it,' he said, moody and hating to admit that he needed me. 'You people at St Jude's are the brainy ones. You know the right people; you're in the right place at the right time.'

'OK, I'm involved,' I admitted. 'But only on the margins and something is telling me to keep it that way.' I wouldn't share with Jayden that I'd been freaked out by imaginary fingers scratching at the window, or any of the other creepy things that had happened lately – the fake Facebook pictures, the dead robin, the notes, the emoticon hearts. Somehow I felt he wouldn't make the most sympathetic of listeners.

'But I asked you and you're here,' he said stubbornly.

'Because I talked to Alex and I felt sorry for him.' I watched Bolt trot ahead, detour around the *Closed to pedestrians* sign and scoot under the police tape, making a neat pattern of prints in the snow. 'Anyway, I don't think he did it,' I added.

Bolt sniffed at a heap of shifted snow then cocked his bandy leg to pee against the white forensic tent. 'I hope no one's working inside there,' I commented.

Jayden shrugged. 'So exactly how did it go – your conversation with Alex?'

'I was walking in the school grounds, Alex was on his bike. He fell off. I didn't recognize him at first so I ran up and asked what he was doing on private property.'

'Yeah, Alyssa – a guy falls off his bike and you tell him he's trespassing. Typical.'

'We could stop right now,' I said angrily. 'I could walk away.'

Jayden's scowl deepened. He tilted his head forward then looked up at me from under knotted eyebrows. 'Sometimes you come across as a hard bitch, you know that, Alyssa? Anyway, forget I said that – you still owe me one.'

A favour for him stopping Harry Embsay from throttling me. It was totally true that without Jayden and Bolt I wouldn't still be alive, but somehow with Jayden it didn't pay to show gratitude. 'You saved me, now you want me to help you get your mate out of jail. OK, I'll try.'

Still glaring, he waited for me to come up with something.

'Do you know why they arrested him?'

'Socos picked up fingerprints on the wrench they found.'

'Scene-of-crime officers? Alex's prints?'

Jayden nodded. 'Plus, it turns out he didn't have an alibi for the time Scarlett was killed.'

'But he told me his dad dragged him off to a family party.'

'Yeah, but he made an excuse and left before midnight – the cops dragged that out of one of the cousins.'

'Not good,' I muttered as Bolt disappeared round the back of the flimsy tent. I went through the few facts I'd picked up from my meeting with Alex. 'He didn't mention that. And there's something else that I've been wondering about – which is why didn't Alex try to contact Scarlett on New Year's Day? They'd only been together for a week, but from what I hear he was totally into her. Ursula said he'd practically stalked her for weeks before she agreed to go out with him. So he would want to talk to her, send texts, meet her every chance he got.'

'How do we know he didn't?' Jayden asked the same thing Sammy Beckett had at Ainslee station.

'We don't.' For the first time I heard scuffling noises from inside the tent then the sound of Velcro being unfastened. A figure in white overalls emerged and yelled at us.

'Is this your dog?' the police forensic woman demanded.

Bolt reappeared, still sniffing and peeing against the side of the tent.

'Call him, Jayden!' I muttered under my breath.

'He's contaminating a crime scene,' the woman warned. 'If this is your Staffie, grab him before I get our dog handlers to come and deal with him.'

'Call him!' I hissed.

'Heel!' Jayden said between clenched teeth, and Bolt obeyed.

'Let's go,' I told him, turning back the way we'd come. I was eager to leave because the place where Scarlett had died was seedy – high walls and rotting fences to one side, the frozen canal to the other – and it was all too easy to picture her lonely, dark, violent death. They'd found the wrench used as a weapon, which of course had further implicated Alex. 'Did they find her phone to see if Alex did try to make contact?' I wanted to know.

Jayden shrugged. 'How would I know? Come on, Alyssa – you're the brainy one and you're not giving me anything!'

'What do you want? You want me to *invent* something just to get you off my back?'

Then suddenly I stopped. I heard Alex's voice again and

I saw the stricken, wounded look on his face.

'The first I knew about it was the cops coming knocking at my door, not telling me what it was about, asking when did I last see Scarlett? I say, in Starbucks in the shopping centre at one o'clock on New Year's Eve – why?'

'OK, maybe there is something I can do,' I decided.

Trotting ahead, Bolt had stopped at the worn stone steps we'd used to come down on to the towpath. He turned and panted, waiting for Jayden to tell him what to do.

'Stay!' Jayden called, then turned his attention back on me. 'About effing time, memory girl.'

I pressed my lips together and tried not to retaliate. 'I'll be in touch later today,' I told him.

'One more thing before you go.' He eyed me suspiciously, as if I was the one who was totally to blame for Scarlett ending up in the canal and for his mate being held in custody. 'There's a kid at your school I think you should check out.'

'At St Jude's?' Immediately and illogically I locked into the existing fear that it was someone I knew well who was behind the Facebook pictures, the dead bird, the sick challenges. It was a gut feeling and I still didn't have hard evidence for any link with Scarlett's death, but my skin began to prickle as I realized that Jayden might be about to deliver it. 'Who?'

'Will Harrison,' he muttered, hardly moving his lips.

I had to lean in and ask him to repeat the name.

'You heard me – Will Harrison.'

My heart gave a small jolt. 'Why – what's the connection?'

'Not many people know this, but he's one of Scarlett's exes.'

Another jolt, a tingle like an electric shock. I stared at Jayden.

'I checked it out with Ursula – she gave me the details,' he insisted. Then he turned his attention to Bolt, who was sniffing and cocking his leg, rummaging in amongst the tattered pages of an old newspaper blown into a smelly corner under the stone steps. 'Fetch!' he said when he saw his dog sniff at what looked like a length of string lying in the snow.

Bolt didn't hesitate. He picked it up and carried it between his teeth towards Jayden, then dropped it at his feet. There it lay on the dirty snow – not a length of string but a lost or discarded cable from a phone charger.

Neither Jayden nor I had noticed the forensic officer follow us along the canal path, but Bolt did. He curled back his lips, bared his teeth and snarled.

'Don't even think about picking it up,' she said, swiftly producing a plastic bag and scooping the cable into it. 'Inspector Ripley will be very interested in this. She may even want to thank you in person – watch this space.'

Swearing, Jayden took the steps two at a time, but when he reached the top a uniformed officer stood in his way. He forced Jayden to give his name and address, a process like pulling teeth as it turned out.

I gave my details without any problem and answered questions about what we were doing and why.

'I don't see you leaving any floral tributes,' the uniform said drily. 'No misspelled, heartfelt messages of regret.'

Jayden upped his tally of extreme swear words and was cautioned by the officer.

Bolt emitted a long, low growl.

In turn I was cautioned about the company I chose to keep. On the whole, I reckon we were both lucky to walk away with no more than the equivalent of a referee's yellow card and a warning to stay out of trouble in future.

'I'll text you later today,' I told Jayden as he swung off towards the centre of town.

Greenlea Shopping Centre was twenty-five years old and jaded. It didn't have two tiers of designer shops or a soaring glass roof, and if the architect who designed it was still alive he ought to be ashamed.

I walked through the wide entrance and up a slope towards H&M, with Boots on my left and a tired-looking department store on my right. Past that, I turned right towards Monsoon, and quickly came to a covered courtyard with a Caffé Nero and a Starbucks side by side.

'Skinny latte,' I told the girl behind the counter at Starbucks. She took the order and asked my name while I read her badge. She was called Lucy. I paid for the coffee then shuffled forward to collect my drink made by a young guy who'd stopped vacantly unloading clean mugs into the station by the till. 'You weren't working during the day last Thursday by any chance?' I asked as casually as I could. 'Lunchtime of New Year's Eve.'

Karl (I read his name badge) looked long and hard at me. 'Why?'

'A friend of mine was in here.'

'Last Thursday, hmm, let's see. Your friend wouldn't be Scarlett Hartley, would it? The girl who got herself killed?'

I nodded. So much for my casual sideways approach.

'You're wasting your time. I don't know anything.'

'It's OK, relax. I was just wondering if Scarlett came in here a lot, and if you know who she used to come in with.'

Luckily for me sullen Karl was elbowed out by gobby Lucy, the girl who had taken my order. 'Can you believe it!' she gushed. 'The poor kid was in here during the day, happy as anything. Next thing we knew, they'd fished her out of the canal.'

'So who was she with?' I prompted, only to be ignored.

'And the way he killed her with the metal thingy – really nasty. And I was chatting with her saying hi, how was her day, not knowing what was going to happen . . .' Lucy shuddered. 'What did you ask Karl? Oh yeah, did she come here often. Well, she would get together with a bunch of mates after school and, yeah, at the weekends. And you know what I heard – they arrested the kid she was here with on Thursday. That's right, isn't it? She came in with Alex Driffield.'

Bored as hell by his job, life, the whole universe, Karl had already gone back to unloading crockery so my chatty informer rattled on down the track without him.

'She was happy, they both were – everything was cool.

You'd never think there was a thing wrong. They just sat and drank coffee, used their phones to text, chatted. I didn't really notice them until I heard Alex stand up and start to yell.'

'At Scarlett?'

'No, at another kid who came along and didn't order anything – he just went right up to their table and whatever he said – I didn't hear it – made Alex jump up and start shouting.'

'What did he look like, this new kid?'

'I don't know. I didn't get a good look. The place was crowded and he had his back to me.'

'Tall or short?'

'Tall – definitely. He had a big scarf and a hat, a grey one. When Alex kicked off and everyone started staring, he ran off past Monsoon, back towards Station Road.'

'What did Scarlett do?'

'She must have said for Alex to sit down and cool it, which he did. He looked kind of embarrassed – they both did. We were busy with customers at the time so I didn't think much of it.'

'But you've told the police?'

'Yeah, after they put out the appeal. I went to them cos I thought this stranger guy who upset Alex might be important.'

'He was wearing a hat? Could you tell what colour his hair was?'

'Fair,' she said with a frown. She thought some more. 'Yeah, definitely blond – I could see that much.'

She paused again and gave suspicious, surly Karl a chance to come back at me.

'What are you, anyway – a journalist?' he asked.

'No.'

'So why all the questions?'

I gave Karl the truth, so far as it went. 'I told a friend I'd try to help so that's what I'm doing.'

'Did you see my iPad – is it in our room?' I asked Galina, who was standing at the top of the stone steps by the portrait of Lady Anne. I'd come back from Ainslee and met up with Jack in the technology centre where we'd chatted through my meeting with Jayden and my subsequent drop-in visit to Starbucks. 'I thought I left it in the classroom after English this morning, but I looked and it wasn't there.'

'Not in room.' She spoke awkwardly through her lip stitches and swelling. 'I go now to after-school tutorial with Bryony, sorry.'

Which left me and Jack walking on under Anne's silent, centuries-old gaze to search in my room for the iPad – on the table, under the bed, amidst Galina's clutter on the windowsill.

'It's not like you to lose things,' Jack said, taking a look in my bedside cabinet.

I sighed and sat on my bed. 'Do you think I'm a hard bitch?' I asked suddenly.

He sat beside me. 'Where did that come from?'

'Jayden – that's what he told me.'

'Jesus – Jayden isn't exactly the one to talk. Pots and kettles and all that.'

'I know. But do you? Tell me honestly.' I knew Jack had found it difficult to get through to me in the beginning of our relationship and I'd tried at the time to explain why I found it hard to show my emotions – well, you would if you'd got my family history. Remember, I'd lost my mum and dad and learned how to bottle up grief at a very young age.

Jack leaned in closer and tilted my face until I was looking into his eyes. He stroked my chin with his thumb. 'Do I even have to tell you?'

'Yes, please.'

'OK, Alyssa – you're amazing. Don't listen to Jayden or any of the others because they don't know you, and I do.'

'Yes,' I whispered.

'I know that you're the most gorgeous girl I've ever met. Plus you care about people and you always tell me the truth . . . You want me to go on?'

I nodded.

'If the others can't see the real you, that's their problem. I can.'

He waited for me to say something, but I just kept on nodding and trying to stop tears from welling up.

'I love you,' he said simply.

We were alone in my room and broke all the school rules. He held me tight and we kissed. Our kisses took over from words, and my longing for Jack swept through me as it always did. I loved his lips pressing against my mouth and neck. I gave myself up to him.

'Here it is,' Jack said as he fished the iPad out from under my pillow. We'd spent an hour in bed together and now we were getting dressed. 'How did it get under there?'

'Someone hid it?' I suggested.

Jack handed it to me. 'You're sure you didn't put it there? . . . OK, you didn't!' He put up both hands to defend himself as I attacked him with the pillow.

'Why would I hide my own iPad?'

'OK, but Galina might – just to annoy you.'

'No, we're best buddies now.'

'Yes, Alyssa. You can be my friend,' she says with melting, puppy-dog eyes.

'She's super-rich and lonely. She loves her dad but not her stepmother. Someone probably tried to kill her in Monaco and now she's convinced that her bodyguard wants to kidnap her, but the police don't believe her. You can understand why I'm feeling protective.'

'See – heart of gold,' Jack reminded me. 'Zara, Eugenie, Connie, they're all jealous because Galina's so bloody hot. You're the only one on her side.'

With alarm bells still ringing in my head, the first thing I did was check my inbox. There was only one new message and the sender's email address was cockrobin@gmail.com.

'Oh God!'

My legs went weak and I sat back down on the bed. I realized that the guy must have found my iPad in the classroom and had been about to return it to me. But then he'd had the warped idea of sending me another message –

Tut-tut – still no warmer? – and hiding the iPad to cause maximum stress. He could've been typing in my room, maybe even sitting on my bed . . .

Jack saw my reaction and took the iPad from me. He read the message out loud. *'Hi again, Alyssa. Tut-tut – still no warmer? In fact, maybe even colder. I'm disappointed in you.'*

'Listen.' Jack insisted on reading the rest. *'First Scarlett, now you. I'm doing all I can to join the dots, make the comparisons and point you in the right direction, but you're just not paying attention. I care about you, Alyssa. I want to warn you. I don't want to hurt you.'* Jack stopped reading and swallowed hard. 'For fuck's sake!'

I snatched the iPad back to see how the message ended. It was a quote from 'Killing You Softly', an old song from the seventies – something I'd heard Aunt Olivia play, but not quite the right words.

I murmured as my eidetic memory conjured up the lyrics whether I wanted it to or not. I stood up and obsessively checked everything in the room as I went through the words of the song – opened my wardrobe and looked inside, pulled out the top drawer of my cabinet to see if anything had been moved, OCD in overdrive, which is what happens when I'm scared.

'This pen wasn't in here,' I told Jack, 'and those shoes were on the floor, not in the wardrobe.'

'Alyssa, calm down,' Jack said softly.

But the words in my head wouldn't go away – the ones about a man playing on his lover's pain, adoring her one minute then ignoring her, treating her as if she was invisible – a way of killing her softly with his love. 'Killing Me Softly'.

Not 'you', but 'me'. Didn't this psycho realize he'd got the lyrics wrong?

Yes, of course he did. Killing *you* softly was exactly what he meant to say.

'And this isn't my lipstick – it's Galina's.' I stopped long enough to pick up the small gold tube from my cabinet and take off the top. 'See – bright red. It's not my colour. Whoever did this put it there deliberately!'

Jack couldn't stop me from running out of the room and down the corridor, crossing the quad and taking the stairs up to the boys' dorm two at a time.

It was nine o'clock at night – starlit and cold.

'Where are you going?' he demanded as he sprinted through the snow to catch up with me.

'I need to talk to Will. And before you ask – no, it can't wait!'

'Why now? What's Will got to do with this?'

'It's something Jayden told me. I need to talk to him. Are you with me?'

Jack nodded and we knocked on the door of the room that Will shared with Hooper. It was Hooper who answered.

'What's up?' he wanted to know, blinking like an owl in the daylight. He was in his usual baggy grey sweater and beat-up jeans, barefoot and tousle-haired, as if he'd been lying on his bed fully clothed. 'You two look like you had a fight.'

'No – no fight,' I said.

'So why are you freaking out?'

'I need to speak to Will.'

'He's not here. I'm working on something important so he went over to Luke's room to give me some peace and quiet. Are you sure you're OK?'

'Yeah, thanks.' I hurried on, leaving Jack to give Hooper a quick explanation for me breaking yet another rule. When I knocked on Luke's door, it was Connie who answered. She was half dressed or half undressed, I couldn't tell which – anyway she was also definitely breaking the rules.

'Don't ask!' she warned.

'I'm not even interested,' I told her truthfully. 'I'm looking for Will.'

'Here, miss!' he called from inside the room like a kid in class answering a register.

I went in and found Luke, Marco and Will sitting cross-legged on the floor with Zara and a pack of playing cards. Again – don't ask.

Jack and Hooper joined us, so now we had me, Zara, Connie, Will, Marco, Luke, Jack and Hooper crammed into one tiny room. There was a low light from the bedside lamp and a muggy, airless atmosphere.

'Yeah, Alyssa – what's up?' Will asked with his back turned and without bothering to get up.

'You might not want to talk about this in front of the others,' I told him. 'We could go outside.'

Cue a new frisson from Zara and the Black Widow, followed by a duet of lilting 'whoo's and 'ooh's.

'Miss, can I finish my game of cards first?' he asked.

'Will, this is important and I'm saying you might want to keep it private between you and me.'

'Whoo!' BWS said again, but this time Zara kept quiet. The tension in the room was as thick and heavy as the air.

Will shrugged. 'Say whatever you have to say – I don't care who hears.'

I was still staring at his broad back and blond crop. 'It's about Scarlett Hartley,' I said slowly and quietly.

I saw his spine stiffen and then he swivelled round, ready to stand up and leave the room with me. But it was too late – Connie moved in and blocked his way. 'I think we all need to hear this, Will.'

He blanked her to look straight at me. 'What about Scarlett?'

Somehow I managed to steady my heartbeat and shrug off the creepy feeling I had about my repeat intruder. 'You two were together when you were at Ainslee Comp – she was your girlfriend.'

'So?'

Will's monosyllabic response was drowned out by the reaction of the others. 'You dated the dead girl?' Zara gasped.

'Whoa, Will, you kept that one quiet,' Luke laughed.

'So?' he repeated. If looks could kill I'd have been dead on the spot.

'So why didn't you have any reaction to her murder? Why did you warn me to stay away?'

'And why didn't you share with any of us?' Connie added,

112

more intense and confrontational than either Zara or Luke.

None of us were expecting Will's next move, which was to launch himself like a rugby full back, not at Connie but at me. He didn't think it through, obviously.

It happened so fast that he actually made contact, knocking me off my feet. I felt the air leave my lungs in a rush as I crashed into the door, slamming it shut and knocking Jack and Hooper out into the corridor. Luke and Marco piled straight in to drag Will off me, giving me space to stand up. I felt the door swing open and saw Jack move in on Will. We were all crushed together, arms flailing, everyone yelling, me trying to calm things down.

'If there's a reason for keeping quiet, now's your chance to tell us,' I insisted. 'You have to – the police have arrested Alex Driffield and I think he's innocent. We need you to be straight with us.'

'*You* think!' Will hurled his comments at me over the general noise. 'Alyssa Stephens thinks Alex Driffield is innocent – holy shit! Now she's got her super-sleuth claws in me!'

Jack didn't wait any longer – he swung a punch at Will, made contact with his abdomen and I watched him bend over double. Luke and Marco did their macho thing of dragging them apart.

'Wait – give Will a chance,' Zara said, while I heard Hooper sprint off down the corridor. 'Come on, Will, we're listening.'

Holding his ribs, Will straightened up. 'So I knew Scarlett,' he began.

'"Knew" in what sense?' Connie was the one who wanted to get this bit straight. 'Come on – no need to be shy.'

'Eff off, Connie, it's none of your business. So I knew Scarlett and, yeah, it affected me when they found her. But what am I going to do – go around telling everyone I was her ex and she dumped me for some other kid who she met on holiday? Look what happens when you guys do find out – straight away I'm suspect number one.'

'Yeah, I get that,' Luke conceded. 'The cops are going to be looking at all of Scarlett's exes.'

'And it wasn't like it was a big thing between us.' Will played down the relationship, which the guys in the room didn't react to but the girls did.

'Maybe not a big thing for you,' Connie pointed out. 'But maybe for her.'

'Didn't you hear what I said? Scarlett dumped me, not the other way round. I wasn't into it and neither was she.'

The Black Widow was the one to back up my original train of thought. 'So why hide it – what's the point? Was it really to stay off the police radar? Cos, if it was, from this point on you failed.'

'Who's going to tell them?' Will used his newly bulked up body to block the exit and set up another challenge.

Connie screwed up her lips, paused then delivered her answer with perfect timing. 'Everyone in this room,' she said. 'When Detective Inspector June Ripley comes knocking, we'll all make a point of telling her what you didn't want us to know.'

chapter six

It turned out June Ripley was as impressive and scary in person as she had been when I'd seen her on the small screen.

'Thanks for the coffee, Molly,' she said as I went into the bursar's room and sat down opposite her. Smaller than I'd pictured, she was clean cut and polished in tailored trousers and the same black jacket that she'd worn on TV, with a heavy silver necklace over a high-necked cream sweater. Her movements as she reached out to take the cup were quick and precise.

Molly checked with me to see if I wanted coffee too.

'No thanks.' I waited as calmly as I could, running through last night's exchange of texts with Jayden.

Nothing useful from this end, I'd said. **Alex had an argument in Starbucks last Thursday, but I can't fit it into the picture yet.**

He'd texted me back. **Cops called at my house. Phone charger cable we found was used to strangle Scarlett before killer hit her on head. Thought you should know.**

So now, in the weak wintry sunlight, sitting opposite June Ripley, I expected a follow-up line of questioning.

She studied me closely and for ages didn't say a word, though it felt as if she was dissecting me on a mortuary slab. I tried not to fidget and to concentrate instead on the melting snow on the lawn outside Molly's window. Then the connecting door between the bursar's room and Saint Sam's office opened and the principal joined us.

Dr Samuel Webb deserves some space here. He runs St Jude's and gives himself totally to the school's nothing-but-the-best ideal. To do this he sacrifices any personal life that he might ever have had – well, none of the students know that stuff because he keeps it so much in the background that you just assume it doesn't exist. No wife, no kids, no family photos on his desk, not even a pet dog, but he's an excellent PR man: 'Results prove that St Jude's offers the highest quality preparation for the baccalaureate examination in the UK. We offer our students the opportunity to develop both scholastically and as individuals.'

You name it, Saint Sam has it covered.

Incidentally, he got his nickname because he never loses his temper, is always on-message, plus his male baldness pattern makes him look like a medieval monk.

So when he joined June Ripley and me in the bursar's office, Saint Sam smiled calmly and emptily at me. 'The inspector is here as a result of yesterday's incident by the canal,' he explained. 'There really is nothing to worry about, Alyssa, as long as you answer a few simple questions.'

'That makes it sound a little bit formal,' June Ripley interrupted. 'I'm really not here for answers – just to thank you for helping us to find the phone cable. It belonged to the dead girl, Scarlett Hartley. I'm sorry if this upsets you, but I can tell you it was used to apply pressure round her neck.'

'I didn't find it,' I interrupted with a shiver. 'It was Jayden's dog.'

'Yes – Jayden Johnson – I saw him last night. Well, whatever. The cable is with forensics now and will form an important piece of evidence.'

I thought it was a long way for June Ripley to drive from her office in Ainslee just to thank me for this, and I was still feeling dissected by her sharp gaze. All I could do was sit it out and see what came next. Meanwhile, Saint Sam smiled and hovered.

'Jayden didn't give me a good reason why you and he arranged to meet by the canal yesterday afternoon,' Inspector Ripley said, quick and direct. 'I'm assuming he's a friend of yours.'

'He is.'

'And a friend of Scarlett and Alex.'

'They all went to Ainslee Comp together.'

'Jayden told me Alex wouldn't have had any involvement in Scarlett's death. I guess you share that opinion.' She said this without any rising inflection – a statement, not a question. 'People who know Alex seem to like him. He's very popular.'

'I do like him – yes.'

'And the meeting with Jayden at the crime scene – it was to show respect to Scarlett.'

This time I didn't have time to respond before suddenly and without warning the inspector veered into fresh territory. 'Tell me about last night, Alyssa.'

'What about last night?'

'The missing iPad for starters.'

'It's OK – I lost it then I found it under my pillow.'

'But there was a threatening message.'

First Scarlett, now you. I'm doing all I can to join the dots, make the comparisons and point you in the right direction and you're just not paying attention. I care about you, Alyssa. I want to warn you. I don't want to hurt you . . . Killing you softly . . .

I nodded at Inspector Ripley. 'How did . . . ?'

'. . .We know? Jack Hooper talked to Molly. He's the one who ran to fetch her when Will Harrison was causing trouble. Jack thought the situation was getting out of hand, but from what I hear by the time Molly arrived things had calmed down.'

'True,' I told her. 'I guess Hooper told you what the row was about?'

'About Will concealing his relationship with Scarlett – yes. Don't worry on that score either. I already knew about that . . .'

'From Jayden?'

She nodded. 'Jack Hooper also told us he was worried about you.'

I frowned and glanced up at Saint Sam who had stood in my sight line, just behind June Ripley.

'Alyssa, Jack says that you've been the victim of some fairly unpleasant practical jokes, culminating in yesterday's threatening message.'

The lyrics of 'Killing Me Softly' blasted their way back into my mind and I shuddered.

'Someone broke a couple of panes in your window,' the

inspector went on. 'They left a dead bird on the windowsill. Molly brought the glaziers in to fix it. Apparently they told her the panes couldn't have been broken from the outside and it couldn't have been done by the bird accidentally getting into the room then trying to escape. Considerable force had been used to break the glass.'

I took a sharp breath and glanced at the bursar.

A series of images replaced the song lyrics. They flashed through my head, as clear and vivid as single frames from a movie – still photographs snatched from a fast-running action sequence.

Poolside photos, shiny sunblock on tanned flesh, a red and gold bikini.

Dead bird on my windowsill, poor little robin redbreast.

Note between bottles scrawled in red felt tip – Who killed cock robin?

Red hearts from an unknown number.

A mislaid iPad, an intruder in my room, 'Killing You Softly', Galina's red lipstick on my cabinet. And Scarlett! Knock off a 't' from the end of her name and scarlet equals a vivid shade of red. This is what the killer had been teasing me about and telling me all along.

A spike of fear ran through me as I made the connections.

Inspector Ripley read the signals. 'What is it, Alyssa?'

'Every time he – whoever he is – does something, he leaves a signature.' Grasping the edge of Molly's desk, my knuckles turned white. 'There's a theme to all this – it proves that it's done by the same guy and he's playing a game with me.'

'What kind of signature?' Ripley's attention was razor sharp.

'More of a colour than an actual signature,' I explained as I finally made the connection. 'Red – he always leaves me something red. He makes the link with Scarlett's name'.

'I looked in my contacts list and I couldn't recognize the number.' That lunchtime Jack walked with me in the school grounds. With snow still on the ground, no one else was out there so we had the lake and the woods to ourselves. 'Alyssa, did you hear what I said – I couldn't find out who sent the hearts message?'

'Yeah. Well, he was never going to make it that easy,' I sighed. The snow had melted in random patches, uncovering areas of flattened, yellowish grass and there was still a film of ice on the lake. I was wrapped up in a big plaid scarf and heavy jacket, wearing my uniform with black tights and Uggs. Jack braved the weather without jacket, scarf or gloves.

We were alone, walking with fingers interlaced, reluctant to talk about bad things but knowing that we had to.

'You know what else Inspector Ripley told me – after I told her about the red theme?'

Side by side, we walked on between the trees, raising rooks from the tops of bare trees, sending them flapping and cawing noisily into the leaden sky. 'No, but you'll tell me – right?'

'She backed up what Ursula said – the principal at Ainslee Comp confirmed that Scarlett Hartley did have the same type of memory as me. We definitely shared the eidetic curse of not being able to forget a smell, a sight, a sound.'

'So what are they implying?'

'The similarity is too strong to ignore. It has to be significant.'

'Are they saying that the killer's finished playing his sick game with Scarlett and is moving on to his next victim?' Jack stopped on the track close to where I'd run into Alex before they arrested him. 'From Scarlett to you?'

'It seems I'm his new target,' I confirmed.

'And they're saying that he played these sick jokes on Scarlett before he killed her?'

'I asked Ripley that but she wouldn't tell me.'

'Why not?'

'Because, when you think about it, those are details of the Scarlett investigation that a cop isn't going to reveal.'

'So what is she going to do to protect you – anything?'

I shook my head. 'Nothing much. You know what the police are like – she said they can't do anything until a crime has been committed. You can have a stalker following you around for months, and if you tell them about it that's what they'll say – no action until stalker guy moves in with actual threats, or else he breaks into your house to steal your underwear – whatever.'

'This guy did break in,' Jack pointed out. 'He was in your room when you weren't there – more than once.'

'He didn't touch my knicker drawer so it's not serious enough, apparently.' I gave Jack a hollow smile, shrugged then went on. 'Dead bird, weird messages sealed with love and kisses – they could still be classed as minor bullying, and we all know how common that is.'

Jack gave an exasperated sigh. 'So what about Saint Sam – did he take any of this seriously?'

'He was the same as Ripley – he underplayed it.'

Dr Webb had acknowledged the crucial memory similarity between me and Scarlett, but then he'd pointed out that Scarlett's death very possibly had nothing to do with her exceptional memory and, besides, our background circumstances were totally different.

'Scarlett was permitted to roam the streets during the early hours of New Year's Day but security here at St Jude's is tight,' he'd told the inspector. 'Students have to be back by midnight. Each and every visitor has to report to Reception on arrival and we have CCTV cameras covering all areas of the school, both internal and external.' Some of which isn't reassuring when you stop to think about it – for instance, which killer in his right mind would present himself to Carol Jenkins in Reception?

'He's underplaying it because he doesn't want the whiff of scandal getting up parents' nostrils,' Jack realized. 'In the end, what did Ripley say?'

'That they'd definitely keep an eye on things, whatever that means. Then she said goodbye to me and asked Molly to send for Will. He's still in with them, I guess.'

With a slight shake of his head, Jack dropped my hand and walked on through the woods.

'What's wrong?' I asked, catching up with him on the brow of a hill where we had glimpses between the bare branches of the frozen Cotswold countryside stretching out below us.

'Will Harrison was way out of order last night,' he acknowledged. 'And I've got the bruises to prove it. Plus, he did go out with Scarlett and she did dump him, which gives him what looks like a motive.'

'But?'

'I don't know – somehow it doesn't feel right.'

I bit my lip and thought hard. 'But we need more than a feeling.'

'I mean – is he the type who would kill Scarlett and move straight on to targeting you?'

'Yeah, is he weird enough?' I knew what Jack meant – Will seemed like a regular guy and had plenty of social skills. True, he had a short fuse and went in for violent reactions, but he didn't come across as secretive and psychopathic. Then again, Jack and I were no experts and, besides, there was the bruise under Will's eye when he arrived at the start of term.

'Did he really get that bruise from working out in the gym?' I asked as we walked on.

'It happens.'

'Or did he get it from a canal-side struggle with his ex-girlfriend?'

'I don't know,' Jack sighed. 'I just don't have a clue.'

It turned out, neither did June Ripley.

She talked to Will for more than two hours before she let him walk out of Molly's office. He wouldn't tell anyone what they'd discussed but it seemed she hadn't learned anything that would lead her to release Alex and take Will down to the station instead.

So he was still walking around the school campus the next day, getting top marks from Justine for his translation of a Maupassant story, chatting with Marco and Charlie (officially now 'an item' according to her) over lunch, and later in the afternoon hurrying to get changed for the five-a-side football match against his old school.

I know this because he bumped into Hooper and me as we made our way across the car park towards the sports centre.

By the way, don't imagine for a nanosecond that Hooper was in the St Jude's team. No – the closest he ever comes to a pair of football boots is when he passes the window of the sports shop in Greenlea Shopping Centre, on his way to Waterstones.

'Why do I have to watch two teams of five guys kick a ball around for no good reason?' he complained.

'Because!' Because I wanted to pick Hooper's brains while we watched the match and find out exactly why he'd decided to involve Molly in breaking up the fight between Will, Marco and Jack when it would've been more normal to let them sort things out between themselves.

Will must have resented Hooper's interference too because he jogged up from behind and swung his bag in a rising arc from his shoulder as he passed. The rucksack hit Hooper smack in the face and made him stumble sideways against me.

'Oops, sorry – accident!' Will said in a sing-song falsetto, stooping to pick up an aerosol can of deodorant that had fallen out of the bag. He didn't linger to check if Hooper was OK.

'Not big and not clever,' I muttered, noticing as Hooper straightened up that a strap from the rucksack had brought up a red weal across his cheek.

'No, it's OK – no problem,' Hooper mumbled as we reached the sports centre and climbed the metal stairs to sit in the mezzanine area. Down below, in the main playing area, Jack, Luke and a couple of other kids in St Jude's kit of red shirt, shorts and socks were already practising passing the ball.

'It's not OK,' I insisted. 'Will can't keep on throwing his weight around like that.'

'He can and he does,' was Hooper's comment. 'Anyway, look what fell out of his bag, along with the deodorant.' He held up a phone for me to inspect. 'I grabbed it before it hit the ground.'

I thought for a while about the implications of inadvertently getting our hands on Will's phone. 'Pity he didn't hang around long enough for you to give it back, huh?' I said with a significant look.

'Yeah. I'll do that later.'

'So, Hooper, are you thinking what I'm thinking?'

'I don't know what you're thinking,' he said with the shadow of a smile. 'What *I'm* thinking is that there might be messages on his phone that would interest us, or if not there will be a list of contacts on this phone and it would be

125

interesting to see if Scarlett is still there.'

'Because that would suggest she and Will were still in touch.' This was good, I decided – even if prying into someone's messages and contact list was bad in the ethical sense, 'good' in this case was where the end justified the means. 'And if they were, it means Will is being economical with the truth. It would prove he was still in the frame as far as the police are concerned.'

'So shall I?' Hooper asked, switching on the phone and letting his finger hover over the contacts icon.

'Yes – check the messages first.'

Which is what we did, scrolling back through messages from Will to Tom Walsingham about today's five-a-side match, telling Tom that he, Will, had been picked to play against his old team, and asking who was going to replace Alex in the Ainslee Comp team. Further back, in early January, there was a series of messages to Will's brother, Henry, about family stuff, plus a couple to Sammy, again about football, and further back still, sent on 28th December, Hooper and I found what we were looking for.

Scarlett we read. Hooper dabbed his finger on the screen and opened the received messages.

Really need to see u.

Answer my texts!

Where r u? We need to talk.

'Twenty-eighth of December,' Hooper said slowly and deliberately.

'Scroll down,' I told him, and he searched for any messages that Will had sent to Scarlett. We didn't find any.

'So she's trying to get him to contact her and he's ignoring her,' Hooper commented. 'Didn't *she* ditch him? Wasn't it that way around?'

'Yes, last summer. So why suddenly does she want to talk to him just after Christmas?'

'Maybe she realizes Will's the one after all.' Being a writer of fiction like his dad, Hooper likes the notion of big romance – rejection and repentance, broken hearts all round.

'But at this point she was going out with Alex,' I reminded him. 'You'd think she would have kept the lid on any feelings she might still have for Will. Life gets too complicated otherwise.'

'Unless . . .' Hooper's imagination fired up and he got a glint in his eye. 'Unless something Alex says or does is screwing her up, making her really confused and unhappy.'

'Like Alex telling her he can't go to the New Year's Eve party?'

'Exactly. And so she turns to Will, who she still counts as a friend. But he's smarting from the rejection – we all know Will has a big ego and a short fuse. It would take him forever to drop a grudge against his ex.'

In the sports hall below, the Ainslee Comp team trotted out in their blue and white kit, Tom at their head. A referee in a black tracksuit soon followed them from the changing rooms.

'So Will ignores Scarlett's pleas for help.' Taking the phone from Hooper, I scrolled through 29th and 30th

December, on into 31st to double check that Will hadn't replied.

The referee blew his whistle and the match began. Trainers squeaked on the polished wooden surface; the ball was kicked out of touch and thudded against a side wall. Loud claims were made for the throw-in.

'No – there's nothing from Will to Scarlett,' I muttered as I scrolled on.

Hey, Marco – fancy a game of footie? I read.

Marco had sent a reply. Maybe. When?

Friday. After school. Sports hall.

So far, so normal, except that Marco had sworn to Jack and me that he refused to play soccer because he wanted to do the opposite of what his dad was pressurizing him to do. Anyway, the arrangement was made and the proof was in front of our eyes – Marco playing for St Jude's alongside Jack, Will, Lee Irwin (IT prodigy) and Danny Wells (chemistry genius).

'Here – pass to me!' Lee yelled at Danny. He received the ball, trapped it under his left foot, turned towards the goal and took a shot.

Goal! Our team swamped Lee with celebratory hugs.

I glanced again at the texts between Will and Marco, and in a fit of curiosity switched from Will's messages to contacts and found Marco's name on the pale blue screen.

Marco Conti. Mobile 07763 159080 Option boxes: Send message. Face Time. Share contact. Add to favourites

07763 159080. The synapses in my brain flashed into action and I felt my heart suddenly pump hard and fast.

'What's up, Alyssa?' Hooper queried.

I remembered without looking it up on my phone the row of red emoticon hearts, the unfamiliar number – 07763 159080.

'I do not understand!' Galina threw up her arms in wonder when I told her that Marco Conti had sent me red hearts. 'Why are you sad, Alyssa? A boy like Marco – and you, so beautiful. English rose and Italian stallion – you are perfect together!'

We were in our room. I'd gone there before the end of the five-a-side match to try and work out if Marco's red hearts were still in the category of creep-Alyssa-out clues and found Galina examining her self-dissolving stitches in the magnifying side of her make-up mirror. 'Why so sad?' she said when I told her who had sent the hearts.

'I'm not sad,' I argued.

'No? You look in bad mood.'

'I don't know if Marco is genuine or if he's trying to spook me. Anyway, I already have a boyfriend. I'm confused.'

'Why? It is simple. Marco comes to St Jude's. He knows me and Eugenie, but no one else. He looks around at beautiful girls. He sees Zara and Charlie.'

'And they see him,' I reminded her. 'They pay him loads of attention. Anyway, Charlie is officially his girlfriend now – why doesn't he send her hearts?'

'Maybe he does.'

'OK, maybe. But if Marco is serious, what do I do next?'

To Galina the answer was obvious. 'If you want to be with Jack, ignore them.'

'I do!'

'Easy then. Let Charlie have Marco.'

'But do I mention any of this to Jack?' I wanted to know.

She shook her head and tutted, sighed and said definitely no – don't tell Jack.

'OK, thanks, Galina. Will you come back with me to the sports centre? We could watch the football match together.'

'Are you crazy?' she cried. 'I have more things to do, better things.'

'Such as?'

'I meet someone,' she said, tilting her head to one side and giving a small, coy smile. 'Someone special.'

'Give me a clue. Is it someone I know?'

'Of course,' she answered, still smiling.

'Who is it? Come on, tell me. We're friends, remember.'

'It is secret,' she whispered. 'I get ready. I meet him. Later I tell you who.'

Cool – she must be feeling better, I thought. 'So be good,' I told her as I walked out. 'Don't do anything I wouldn't do.'

You know my fondness for agony-aunt columns, so here's one to contemplate:

Dear Problem Page Pamela. I am in a long term relationship and I love my boyfriend very much. But I also have an admirer who sends me secret messages . . . [OK, delete 'sends me secret messages', insert 'sent me a secret message' – best to be completely accurate] *Do I let my admirer know that I received the message and that I'm not interested in him? In the interests of honesty and openness, do I tell my boyfriend what's happening? Or do I ignore the whole thing and hope that my admirer loses interest? Please help.*

Pathetic, huh? Of course, I would follow Galina's advice about keeping quiet and I'd never write a letter like that. It was just in my head as I rushed back to the sports hall to meet up with Jack.

By the time I got there, I'd made my decision.

'Hi – did you win?' I asked my showered and shiny-clean boyfriend.

'A draw – three–three. Where were you? I thought you were going to watch the match.'

'Coffee?' I suggested, steering him out of the way of Will, Luke and Marco. 'I watched the start then something came up.'

Out of the corner of my eye I saw Will pause by the sports-centre exit and delve into his rucksack. Luke and Marco said something to him then walked on. Will tipped all his belonging out of the bag on to the floor.

'Nothing bad?' Jack asked me.

'No, I had to dash over to my room and check something with Galina – that's all.'

'Cool,' Jack said as he put coins into the coffee machine and it started to hiss and spit cappuccino froth into a paper cup. He smiled at me – oh, that smile! 'We were rubbish,' he told me. 'Will played like an idiot and Marco never passed the ball, just tried to do it all himself. OK, he looks the part, but he's not a team player.'

'*Quelle surprise!*'

'Yeah – really!'

The smile lingered on his lips, the lips that I always want to kiss. 'Coffee to go?' I suggested as the machine filled the second cup. I offered Jack two plastic lids and led the way downstairs.

'Why? Where are you taking me?'

'Your room?' I suggested. Jack was one of the lucky ones – he had a single room at the end of the boys' dorm, his own personal space, and we had two whole hours before the eight o'clock curfew. 'And let's skip dinner.'

The smile turned into a grin as he slid his arm round my waist.

We passed Will at the exit, still unzipping pockets and searching in his bag. 'Hey, Jack, do you have a minute?'

'No, actually.'

'Just call my number,' Will muttered.

'Sorry – aren't you the guy who punched me in the stomach?' Jack reminded him. 'Why would I suddenly want to call your number?'

'I lost my phone – that's why. Just do it, will you?'

Jack shrugged. 'Sorry – out of battery.'

We walked on hand in hand, leaving Will in a major strop until I acted like I'd remembered something and retraced my steps. 'Oh, Will,' I said. 'Hooper was looking for you earlier.'

'Piss off, Alyssa.' Will stuffed everything back into his

bag – football kit, shower gel, deodorant, towel.

'Please yourself,' I told him. 'Hooper said it was important. Oh yeah, silly me – now I remember. Actually, he found your phone.'

Jack's room is just a place to dump his stuff. There are jeans and socks on the floor, a tangle of cables and adaptors trailing from his desk connecting to his TV and iPad, or waiting to recharge his phone. You have to fight your way through all this to get to the bed. The only object he's chosen to display is there on his windowsill – a white ceramic head with areas of the brain mapped out – *'Intuitive, reasoning, selfish propensities, reflective facules,'* etc. Yes, 'facules'.

Before Freud and Jung, they used to measure the bumps on your skull to work out your personality type – thanks to L. N. Fowler of Ludgate Circus, London. He wrote, 'For thirty years I have studied Crania and living heads from all parts of the world and have found in every instance there is a perfect correspondence between the conformation of the healthy skull of an individual and his known characteristics.'

If you had a big bump in your cranium just behind your left ear it meant you were brave, a big bump below and to the right meant you were a sex addict – my twenty-first-century terminology, not Mr Fowler's.

It's a joke now, when you think about it, but Jack liked his ceramic head enough to put it on his windowsill.

Anyway, we stepped through the chaos and sank on to the bed under the eyeless socket of Fowler's head and I knew I was in the best possible place to escape from the so-called real world – here, in Jack's arms. We held each other for a while and let the world melt away, getting physically close and allowing me to forget the taunting messages, the creepy feeling that someone was breaking into my room and watching my every move.

Have I said recently that Jack's smile lights up the room? I guess so. But I haven't mentioned his abs or his sculpted torso or those perfect tennis-player's quad muscles just above the knee. Well, I admired them all again as he stroked my cheek, cupped my chin between his hands and softly kissed my lips.

But when the kissing stopped Jack lay on his back, arms behind his head, looking thoughtful.

I turned on to my side. 'So?' I asked.

'So?'

'What are you thinking?'

Now here's a rule I've learned since then and it deserves upper case initial letters – Never Ask a Guy What He's Thinking. It'll end badly, believe me.

'Nothing,' he said, without giving me eye contact.

'Yes – you've got something on your mind.'

He shook his head. 'It's nothing. Forget it.'

'Have I done something wrong?'

Retrospective rule number two – Never Invite Blame. It'll end even worse.

'Honestly, Alyssa, I don't want to talk about it.'

I guess I fell into a small panic at the idea that Jack was hiding a problem from me so I went on digging the hole. 'Something I *said*?' I asked.

Jack sat up and propped a pillow behind his back. 'No – if you really want to know, it's something Hooper told me after the match.'

'What?'

'He said you found out who texted the hearts message.'

Thanks for nothing, Hooper! 'It was Marco,' I muttered. 'I recognized his number on Will's phone.'

'Yeah – Hooper said,' Jack interrupted. 'So when did you plan on telling me?'

'I didn't.'

'Why not?'

'Because it's not important.' I tried to sound calm, but inside I was flailing in deep water, far from shore like a woman who can't swim. 'Not waving but drowning' – as Stevie Smith once wrote. She was a poet-contemporary of my own lion aunt, Lady Caroline Stephens, code breaker at Bletchley during the Second World War. Stevie admitted in the poem that she was too far out all her life, not waving but drowning.

'Not important when Marco Conti sends you a loved-up text?' Jack countered.

'OK, then – it matters. But I didn't tell you because I thought it would upset you. And I was right – it has.' By this time I was swinging my legs over the side of the bed, struggling into my clothes.

Jack did the same. 'I wouldn't have kept it secret if it was the other way round – I'd have come clean,' he insisted.

'Why are we fighting over this?' I wanted to know.

'Because you asked me what I was thinking and I told you.'

'And you should be pleased, not angry.'

'How do you work that out?'

'Because now we don't have to worry about the red hearts being one of the clues, part of the trail set by the killer,' I explained. 'It's just Marco being stupid. Now, can we stop arguing?'

'Yes, if you swear here and now that you didn't do anything to encourage Conti to send that text.'

In Stevie Smith metaphorical terms I was back on dry land, striding out of the water and, hands on hips, standing up for myself. 'Jack, wait – did I just hear that properly? You're suggesting that I led Marco on?'

'I didn't say that,' he answered sullenly.

'You implied it. I can't believe it would even enter your head.' I was standing up and fighting back, ready to walk away. 'Let me spell it out – Marco sent a stupid message. I deleted it.'

Picture it – my bare feet shoved into Uggs, jacket zipped, door slammed behind me. End of episode where Alyssa loses it with Jack and immediately regrets it.

By the time I'd crossed the quad with its shitty little heaps of dirty, melting snow and climbed the stairs to my room I felt hollow, as if all my insides had been gouged out of my body. I ran down the long corridor, past Zara and Connie's open door, ignoring Eugenie as she came out of her room and flinging open the door to Room twenty-seven.

Jack and I had argued over nothing – I needed to bury my head under my pillow and not talk to anyone until my innards were back in place and I was calm again, which might be several days, the way I was feeling right then.

Eugenie must have realized something was wrong because she followed me into the room. 'Alyssa, are you OK?'

'No!' I groaned, curled up on my bed in foetal position.

'Don't tell me – you and Jack are over.'

I sat right back up in shock. 'No. What makes you think that?'

'I saw your face – you looked tragic. That can only mean you two had a terminal fight.'

'Not terminal,' I protested weakly.

'But a fight?'

Nodding, I made the effort to clear the mess on Galina's empty bed and create room for Eugenie to sit down. 'Jack's jealous of Marco.'

'You're kidding,' Eugenie gasped. 'What about Marco and Charlie? Aren't they an item?'

'Don't ask me. Anyway, Jack sees Marco as a threat.'

'As any guy would,' she acknowledged. 'But don't worry – it's good that Jack's jealous.'

'It doesn't feel good.'

'Not right now, I agree. But it doesn't take a rocket scientist to work it out – jealousy basically means that he cares.'

'OK, keep talking.'

'If he didn't care about you, he wouldn't mind who you

spent time with or who you got text messages from.'

'How come you know about the text – yeah, don't tell me – Hooper.'

'Hooper,' she echoed. 'And, aside from all that, you should be flattered.'

'That Marco sends me a message?'

Raising her mass of wavy red hair from the nape of her neck, Eugenie elaborated. 'That he chooses you over Charlie. She throws herself at him and he ignores her. It's you he's interested in, Alyssa.'

'And I don't care. Charlie can have him – I've got Jack.' That's what it boiled down to, however simplistic it sounds.

'Cool.' Eugenie felt we'd cut through the crap and got where she wanted me to be. 'Anyway, I was looking for Galina. Do you happen to know where she is?'

I shook my head. 'She said she was going out to meet someone.'

'I called her to talk about buying one of her handbags at mates' rates but she's not answering.'

'Sorry, I can't help.'

Eugenie took out her phone. 'Look, there's a picture of it here on the website – the little clutch purse in nude patent leather. Do you like it?'

'Yeah, it's cute.' Noticing that Galina had ditched her own phone on her pillow, I picked it up and saw missed calls from Eugenie. 'That's why she's not answering,' I pointed out. My mind was still snarled up in the traffic jam of thoughts and feelings following on from my fight with Jack, so I wasn't paying much attention.

'Who *ever* goes anywhere without their phone?' Eugenie was suddenly concerned.

'You're right.' Now I was alert, checking Galina's phone and noticing that the battery was low. Automatically I looked around for the cable to recharge it, but had no luck.

'Does she often go AWOL?' Eugenie wanted to know. 'I mean, it's past ten o'clock, it's the middle of winter and it's blowing a gale outside. I've looked everywhere.'

Something else was missing and it only occurred to me at this point. 'And where are Sergei and Mikhail? Were they at dinner? Did you see them hanging around?'

Eugenie shook her head. 'But then Galina wasn't at dinner either, otherwise I would have mentioned the bag face to face.'

I saw that the phone battery was down to ten per cent and kept on looking for the cable. Then Eugenie took it from me and listened in to Galina's voicemails to see if they told us where she was and who she'd met. Her eyes widened and her face changed from puzzled to shocked. 'Quick, Alyssa – someone just asked for you on Galina's phone. It sounds like the start of a message.'

I snatched the phone back in time to hear a man's voice. 'Hey, honey,' it said in an American accent that I straight away knew was fake. 'I missed you – where have you been? OK, I understand – you were making out with Jack and didn't want any interruptions. Listen – I know you're not expecting to hear from me on Galina's phone, but I do love to surprise you and I knew you'd pick this up sooner or later.'

A guy's voice with a fake Texan drawl, using an app which slowed it down and distorted it. I felt my skin begin to prickle. 'Are you still there, Alyssa? Yeah, it's me again. Listen, darling, I'm doing all I can to help you . . .'

'I can't listen to this!' I said as I threw down the phone.

Eugenie picked it up again and gave me a whispered report. 'He says he's disappointed in you again. He keeps giving you clues, but you let the trail grow cold. What's a message for you doing on Galina's phone, anyway?'

'I don't know, but save it – don't delete it!' I gasped.

'He says never mind that you let the trail grow cold, he still loves you, especially when you're angry.'

'Press SAVE!' I heard cold fingers scratching at the windowpane, saw the robin lying dead on the sill – they flashed back into my mind as vividly as when they first happened. Now there was a new message, a voice telling me he loved me, and on top of this Galina was gone.

chapter seven

Raisa lived in a rented cottage in Upper Chartsey.

I didn't know this until I retrieved her landline number from Galina's phone before the battery finally gave out.

'Hold on – maybe we shouldn't panic,' Eugenie said.

'Then again, maybe we should.' After the events of last year and given what had happened so far this term, I decided to call Raisa on my phone. 'Hi, it's Alyssa Stephens here. I was wondering if you knew who Galina was meeting tonight.'

'No.' The answer came slowly, as if I'd woken Raisa, or as if she had trouble interpreting what I'd asked. 'I think she is in school.'

'That's the point – she's not here and she went out and left her phone in our room, which makes me worry that she left in a hurry.'

'Say this again,' Raisa interrupted.

'Sorry, I'll speak more slowly. I'm worried about Galina. Do you know if she went into Ainslee with a friend to see a movie or something?'

'No movie.'

'So when did you last see her?'

'The afternoon. I brought clean dress from dry cleaner. She says she stays home tonight; she doesn't need me. I come back to my house.'

'OK, thanks.'

I was about to end the conversation when Raisa came back with questions of her own.

'She is not in room? She is not with school friends?'

'No, I'm afraid not.'

'She is unhappy?'

'No, not that I know of. Not since she ran away from Mikhail and he busted her lip. Since then she's been OK – not crying or anything. And she said she was meeting someone. Someone she knew.'

'*Lyublmaya moy*,' Raisa murmured sorrowfully. 'I worry now. I take taxi. I come to school.'

'No, don't do that,' I decided. 'Let me make a proper search. I'll call you back.'

Eugenie heard the plan and was out of the door ahead of me. We tried the obvious places again – other rooms along the girls' corridor then out across the quad to knock on the boys' doors.

We didn't get far before Bryony joined us.

'Sorry to be a jobsworth, girls,' she said at the top of the stairs, 'but it's my solemn duty to remind you that the boys' dorm is out of bounds after eight o'clock.'

Of all the staff, Bryony was the one I'd have chosen to be on duty that night. She doesn't give out any crap about rules unless she absolutely has to. On the other hand she quickly picks up a problem and helps when something serious is happening. Tonight she was warmly wrapped in a long black coat with a soft cream beret covering her dark hair.

'Galina's gone walkabout,' Eugenie told her. 'There was something weird on her voicemail.'

Bryony took us back down the stairs into the quad, where we stood under a starlit sky. The light from the full moon was strong enough to cast shadows and to pick out the masonry over the arched doorways and windows. Two gargoyles carved in stone – one grinning, one sticking out its serpent-coiled tongue – squinted down at us. 'What kind of weird?'

'Some guy left a rambling message for Alyssa – on *Galina's* phone.'

'Let's focus on Galina for now,' I interrupted. 'She told me she was meeting someone, but I talked with Raisa. She said Galina didn't plan to go out this evening. Galina left in so much of a hurry that she forgot her phone. And there's something else – Mikhail or Sergei should still be on duty and they're not.'

'Yes, it's true – I haven't seen either of them,' Bryony confirmed. 'Let's think this through. OK – given what happened to Galina earlier in the week, I think I should tell Dr Webb right away.'

I stayed behind in the quad while Eugenie and Bryony hurried down the drive to the principal's house, which was close to the main entrance. Having heard the voices and footsteps on the stone flags, Luke opened his window and called down.

'Alyssa?'

'Yeah, it's me. You haven't seen Galina by any chance?'

'Not lately.'

'Could you ask everyone in the boys' corridor for me?'

'Marco, Alyssa wants to know where Galina is,' Luke spoke over his shoulder. Seconds later, Marco appeared in the quad with bare feet, in T-shirt and jeans. Luke leaned out of the window again. 'Sorry about Marco. I don't know what got into him. I just mentioned your name and he was like a greyhound out of the traps,' he apologized.

'Marco, can you go back in and find out if Galina's up there in someone's room?' I insisted as patiently as I could.

'What's wrong?' Marco asked, full of concern. 'Are you in trouble?'

'No – not me. It's Galina. I want to know where she is.'

'Alyssa, you're freezing.'

'I'm fine.' I turned and yelled up at the window. 'Luke, will you hurry up and look for Galina for me?'

Luke disappeared but Marco didn't move. For a second I thought he was going to put an arm round me to shield me from the cold. He stood so close I could feel his body heat. 'Bryony will be back soon,' I told him. 'She's gone to fetch Saint Sam.'

'You're shivering.'

'We have to find Galina – it's important.' I'm tall, but Latin lover boy Marco is three or four inches taller, so I had to tilt my head back to speak to him. As I did this, I noticed over his shoulder that Jack was standing at his window, watching us. I swore silently to myself.

'Come inside,' Marco invited. 'At least wait where it's warm.'

I shook my head and stepped away. Luckily Bryony and

Eugenie were soon back, with Saint Sam in tow.

I gave him the facts and he acted fast, calling Molly and asking her to check CCTV footage in her office while he called the police. Bryony insisted that Eugenie and I go back to our rooms before we caught our deaths. There was nothing else we could do – it was out of our hands, she said.

'But, Alyssa, don't stay in your room by yourself tonight,' Bryony insisted. 'Eugenie, you'll make sure she doesn't?'

It was agreed – there was a spare bed in Eugenie and Charlie's room and I'd spend the night there.

'Give me five minutes while I go and fetch my toothbrush and PJs,' I told Eugenie. I needed breathing space and a chance to make a last check of the room. I didn't know what I was looking for, but there might be something I'd missed.

I went up and at first I thought everything was as I'd left it when Eugenie and I had dashed out. I picked up Galina's phone and didn't find any new messages – only a final warning that the battery was about to die. Hoping that someone else might have a compatible charger, I put the phone down again on Galina's bed. Then slowly the prickling sensation of dread crept over me – a sense of interruption or intrusion – the feeling I always got when I found a sinister message or a threat. I began to notice small things that felt wrong – the wardrobe door hung open and I always, always kept it closed. The duvet was crumpled, as if someone had been sitting on the bed, and my blue PJs weren't under my pillow in their usual place. Remember, I'm a methodical girl.

145

The bastard had been here again! He wasn't here now because there was nowhere in this small room he could hide. But he'd definitely been in and I suspected he'd left me another 'gift', a memento of his visit.

I took a deep breath and threw back the duvet, but didn't find anything. Then I quickly went through the clothes in the wardrobe until my phone rang. I jumped, dragged it from my pocket and threw it on to my bed as if it might bite.

I read the screen – 'Blocked number'.

Don't answer it!

It rang out and I waited, hardly daring to breathe. Then the voicemail alert beeped – one new message, which I steeled myself to listen to.

'Hey, Alyssa. Don't you know I can read your finely tuned mind? Right now you're thinking maybe the Russian mafia succeeded this time around. They snatched Galina. C'mon now, 'fess up.'

Oh God, it was the same fake Texan drawl with the slow distortion, each word drawn out, with long gaps in between. It was so JR from *Dallas* that it would have been funny except that my skin crawled with disgust. I felt the walls close in on me and I jumped at my own fragmented reflection in the leaded window.

'Well, how wrong can you be? But I feel for you, darling, I really do. So here comes another clue. Forget the Russians. Use that fabulous memory talent of yours and focus closer to home.'

There was a sound in the background – a door opening

and a girl's muffled voice – then the message ended abruptly.

Breathe! I told myself. Think. This is someone close enough to know what's going on from minute to minute and arrogant enough to take big risks. He's leaving clues, setting a challenge.

Or 'she', I realized. Why does it have to be a 'he'?

Because of the fake voice, the deep drawl.

But it's distorted by a special phone app. It's slowed down from a normal pace, impossible to recognize.

I was breathing, thinking these things through, when a message alert came up on my phone – number blocked again, and this time there were no darlings and honeys, no deliberately cheesy love and kisses.

'Better catch me quick, memory girl,' I read. 'You think this is bad but it's going to get worse – one hundred per cent guaranteed.'

We handed Galina's and my phones straight to the police when they showed up just before midnight. They tracked down the creepy messages and calls to different numbers – all from pay-as-you-go or stolen phones, as it turned out.

Inspector Ripley arrived with an older plain-clothes guy, Sergeant Jimmy Owen. He was skinny with hunched shoulders and looked as if he'd tried to give up smoking for decades but failed. His lined face and tired eyes behind heavy-rimmed glasses were a big contrast to Ripley's bright and bushy manner.

'We wouldn't normally respond to a missing persons call until more time had elapsed,' she told Saint Sam, Molly and me in the principal's office. 'But, given what's happened lately, we didn't want to wait.'

'We appreciate it,' Sam said smoothly. I know that he never reveals what he's thinking, even when someone has interrupted his viewing of his favourite Saturday night Dan Snow documentary on BBC4. 'I'm hopeful that everything will work out fine, but of course I have ultimate responsibility for the safety of pupils at St Jude's and it would have been negligent of me not to inform you of Galina's disappearance.'

You think people don't talk in officialese in real life, but I assure you they do – at least, Saint Sam does.

The smoker cleared his throat and invited the principal and Molly to come next door and provide more details – Galina's age and appearance, a photograph from her file, contact number for her parents and so forth. This left me with Ripley.

'This latest thing with Galina has upset you a lot, Alyssa.' As usual, not a question but an observation.

'Definitely. I've been worried about her ever since Tuesday – you know, when she told me she was trying to get away from Mikhail.'

We're outside the churchyard on Chartsey Bottom Main Street.

'Leave me!' Galina yells at Mikhail. 'I tell my father what you do!' Then some Russian insults and a sprint towards Jack, Marco and me, with Mikhail lumbering behind.

'Back off, buddy!' Jack warns.

Galina runs through the lych gate, Marco stands in Mikhail's

way. There's a fight while Galina runs on into the church porch.
I find her there, trembling and hiding her face in her hands. Then
I see the blood.

'He did it,' she sobs. 'Mikhail, he did this.'

'In the cafe?'

'No, outside village, on small road. I ran away.'

Eventually Jack wrestles Mikhail to the ground. Marco stamps
on his chest and says nothing.

'Not an accident,' Galina sobs. 'He punches me. He tries to
kidnap me.'

I relived these details and shared them with Ripley.

'That's remarkably detailed,' she commented when I'd
finished. She didn't sound admiring, more suspicious, as if
I might have made it all up and rehearsed it to make myself
word-perfect.

'And true,' I insisted quietly.

'Ah, yes – the total-recall facility. What's it really like,
Alyssa, to have your kind of memory?'

'It's like hard-disk overload,' I tried to explain. 'Eidetics
never get a break from remembering things they'd rather
forget. Sometimes I just get information overload and crash.
I turn into a sort of zombie – my mind goes dead, there's
nothing there.'

'So I wouldn't want it?' she decided.

'Not if you want to stay sane – no.' I thought for a while
then revised what I'd said. 'Actually, in your job – yes, you
might.'

'Anyway, it's interesting, what you just said. Scarlett's
mum told me the same thing – that having total recall was

a curse rather than a blessing for her daughter too.'

'You see – we're freaks.'

'It's rare but I wouldn't call you freaks. And it helps me, for sure. I know I can rely on you.'

'That's cool,' I told her. 'What else do you want to know?'

'Plenty. But what do you say we get out of here and go for a drive? It might do you good to get away from school while we carry on talking.'

Without waiting for an answer, Ripley went to tell Sergeant Owen she was taking the car.

'OK, boss.' He sat out of sight in Molly's room but I could tell by his voice that he wasn't happy.

'Half an hour,' Ripley promised as she led me out and sat me next to her in the unmarked police car parked outside the main entrance.

Before I knew it we'd sailed off down the drive, out through the gates and along the lane leading to Hereward Ridge.

'So carry on,' she invited as she adjusted the heating. 'I'm interested in hearing more about what people might have told you about Scarlett Hartley.'

'Not much. It's mostly what I read in the paper and saw on TV. A little bit from Jayden and his girlfriend, Ursula.'

'Oh yes, Jayden Johnson,' Ripley smiled. 'He's an interesting kid. Totally focused, just like you, Alyssa, but it manifests itself differently.'

'Yeah, Jayden's cool.'

'How about Ursula?'

'I like her too. She's the one who told me that Scarlett

went out with Matt Brookes and Sammy Beckett before she and Alex were an item – I'm not sure for how long or how serious those others were. And it turns out Scarlett went out with Will Harrison while he was at Ainslee Comp, but she dumped him some time last summer.'

'Thanks for that.' Ripley seemed to be making careful mental notes then switched subjects as the car swept up the dark hill. 'Moving on again – tell me how you're dealing with the bullying and the messages you've been receiving.'

'They creep me out more and more,' I admitted. 'Whoever this guy is, he's now telling me that Galina isn't the end of it, that it's going to get worse.'

'Yes, that's what I picked up when Dr Webb called the station.' Ripley pulled into a small lay-by overlooking the valley so she could fully concentrate. She switched off the lights, but kept the engine running.

'He left a message on Galina's phone. He said to forget the Russians and concentrate on the clues.'

'So he's threatening to raise the bar?'

I nodded. 'Is this what happens? Is it normal?'

'Nothing is normal about stalkers – believe me. I've seen all kinds from ones who occasionally shadow celebrities and send them pathetic proposals of marriage to those who stalk their victims every single minute of the day without ever saying a word. They stay in the shadows and are the most difficult to deal with.'

'And I know you're probably not supposed to share this, but can you tell me if someone did the same thing to Scarlett?' I pressed for an answer to the question that

Jack and I had wondered about, even though I wasn't really ready to handle this if the answer turned out to be yes. 'Did he set her challenges to see if she could work out who he was?'

Ripley shook her head. 'I'm not saying no,' she quickly put in. 'I'm saying we don't know. Naturally, we've asked her friends about it but so far there's not much hard evidence.'

'"Not much hard evidence",' I sighed as Ripley turned on the lights and did a three-point turn to face downhill. That meant they hadn't been able to trace Scarlett's missing phone or pick up any email messages. 'So now, what about Galina? From what I know about abductions, the first forty-eight hours are crucial.'

My friendly inspector let the car cruise downhill. 'That's true. That's when we gather forensic information, interview witnesses and so on. After that, the pace of investigation slows down and we enter into more of a waiting game.'

'So what are you waiting for – a ransom demand?'

'Yes, or at least some contact with the kidnapper. Something that leads us forward into the next phase, which is usually a negotiation for the victim's release.'

'But this is contact with the kidnapper!' I pointed to the phone lying in the CD compartment of Ripley's car. 'OK, so it's not a straightforward ransom demand, but actually it's worse!'

'*Better catch me quick, memory girl. You think this is bad but it's going to get worse – one hundred per cent guaranteed.*'

'Before the threat turns into a reality,' she agreed. 'We

152

can check the phone for prints. And, remember, it's only been a few hours so we can still hope that Galina will show up of her own accord.'

Ripley didn't say this to reassure me, she said it to test me out and carefully watched my reactions.

'She won't,' I said as a shiver ran down my spine and the car coasted down the hill.

'No?'

'Scarlett didn't, did she?'

'And you're convinced this is a parallel situation? Same perpetrator, same mode of operation?'

'Yes, carbon copy, minus the perfect recall, of course.'

'So we'll search the canal for another body.' Ripley shrugged then hunched forward over the steering wheel, as though it was too late at night and the gruelling nature of her job was finally getting to her. 'Sorry, Alyssa – ignore that. It was unprofessional.'

'We have to find Galina,' I said again, studying her profile. 'We need to trace Mikhail and Sergei, find out when they last saw her, check Ainslee Westgate to see if she took a train, make contact with her stepmother. You never know – Salomea Radkin might have some information that we don't.'

The inspector turned to smile at me. 'We make an unorthodox team, you and I. So who else should I talk to?'

'Try the stepmother,' I repeated. 'You never know – Mrs Radkin might come up with something.'

Ripley agreed and we drove back to St Jude's like two

female detectives in a popular cop series, *Ripley and Stephens*, alert and on the ball, exuding girl power.

Next morning, the police were crawling all over St Jude's and it was hard for anyone to go on with life as normal.

Jack made a brave effort, though. 'Take a look at Nadal's forehand,' he told me. 'See the footwork he puts in to get him into exactly the right place to play the stroke.'

Yes, Jack and I were talking again. Or, rather, I was with him in the technology centre and he was studying a training video featuring his favourite tennis player of all time. I stood at the window, watching another police car arrive. I saw Raisa and two uniforms step out then walk swiftly towards Saint Sam's office.

'I'm not boring you, am I?' Jack checked. 'Tell me to stop if I am.'

'No, please – I'm listening.' I urged him to go on, wishing that Nadal's forehand was all we had to worry about in the foreseeable future.

'Compare Nadal with Djokovic,' Jack said. 'They both have incredible athleticism, but totally different body language. Look how scarily cool and focused Djokovic is. With Nadal, there's more emotion.'

I left the window and joined him at the computer. 'Talking of emotion . . .' I began.

Jack pressed the PAUSE button and glanced up at me. 'Yeah, I know – we're both still feeling bad. I've already said I was an idiot. I'm sorry.'

'Me too. I'm sorry if I did anything to give you the

154

wrong impression about me and Marco.' I could mention relationship rule number two again here – don't apologize for something that is in no way your fault. But that's in an ideal world and I was so relieved that Jack had come over to me at breakfast and sat down like nothing had happened that I happily broke my own rules.

Jack smiled and kissed me. We were good again. The line of Marco hearts and Jack's recent view of Marco and me almost going into a clinch in the cold quad – I saw that he wanted to show me that both incidents were history.

'Raisa showed up in a police car,' I told him. 'She looked upset.'

'Still nothing about Galina?'

'No.' I'd spent the night awake in the spare bed in Eugenie and Charlie's room, my overactive mind hopping between Galina's disappearance and Scarlett's murder, constantly looking for the missing link, wondering who was the shadowy figure connecting them – someone right under my own nose, someone in plain sight.

'You look shitty,' Charlie had told me when she woke up, offering me Touche Eclat to hide the shadows under my eyes.

'Thanks – I *feel* shitty,' I'd told her. Not waving but drowning again, until Jack had sat down next to me in the refectory and made me eat something instead of drinking litres of coffee. He'd said sorry for being an idiot.

'It's because I care,' he'd explained.

Wow, Eugenie – top marks for you in relationship counselling!

'Where's Galina's family?' Jack wondered. 'Why is it all down to the maid to fill them in about the disappearance?'

'Her dad's in New York doing shady oligarch deals. She doesn't get on with her stepmum.'

Jack sighed. 'Is there a single family at St Jude's that's not totally dysfunctional?'

'Yours?' I volunteered.

Jack's parents were still married, a miracle when you have crazy wealth like they do. His dad's an international property developer, his mum's a gallery owner and they have homes in London, the Caribbean and Switzerland. Jack's their only child. When they found out at the age of seven that he had an IQ of 138 and was a maths genius, they said OK, we'll send you to St Jude's Academy, but it's not going to be all work and no play. That's why they started tennis lessons for him and discovered he was exceptional at sport too.

The other miracle is that Jack didn't let it all go to his head. He's modest and laid-back, funny and genuine, and I love him. You already know that.

'Hey.' It was Charlie who broke up our reconciliation session by delivering a message from Saint Sam. 'Would you two please quit chewing each other's faces. Alyssa, they want you in the principal's office right away.'

'I'll wait here for you.' Jack blushed and went back to his training video as I dashed away.

Poor Raisa – her eyes were red and swollen and her round face a picture of misery as she sat in one of the red leather chairs in Saint Sam's office. Molly was with her, offering tea and sympathy.

'Dr Webb has been called away to speak to Inspector Ripley,' she told me when I joined them. 'He won't be more than five minutes.'

'Do you know why they want to see me?' I asked.

'I think they're still at the stage of gathering as much information as they can about Galina's disappearance and Inspector Ripley particularly asked to speak to you again.'

Mention of Galina's name set Raisa off on a fresh bout of crying. Molly handed her a box of tissues.

'Too many bad things,' Raisa wept. 'Always bad things for my little girl.'

'It's not your fault – you've always taken good care of her, I'm sure.' Molly spoke softly. 'For how many years now?'

'Ten years she is my *lyublmaya*, my beautiful girl. You should see her then – so pretty. I am with my Galina all this time. I see her happy; I see her sad. I cannot stop the bad things.'

'No one can,' Molly empathized. 'But we have to stay positive and let the police do their work. We hope that Galina will be found unharmed.'

'My girl,' Raisa sobbed quietly. 'I tell them, I say after boat accident – her father's enemies, they are to blame. I make them listen. Since then we have Sergei and Mikhail with her always. It is not enough – I tell Salomea, it is not enough.'

'Let's wait and see. If Galina has been kidnapped, in the

157

normal way of things it can't be long before the people who took her will make contact with the family. There'll be a ransom demand, conditions laid down.' Molly pronounced the conventional wisdom, without knowing the full details about my stalker's menacing phone calls, which would turn a common or garden kidnap situation into probable murder.

That's the point, I thought, hearing footsteps approaching down the corridor. This doesn't feel normal to me – it feels crazy. And Ripley already knows that if I can tell them anything useful it won't be about Russian thugs intent on getting to Anatoly Radkin through his daughter – it will be about the psychopath who's leaving me messages on stolen mobile phones.

The footsteps stopped outside Saint Sam's office and, after a brief conversation, the door opened and a slender blonde woman appeared.

'Salomea!' Raisa sprang up from her seat, letting a bundle of used tissues fall from her lap.

Galina's stepmother was ballerina-slender and small-boned with amazing cheekbones and hair swept up into a dancer's ponytail. She was wearing a large, copper-coloured pashmina over a black jacket and trousers, with high black ankle boots and a bag that cost at least twice as much as the ones advertised on Galina's website.

I'd been expecting distance and elegance, coolness and grace, so I was surprised when this birdlike woman rushed over to hug Raisa. She soothed her in Russian and sat her down on her chair.

'We will find her,' she promised in English in order to include Molly and me as well as Galina's weeping maid.

'That's what I've been telling her,' Molly agreed. She waited while Salomea bent over Raisa and spoke rapidly, then she suggested more cups of tea.

'No tea, thank you.' Salomea drew up a chair next to Raisa. 'Anatoly knows what has happened,' she explained. 'He will be here as soon as he can. And you know, Raisa, he solves all problems.'

Raisa nodded through her tears.

'I came as quickly as I could,' Salomea told us. 'Anatoly wanted me to be here to answer questions – to do anything I can to help.'

All this was unexpected, I admit. I had Salomea down as wicked stepmother asking the mirror who was the fairest of them all and spitefully packing Galina off to a remote Cotswold location in case the mirror came back with the wrong answer. 'You, O Queen, are fair, but Galina is fairer still.' Instead, what I saw was an animated, caring woman who seemed genuinely distressed over her stepdaughter's disappearance.

'Mikhail is to blame,' she decided as she stood up and paced the room. 'It was his job to stop something like this from happening. And yes, Galina didn't like having him and Sergei around all the time, but it was for her own safety.'

'Actually, it didn't turn out that way,' I reminded her. 'The truth is Galina swore that Mikhail attacked her a few days ago.' Speaking for the first time since Salomea came into the office, my voice sounded flat and ordinary amidst the torrent of emotion-driven opinion pouring from Salomea's lips.

'No!' she protested. 'That was a story Galina made up.'

'Really? You don't believe he punched her and cut her lip?'

'Mikhail denied it. He said she tripped and fell.'

'Do you believe that?' I asked Raisa, who shrugged then came down on Mikhail's side.

'So it comes down to whose version you trust,' I said, digging in my heels and refusing to budge.

It was Salomea who had to back down. 'I'm sorry now that I didn't pay more attention. I said it couldn't be true – Mikhail knows how much power Anatoly has. His influence is very great. Mikhail would never dare.'

'I believed Galina's version, not his,' I insisted quietly.

And right there and then, Sergei's conversation on the phone flew into my mind.

I'm walking into the quad with Will, my multilingual suspect. Not that he knows that I'm suspicious about the bruise under his eye or the grudge he might still hold against Scarlett.

We pass lean and hungry Sergei, talking on the phone. I pick up the names Galina and Salomea amongst the flow of rapid Russian.

Will, my translator, tells me that Sergei is telling Salomea that things didn't work out, he wasn't happy.

I stare at Sergei, wishing that I could understand the nuances, reading his expression as part scared, part angry, as if offering excuses to his employer that he feared wouldn't be acceptable.

His eyes flick towards me and Will as we pass by, but we're of no interest. He turns his back.

My memory shunts sideways to another event.

I see Sergei's back view again. It's a little earlier in the week. When would that be? Oh yes, on the platform at Ainslee Westgate. I'm standing under the station clock, waiting for Jack to step off the Paddington train. He's not going to arrive. He's missed the train. My lovelorn heart aches.

So I hardly notice Sergei rush by. I see him from behind, fighting his way against the flow of passengers alighting from the Paddington train. He reaches the ticket barrier and waves to attract the attention of a slim, fair-haired woman. She comes through the barrier. They embrace passionately and disappear into Costa together.

I see the woman again, as clear as day, dressed in a black, full length coat and high black ankle boots. High black ankle boots. She's slender with a dancer's grace. She's in Saint Sam's room now, wearing the same boots, looking straight at me.

I didn't have time to recover from the shock of this before Ripley and Saint Sam came into the room.

Ripley introduced herself then brought Salomea up to date with police progress. 'We have CCTV footage of Galina leaving the school by the main gate at 9.30 p.m. She's in uniform, alone and on foot and she's not carrying a bag, which suggests she didn't intend to go far.'

'Did she actually make it to her planned meeting?' I wanted to know.

'We can't be sure. We certainly didn't get it on camera. As I say, she was wearing her uniform with a big ski jacket over the top. We can see her feeling in her pockets for something.'

'Probably her phone.'

'Yes. She pulled out the charger cable, but that was all. Then she glanced at her watch a couple of times. After the second time, she broke into a run, so that does suggest she was late for a pre-arranged meeting. But then, as soon as she's clear of the school grounds, we lose track of her movements.'

'And Mikhail – he was on duty last night. Have you spoken to him?'

Ripley shook her head. 'So far we haven't been able to trace either him or Sergei. I've got people working on it and we'll let you know as soon as we catch up with them.'

I looked keenly at Salomea to see how she reacted to the mention of Sergei's name. A small frown creased her smooth brow before she turned her attention back to Raisa while I tried to catch Ripley's eye, which I finally did.

'Was there something else you wanted to talk me about?' I asked.

'Yes, Alyssa. Shall we go through to Molly's office?'

I followed her and closed the door behind us.

'First off,' Ripley began, sitting me down at the glass-topped desk and perching on it herself, arms folded and legs outstretched. 'Tell me how you slept.'

'I didn't.'

'You want my advice? Pace yourself. Step back a little. Don't think that you're the only one with the answers.'

'Sorry – do I do that?'

'That's how it looks to me.'

'And I'm getting in your way – is that what you're saying?'

'No, don't be so touchy. Just take it easy, otherwise you'll crash and burn. Sorry – I'll step out of mummy mode and stop talking about you getting a good night's sleep, blah blah.'

'That's OK,' I told her. 'I appreciate it.'

'Anyway, since we spoke last night, I've listened several times to the message and I agree with you – the threat is definitely increasing.'

'That is so not good news,' I groaned.

'I agree. This isn't the usual cyber bullying – "You're dead if you steal my boyfriend/girlfriend", plus personal insults and laughing at you because you're fat or you're Billy No-mates. That kind of stuff.'

'No – this is definitely different.'

'So we're trying to unscramble the voice and let experts look at it. Meanwhile, we have to investigate all the guys here at St Jude's. I mean *all* of them.'

I paused to think this through.

I hear fingers scratching at the window pane, I run my hand over a feathered corpse, I hear a voice telling me he loves me, killing me softly.

Ripley spoke over my mental action replays. 'You know that it takes a seriously warped personality to play this kind of mind game, setting challenges and, if we're right, acting out one murder and planning a second and possibly even a third. So tell me, does anyone in your group of friends spring to mind?'

'No, everyone I know seems too normal.'

'Seems?' she echoed.

'Yes, and that applies to kids at Ainslee Comp as well, like Alex Driffield for instance, who is a genuinely nice kid.'

'Anyone else we should exclude or, more importantly, include?'

'I've thought maybe it could be Will Harrison – that's a possibility. But it's a hunch based on two small facts.'

'Namely?'

'That he came back to school with a black eye and that he and Scarlett were once an item. Honestly, I jump from person to person – other old boyfriends of Scarlett's, someone in the shadows who I don't even know about.'

Ripley lifted a hand to slow me down. 'OK, those are the people we might line up for Scarlett's murder. But now switch to Galina. Who do you have in mind in that situation?'

I took a deep breath then began again. 'It could be Mikhail because – well, because.'

'He looks the part?' Ripley prompted. 'And because he tried to kidnap her – allegedly.'

Yes, but stalker guy said to forget the Russian mafia – it'll take us down the wrong track.'

'And we believe him?' She was dubious.

'In some twisted way, yes I think he's telling the truth. But then I'm not certain – it could be a double-bluff.

Suddenly I'm thinking it might not be Mikhail but it could be Sergei.'

'Why the shift of focus?'

'Because it turns out that he and Salomea are lovers.'

'Stop!' Ripley made it clear she couldn't keep up. 'How come you didn't mention this earlier?'

'I ran through a few things when I first met Salomea, back there in Dr Webb's office. I tried to remember where I'd seen her before and it came to me – it was at Ainslee Westgate, with Sergei. They met and kissed, and not just friends kissing, unless that's the Russian way of greeting. Anyway, you should ask her.'

'I will,' June agreed. 'Thanks, Alyssa.'

'Think about it, though. Say Salomea has a relationship with Sergei behind Anatoly Radkin's back. Anatoly most likely gives him and Mikhail the job of protecting his daughter on her suggestion without properly vetting either of them. And it's possible they do have connections with less scrupulous elements inside the Russian government. I don't know – my head is in such a mess.'

'Salomea as well as the two guys?' Ripley cut in.

'Yes. That would be really bad news for Galina's dad, wouldn't it? He's married a woman who secretly works for a government who wants him dead and meanwhile she's having an affair with the bodyguard and together they arrange to kidnap Galina.'

'However hard I try, I can't see any way that this would link up with your stalker or with Scarlett's murder,' Ripley decided. 'But I will check out the relationship between

Salomea and Sergei – that in itself shouldn't be too difficult. And I can see it might throw up interesting new angles on Galina's disappearance.'

'Cool,' I murmured.

'Like I said, you do look tired, Alyssa, and we should probably finish now.' She paused before rounding off the conversation. 'Just give me a few more moments to think aloud here. For a start, Scarlett died on New Year's Day, which I take it was before Galina and her bodyguards arrived at St Jude's?'

'Yes, they got here just two days before the start of term.'

'And Scarlett's killer would have had to have been around before that. OK, good. And thank you. We really will wrap things up now.'

She walked purposefully towards the door but I stopped her before she made her exit. 'At least we know that Alex isn't involved,' I reminded her.

'I'm saying what's wrong, what's wrong? And my dad is in the hallway behind me, dragging me back and telling the cops that I was only a kid and they couldn't throw their weight around like this and why the hell were they asking all these questions? And then they said they were sorry to inform us that Scarlett was dead and it was like I walked off the edge of a cliff and just fell and kept on falling.'

I see Alex's pale, stricken face streaked with tears and mud. I cannot believe that he's guilty.

'This has all been happening since you arrested him, so he can't possibly be the killer.'

With one hand on the door handle, Ripley gave a tiny

shake of her head. 'It's too soon to draw conclusions,' she said.

Connie was with Jack when I went back to the technology centre to find him. She'd commandeered his attention as only she can and switched him from his training video to her social networking.

I was feeling exhausted after my session with Ripley and not ready for Facebooking or Tweeting. I almost turned back but Jack spotted me and used me to scramble free of Connie's web.

'She's showing me an app on her phone,' he explained. 'It makes short videos which you can post on to Twitter.'

'It means you can share a video version of any big moment in your life,' Connie enthused, aiming her phone at me. 'Births, marriages, deaths – you open up your app, point your phone and shoot.'

'Don't film me,' I protested.

'Chill, Alyssa. Look – you press your screen to start filming and lift it to stop. Press again then lift, and so on. Then you post it on to your feed. And voila!'

'OK, that's cool, Connie.'

'Say it again – this time like you mean it.'

'I do – I mean it. Digital technology is amazing. But I don't tweet so it's not for me.'

'Don't tweet?' she echoed with a shocked look.

Seeing me wilt under pressure from Connie, Jack stepped in. 'Actually, why don't you post the video of Alyssa on to my phone?'

'No way – I look a wreck!' I wailed.

'You never look a wreck,' Jack grinned, and he kissed me in front of Connie.

'Jeez, you two – get a room,' she grumbled, posting the chopped-up footage of me shielding myself from her lens for all Jack's followers to see. 'Take a look at some of the others. Here's one of Harry Styles getting ready for a concert – that has fifty thousand followers. And here's a video of you, Jack – you're lifting weights. Two hundred and five followers. Don't suppose you know who sneaked that in. Oops, here's one saying "check out how drunk this girl is" – not nice.'

'You see,' I said to justify my non-participation, 'that's the issue with apps like this – it's the privacy thing.'

'I guess it can get a little nasty,' Connie admitted, her enthusiasm starting to wane as she came across more content she didn't like. 'Up-skirt shots like this and girls staggering out of clubs to be sick in the gutter.' She frowned then backtracked and replayed the last piece of footage. 'Is this for real?' she asked.

Drawn in by her shocked tone, Jack and I looked over her shoulder. There was a prefacing note containing five short words that were already branded on my brain – 'Catch me if you can' – then a brief long-distance shot of a girl in uniform walking in the dark. Cut. Next sequence of the girl's face smiling, close up. Cut. The same girl's expression changes. Eyes widen, pupils dilate, she opens her mouth to scream. Cut. Final sequence – the girl lies curled up on the back seat of a car. Mouth taped, hands tied behind her back with what looks like cable from a phone charger cutting into her flesh. End of video.

Connie dropped the phone. It clattered on to the table then skidded sideways. Jack caught it before it fell to the floor.

'That was footage of the guy kidnapping Galina,' Connie whispered. 'The bastard filmed it and put it up online for the whole world to see!'

chapter eight

'She *smiled* at him,' I remembered.

It was early Sunday. Jack and I cycled side by side along the bridle path leading to Hereward Ridge on a cold, clear morning. A hoar frost lay on the branches of overhead trees and covered the slopes overlooking the meandering river and ruined abbey below.

'Galina smiled at the guy who abducted her.'

'That means she knew him – right?'

Whumph! We hit a tree root that snaked across the track, shot out of our saddles, wobbled and came to an undignified halt.

'Oops, are you OK?' Jack asked. I nodded and let my thoughts race on. 'Galina had arranged to see her abductor and when she realized she was going to be late, she started to run. Then when she did meet him she looked pleased. So, yes, she knew him.' Setting my bike upright and getting my thoughts in order, I prepared to pedal on.

Jack hopped nimbly back on to his bike. 'But it's someone from outside St Jude's.'

'Why does it have to be?'

'Because she left by the main gates. She was out of school grounds when it happened.'

'Maybe because they knew they'd be caught on CCTV if they met close to the school. If you wanted to keep your relationship with me secret, you wouldn't meet where there are cameras, would you?'

'Why would I want to keep us a secret?' He grinned then whizzed ahead of me along the bumpy track.

'No, but if you did . . . ?'

'OK, we'd meet up in the village, I guess.'

We cycled on through the wintry morning and my brain was brought back to life by the cold wind after yet another sleepless night tossing and turning in my narrow bed. Whispers had filled the room.

Me saying to Galina, 'Will you come back with me to the sports centre?'

Her saying, 'Are you crazy? I have more things to do, better things.'

'Such as?'

'I meet someone.' She tilts her head, gives a coy smile. She's so beautiful it's unreal.

'Someone special.'

'Give me a clue. Is it someone I know?' Who has she hooked this time with her radiant smile, her lustrous hair, her high cheekbones and bee-stung lips?

'Of course.' She's still smiling, radiating happiness.

'Who is it? Come on, tell me. We're friends, remember.'

'It is secret,' she says in that throaty, heavily accented voice. 'I get ready. I meet him. Later I tell you who.'

'So be good. Don't do anything I wouldn't do,' I say in a feeble attempt at humour.

And I hear myself say it again in the darkness, into the emptiness.

'I want to switch me off,' I told Jack as the wind chilled our faces and our bodies grew hot under the layers of T-shirts, sweaters and jackets. 'I wish there was a way to do that.'

'To forget?' he guessed.

'Yes. Remembering is pressure for me, total pressure. I don't know how much more I can take.'

The only thing I can compare it to, if you're wondering why I'm caving in like this on what ought to be a simple, getaway-from-it-all bike ride, is when you have a sudden fight with someone you love – your moody boyfriend or girlfriend, your god-awful parents. Emotions run wild, you say things you shouldn't. It ends with, 'I hate you!' You storm off. You slam doors, you run. Then, later, the storm has died down and you're still trembling, replaying the whole thing word for word, thinking of the things you said or didn't say, trying in vain to work towards a different ending. It's that – the remembering and regurgitating the emotion. That's how life is for me every single minute of every day.

'Come on, let's go,' Jack said, suddenly veering off the main track and swooping across country, down the hill towards the old abbey.

There aren't many places open in Chartsey Bottom on a Sunday – actually, only the Bridge Inn and the tea shop, which stay open for day trippers all year round. Otherwise the whole place hibernates. Curtains across the windows of stone cottages stay drawn, doors are closed, cars sit in driveways covered in white, sparkling frost.

'Shall we stop here?' Jack asked as we passed the Squinting Cat with its hanging sign depicting – you guessed it – a black cat with a squint.

I read the sign on the cafe door – '*Closed*' – and felt it was a metaphor for all the other closed doors I'd come up against lately. I looked up and down the empty street. 'No, it's shut. Let's carry on.'

'What about hanging around to see if we can pick up anything about Galina's meeting with her mystery man from the locals?'

I shook my head. Take a step back, Ripley had told me. Don't burn yourself out. 'No, not right now.'

'So where to?'

'Ainslee?'

'OK. Where in Ainslee?'

You have to laugh – I couldn't do the stepping back thing for more than five seconds. There was always something drawing me in, an itch inside my brain that I could never scratch. 'Canal. Lock-keeper's Cottage,' I replied.

'This is it,' I told Jack. 'I wanted you to see it for yourself, to find out if you get a new angle on things.'

We'd gone down the steps and propped our bikes against the crumbling brick wall then stood on the towpath looking at the remnants of police tape fluttering in the wind. The white tent had been dismantled. The forensic

173

team investigating Scarlett's death had packed up and gone.

Jack stood at the edge of the towpath and silently stared down into the black canal water then at the giant beam and blackened cogs that worked the lock. 'This makes it . . .'

'. . . Real?'

He nodded. 'You read about a murder and see it on TV, but you don't really get it – how scared Scarlett must have been, how hard she must have fought . . .'

'I know.' The wind shifted the tape and made it snake towards us, snagging around our ankles as we stood there. 'We didn't even know her and look how bad we're feeling – helpless, desperate, wanting answers but not getting them.'

'She leaves the party after midnight,' Jack said, staring into the water and doggedly dredging up our few scraps of knowledge about Scarlett's death. 'She's on CCTV outside The Fleece, close to Ainslee Westgate, talking to a guy, but it turns out we only get the back view. She takes a short cut by the canal. Neighbours hear a racket – two people arguing – but they don't do anything about it. There are lots of drunks wandering around in the early hours of New Year's Day. Why be arsed?'

The plastic tape rattled against our legs and Bolt trotted into view, scouting ahead of Jayden, who appeared at the top of the stone steps leading down from the Lock-keeper's Cottage. He took the steps two at a time, lazily and loosely, with his usual air of defiance.

'Coincidence, or what,' he muttered.

'Definitely a case of "or what",' Jack retorted. 'So, Jayden, how long have you been spying on us?'

'You're so funny!' Jayden sneered. 'Why would I spy on you? That's the thing with you kids from St Jude's – you think you're the centre of the universe.'

'How did you know we were here?'

'It's a free country. Can't a guy walk his dog?'

'Yeah, and can't Alyssa and I have a private conversation without you sniffing around?' Jack stooped to untangle the tape from his leg but stood up fast when he came level with Bolt's bared teeth.

Jayden smiled. 'Just walking my dog, meeting my mates.' He looked beyond us to a narrow humped bridge across the canal where three people stood silently watching. 'Hey, Alex!' he called.

Alex. This was new. Ripley had told me no promises, but evidently she'd decided to let her chief suspect go after all.

He split off from the other two – Ursula and Tom – and came towards us so that Jack and I were caught in a pincer movement between him and Jayden.

'You set this up!' I exclaimed. 'You saw us ride into Ainslee on our bikes and you followed us!'

'Chill,' Jayden muttered. 'Oh, Alyssa, when will you learn to trust me?'

As Alex drew near, I noted that he looked even more like the walking dead than the last time I'd seen him. His pale skin had taken on a yellowish tinge and there were dark circles under his eyes.

'What do you want, Alex?' Jack stepped protectively between us, which left me exposed to Jayden on my right flank.

Jayden left us in doubt a while longer, while Tom and Ursula followed Alex off the bridge in a rearguard action. And, don't forget, Bolt was growling and baring his teeth, ready to snap at our ankles.

'You want answers, don't you?' Jack challenged Alex without getting a response. 'You think Alyssa can come up with a magic solution to how Scarlett died?'

Alex didn't reply. He just stared at me with the dead look in his eyes.

'One step at a time – she got you out of police custody, didn't she?'

'Alex got himself out,' Jayden argued. 'He stuck with what he knew, told them the truth. They had sod-all to go on.'

'Except for the prints on the murder weapon,' Jack reminded them.

'Yeah, along with Alex's dad's prints, plus other sets that they can't match up with anyone they know,' Jayden told us. 'Sure the weapon came from the JD workshop but it's no more than circumstantial evidence.'

'Anyway, cool – you're in the clear.' I was relieved and I let it show.

Alex's brain clicked into gear and he gave the briefest of nods. I think I even heard the word, 'Thanks,' slide out from between clenched teeth.

'Come on, you guys.' Ursula pushed her way past Alex until she stood in the middle of things. 'Why are we giving these two a hard time?'

'Because we can,' Jayden grunted.

Bolt padded along the very edge of the towpath, up and down, up and down, staring at the water.

'What I mean is, at least Alyssa's on the case – why else would she be here?' Ursula wondered.

Tom agreed. 'We're all on the same side, working together.'

'So what have you found out – anything new?' Jack backed down from the stand-off with Jayden to liaise with Tom instead.

'Not much, except we found out that Sammy Beckett lives in that house opposite.' Tom pointed across the canal to a small end-of-terrace house with a high fence that had graffiti sprayed all over it. 'He said the cops have been all over him like a rash because someone told them that in a previous lifetime he'd dated Scarlett.'

'Now who would that "someone" be?' Jayden pretended to wonder but stared right at me.

What was it with him, that he was so hostile? Was it genetic, like it was with Connie, or was it learned? Would I ever work it out?

'Sammy said he was interviewed by a Sergeant Owen,' Ursula explained. 'It turns out he had an alibi for the time of Scarlett's murder.'

'He was with a girl,' Tom added. 'From St Jude's, as it happens.'

'Who?' Jack and I demanded in the same breath. That one short word came across as, 'Astonishing, a girl from our high-class school going out with a kid from the local comp – and pigs might fly!'

177

Jayden let out something between a snort and a laugh then kicked a stone into the canal. Bolt crouched and looked as if he was about to jump in after it but then thought better of it.

'Sorry,' I said. 'I didn't mean . . .'

'We all know what you meant,' Jayden interrupted. 'But get this. Plain, ordinary Sammy Beckett who lives in a terraced house and goes to Ainslee Comp is currently hooked up with a member of the aristocracy.'

I stared at him and racked my brains.

'Work it out, mastermind.'

'Eugenie?' I queried. She was the only titled girl I knew who currently attended St Jude's. Daughter of Sir Roger and Lady Mary Clifford, whose bloodline went back to the Tudors, whose ancestral pile was Farfield Court, ten miles outside Ainslee, in the heart of the Cotswolds.

'It was never going to be Sammy Beckett,' Alex told me as he and I strolled along the towpath.

We'd left the others huddled by the lock and taken a walk together to pool what facts we knew and for me to hear how the cops had treated him. Ripley had been cool, he told me. Owen was the one who had given him a hard time. Good cop, bad cop.

'He wanted to know what I'd done after I left my uncle's party on New Year's Eve.'

'He would, yeah.' I'd spent a lot of time wondering the same thing.

'So I told him.'

178

'Are you happy to share?'

'I went home. I'm a saddo, Alyssa – I went home before midnight and watched Jools Holland welcome in the new year on TV.'

'No witnesses – that's a pity. OK, why leave the party early?'

'Saddo again. You want to know the truth? I was missing Scarlett. I didn't want to be there without her.'

'So why not leave your uncle's and hotfoot it over to her?'

'My Uncle Chris lives way out in the country, miles from anywhere. I'm on foot, I've got no spare cash for a taxi. By the time I reach civilization it's way too late to walk the extra distance into Ainslee. So I go home and veg out in front of the telly.'

'And, anyway, I hear you'd had a fight?'

He frowned. 'Yeah. She said I was a wuss for not standing up to Dad. She was so mad she said not to try calling or texting. We'd only been going out for a week. I didn't know what to do.'

'Yeah, I get it. But listen, Hooper and I – it just so happens we found Will's phone,' I informed him then deliberately paused to let this sink in. I waited a long time but all I got was the closed, dead look from Alex. 'Don't you want to know what was on it?'

'A ton of messages from Scarlett,' he muttered.

'You knew she was texting him and he wasn't texting back? Why did she need to see him – have you any idea?'

179

'She told me he'd kept some stuff that belonged to her and she wanted it back.'

'What kind of stuff?'

There was another long pause – enough time for me to turn round and see that Bolt was following us, tongue lolling, breath forming clouds of steam in the freezing air. Suddenly he was a comedy dog, the bruiser bulldog from *Tom and Jerry*, wheezy and bandy-legged.

'Some pictures.'

'Pictures of them when they were going out?' I had nasty flashes of 'me' in a red bikini, which I had to block in order to carry on with the conversation. 'They were personal?'

Alex nodded. 'They belonged to Scarlett. Will should've deleted them.'

'But he refused. That's why she wanted to see him – to persuade him?' Another lightning flash – this time of Alex and Scarlett sitting together in Starbucks at lunchtime on New Year's Eve.

Alex stands up and starts to yell.

'At Scarlett?' *I ask waitress Lucy.*

'No,' she says. 'At another kid who came along.' He says something that makes Alex jump up and swear.

'What did he look like, this new kid?'

Lucy doesn't get a good look at him, she doesn't have any useful details except one.

'Could you tell what colour his hair was?' *I ask.*

'Fair,' Lucy says, frowning as she remembers. 'Yeah, definitely blond.'

There you go – it was ages since I'd had the brief talk in

Starbucks but, as you know, nothing fades. I mean – not a single thing. Tall kid wearing a big scarf and grey knitted hat, blond.

'So you bumped into Will by accident on New Year's Eve?' I prompted Alex. 'You want to tell me what you said to him?'

'Easy. I said, "Delete Scarlett's photos, you bastard!" '

'And?'

'He said sod off, he didn't have them on his phone any more, the lying swine.'

'OK, I get that too. Just one thing, Alex. When you and Will had the stand up argument, did he have a black eye – a bruise just here?' I put my fingers across my right eye socket.

'No.'

'No bruise – you're sure?'

Alex stopped and turned back towards me. 'Where are you going with this? Who cares about a sodding black eye?'

Will turns up at the start of term minus the Louis Vuitton luggage. He's bulked up, blond and nervous when we talk about Scarlett. He has a bruise under his right eye.

I press him for information about the dead girl.

'Quit that, Sherlock, while you're ahead,' he tells me.'

'So he didn't get it working out in the gym over Christmas like I thought,' I mused as Jayden and the others came within earshot. 'Jayden, you were there on New Year's Eve – do you happen to know how Will Harrison damaged his face?'

'He walked into a door?' was Jayden's suggestion, like he couldn't give a damn.

181

'Did he get involved in a fight at the party?'

'Not with me personally. Anyway, he didn't hang around long enough.'

'He left early?'

'Come to think of it – yeah.'

'Was he in a bad mood? Did he argue with anyone?'

'What am I – his keeper?' Jayden was about to go off on a typical one when he suddenly saw where I was going. 'Yeah, he did. Nobody wants to hang out with him since he left Ainslee Comp and his head grew to twice the normal size. All he was interested in at the party was avoiding Scarlett. He didn't stay long – in fact, he was out of there before midnight.'

'And still no bruise?' I checked.

'He was well pissed but there was no facial damage,' Ursula confirmed calmly before a sudden thought lit up her expression. 'Hey maybe it was Will on the CCTV footage – hassling Scarlett!'

'It's a definite possibility,' I said quietly.

'Sammy Beckett – he's cool,' Zara told Eugenie.

Jack and I had cycled home. He'd gone off for a Sunday session with his tennis coach and I'd gathered the girls in the sports-centre coffee bar.

'Very cool,' Charlie agreed.

Eugenie, who has my pale complexion, coloured up bright red.

'Have you taken him home to Farfield Hall?' BWS wanted to know. Rich girl takes poor boy home to meet her parents.

'Ouch!' Zara winced.

Eugenie flicked her hair back behind her shoulders and withered Connie with her scorn. 'Your class prejudices are so twentieth century, Connie Coetzee. And, sure, my parents have met Sammy and they like him.'

We all backed Eugenie and disagreed with Connie, making up our minds that Sammy (who incidentally is cool because, though he may be a statistic-obsessed nerd, actually looks like a young Johnny Depp with that honed, exaggerated jaw line and those big, dark-lashed eyes) was in the clear.

Down below on the indoor tennis court, Jack's coach fired balls from a machine and Jack returned them at a hundred miles per hour.

'So what did Ripley say about the video footage?' Completely unfazed, Connie pushed us forward to another burning topic.

'Ripley hasn't come back to me yet,' I replied. 'It's only twelve hours since I gave it to her. The techies will do their thing and try to trace where it came from. Today's Sunday, so maybe not until tomorrow. Anyway, I expect the guy's an IT geek who's clever enough to block that info, even from police experts.'

Jack's coach called him to the net and the machine tried to lob him. Jack jumped and smashed, sprinted and retrieved from the base line. I stood up for a closer look.

'Any more nasty messages?' Zara enquired. She was with me, leaning on the rail, looking down at the court.

Catch me quick, memory girl. It's going to get worse, one

hundred per cent guaranteed. Killing you softly.

'Nasty doesn't cover it,' I muttered.

'Surreal?' Zara suggested.

'Yes – like we're playing a game where no one tells me the rules or the score.' I stared down at Jack executing a perfect forehand drive. 'The thing is, I'm beginning to realize now that if I lose Galina could die.'

Zara sidled close. 'I'm sorry, Alyssa. I guess there's nothing I can do?'

I shook my head and felt the urge to cry that you get when someone is being especially nice.

Jack picked up balls from the corner of the court, glanced up and flashed me one of his bright smiles.

Thank you, thank you! I smiled back down.

'You want my advice?' Zara said. 'You probably won't take it but I could give it anyway.'

'Go ahead.'

'Deep breath, Alyssa. Are you OK? You're sure you're not going to cry on me?'

'No.'

'So this is what I would do if I were you. I'd step right back from this crappy situation. Hand over everything you know to the police, stay out of it from now on and let them do their job.'

'I can't,' I sighed.

'Why not?'

'I've already said – he's got Galina. He could kill her if I don't work out a way to stop him. How do I step away from that?'

'But think about it, Alyssa. This really isn't down to you. You're getting dragged in, and it's probably too dangerous for you to deal with.'

Leaning on the rail, I closed my eyes.

'You're sure you're OK?'

'Yeah, just dizzy.'

'So I'll quit talking. But remember, we're here for you – me, Eugenie, Connie, Charlie – whenever you need us.'

I took the deep breaths and choked back the tears. 'Thanks. That means a lot.'

'And guess what,' Zara rattled on. 'I've decided to switch from physics to neuroscience in my UCAS applications. I'm more and more fascinated by how this stalker guy's brain works. It's turned me on to neuroscience – trying to understand the brain of a psycho. I've started to read about temporal lobes and synapses. It's incredibly complicated.'

'I think you'll be brilliant at it,' I told her. Then we hugged and I felt a whole lot better.

In your experience, how would you expect an exiled Russian oligarch to look? Here's how I see it. He'd have no hair to speak of and a thick neck, giving him a bullet-headed look, and his grey eyes would be cold and hard. His suit would be hand tailored to cover a thickening waistline. He would ride horses bare chested and go fishing in a raging river like Putin and he would attend film premieres with a trophy wife at his side.

In fact, Anatoly Radkin had the suit and the wife, but a head of thick, dark hair, no paunch and eyes full of concern when Molly called me to meet him in her office on Sunday afternoon.

'This is Alyssa Stephens. She's Galina's roommate,' Molly told him.

Anatoly shook my hand. 'You were the last person to see my daughter before she vanished.'

I nodded and stole a glance at Salomea's face as she stood quietly by the long window overlooking the lawns. Her expression was tight and guarded.

'How did she seem?' he asked.

'Excited. She said she was going to meet someone special, that she would tell me about him later.'

'She hadn't told anyone else?'

'I don't think so. I got the impression it was a big secret and she planned to slip off to meet him without Mikhail or Sergei finding out.'

Anatoly blinked away the two names without comment. 'I'm sorry to ask you so many questions, Alyssa. You have told this to the police and I'm sure that soon they will actively question everyone here at St Jude's, but you understand I'm impatient because I'm very afraid for my daughter. I need to know from you everything that happened on Friday night.'

'It's OK. I'll do all I can to help.'

'And the video footage – you were the one who handed it over to the police?'

'Yes. At first I was totally shocked. Then I started to think it through. It's all cut up into quick, two or three second segments. When the kidnapper first filmed her walking down the drive it was from behind, so that probably means he followed her out of the quad where the boys' and girls' dorms are. Maybe he watched her from one of the boys' rooms and left just after she did.'

Galina's father listened closely and calmly, considering the circumstances. I got the impression that he agreed with what I'd just said.

'The second segment is filmed as she moves towards him, which must mean he'd taken a short cut and got to their prearranged meeting place before her.'

'Or else he'd kept her waiting,' Molly suggested. 'She could have sat for a while – in someone's house, in the cafe in the village.'

I disagreed. 'Inspector Ripley will have checked that out – it'd be the first thing she'd do. As far as I know, no one saw Galina in Chartsey Bottom on Friday night. Besides, the video shows them meeting out in the open, in the dark – there were no street lights.'

'OK, so he took a short cut and overtook her,' Anatoly decided. 'He's ready to film her as she arrives.'

'And she knew him because she was smiling.' I was totally clear about this. She knew her attacker/abductor/potential killer. That was the most chilling thing – Galina's smile of anticipation, lips parted, eyes sparkling as she approached.

'No street lights?' Anatoly repeated.

'No. There were trees behind her, but there was nothing else – no landmark that would help to identify the place.'

'What kind of trees?'

'Oaks. There are lots of those around here, everywhere you look. It was only a couple of seconds before that

187

segment ended then the video cut to a close-up of Galina's face without any background detail, and that's when suddenly she wasn't smiling.'

I stopped, unable to go on until Anatoly pushed me.

'It helps me to know this,' he insisted. 'If you could continue, please.'

Catch me if you can.

Galina is in school uniform, she's eager to meet her abductor, she risks meeting him late at night, in the middle of the countryside. She smiles at him. Cut.

Her lips stop smiling, her eyes widen and her pupils dilate. That's when she opens her mouth to scream.

What has changed? Has he said something to her? Is it something he's done? What makes her change from delight to terror as the camera comes close and her features dissolve into a blur? Does he produce a knife or a gun as he reaches her? Does he put a hand to her neck to throttle her?

She's backing off, screaming, pleading.

Cut to the final sequence. Galina lies curled up in foetal position on the back seat of a car. The car has fancily stitched cream leather seats, which means it's high spec. Galina's mouth is taped with silver duct tape. Her hands are tied behind her back with cable from a phone charger (her own, presumably) cutting into her wrists. Her eyelashes and cheeks are wet with tears, her nostrils flared. She looks up and sideways at her 'someone special', who must be leaning into the back of the car to film her. She is betrayed, afraid for her life, desperate. Cut.

Anatoly listened and considered. I told him everything I knew and he thanked me. 'Galina's mother is in

Moscow. She will be kept informed.'

I stole another glance at Salomea, wife number two or three, the un-wicked stepmother who was nonetheless cheating on a man who appeared in the top twenty of rich lists around the world. She met my gaze and her eyelids flickered.

'Does anyone know what happened to Sergei and Mikhail?' I asked.

Salomea turned to stare out of the window at the gathering dusk.

Anatoly raised an eyebrow. 'My people found them in London. They were on the tube train to Heathrow with tickets for Moscow in their pockets.'

'Your people?'

'I have more than thirty permanent employees in this country, all engaged in various aspects of security – bodyguards for me, my wife, my daughter. They are well trained. It's difficult for Mikhail and Sergei to hide for very long.'

Ouch! 'So you're supposing that they lost track of Galina and panicked?'

'Yes, maybe. They planned to do the first thing that came into their heads, which was to leave the country and head for Russia because they know I can't follow them there. That was the mistake – it was too obvious. I had my men pick them up at the check-in desk.'

It was like having your own personal police force, but without the official codes of conduct or any accountability. Anatoly's 'pick them up' phrase probably edited out a few brutal details that he didn't want me to know, but which Salomea understood all too well. A shudder ran through her slight, ballet dancer's frame as she listened to her husband's account of what had happened to her secret lover.

I took a moment to picture it. Mikhail and Sergei hurry towards check-in. They didn't do their job; they let Galina leave the school undetected. Only one of them had officially been on duty on Friday night, but both were responsible for her safety. Their gut reaction was to run.

They don't reach the self-check-in machines before ripped men in suits surround them and hustle them out of the line. It's discreet so nobody notices as Sergei and Mikhail are escorted from the terminal. A car is waiting.

Anatoly Radkin is the picture of civilized concern as he quizzes me in Molly's office – as handsome as his daughter is beautiful, prompting me for every detail I can remember, backed by an army of well dressed thugs.

'Where are they now?' I asked.

'I don't know,' he replied dismissively. 'They are no longer on my staff.'

No longer part of the story – officially at least. I wondered how long it had taken Sergei to buckle under pressure and admit his relationship with his ex-boss's wife. Salomea must have been wondering the same thing.

I pictured her walking through a desert of hidden landmines in the full glare of her husband's sun. After all, a kiss on the lips in Ainslee Westgate station is unbelievably high risk when you're married to a man as powerful as Anatoly Radkin.

'There's a reward for information,' Anatoly said, maybe or maybe not coincidentally directing his attention to Salomea for the first time since I got there. He went over and put a protective arm round her shoulder. She shuddered and he withdrew the arm. 'So, Alyssa – if you think of anything else . . .'

I didn't need any reward, I told him with a burst of angry contempt that I didn't try to hide. 'Right now, getting Galina back safe is all that matters.'

chapter nine

There's a row of metal lockers in the glass corridor connecting the technology centre to the music room and that's where I found the tie. It was slung over the top of my locker door, hanging like a noose.

Jack, fresh and damp from his shower after tennis coaching, saw me freeze on the spot but it took him a while to clock the red and green tartan noose.

'Why is my door hanging open?' I wondered aloud. Not 'Whose tie is that?' or 'Oh my God, that could be Galina's!' No, what bothered me was that I was sure I'd left the metal door locked and now it was mysteriously ajar.

Jack slid his hand through the noose part of the tie then handed it to me. I read the name tag stitched into the reverse side. Galina Radkin. My heart lurched.

'And a message,' Jack told me as he swung the door fully open. He pointed to a lime-green Post-it note on the inside.

I've said this before, Alyssa. The problem with you is that you keep missing what's under your nose.

I read it and screwed it up, threw it down on the floor. Thumping heart, breathlessness, pins and needles in my arms – the note induced an immediate, full-on panic attack.

Jack rescued the piece of paper then paced up and down the corridor. He stared out at the car park as if the answer lay among the rows of cars.

'He opened my locker!' I wailed, as if violated. The small things become big because it postpones the moment when you have to address the central issue, which was more proof that my stalker was on my case twenty-four/seven, breathing the air I breathed, predicting every move I made. I slung the tie back at Jack and another lime-green note slid out of the lining and fluttered to the floor.

Jack picked it up. '*PLEASE HELP ME*,' he read.

'Is it definitely Galina's handwriting?' was Luke's first question.

Jack and I had taken the two notes and the tie into the music room where we'd found him, Will, Hooper and Connie, instruments in hand, waiting for Eugenie and Marco to begin their singing lesson with Bruno Cabrini.

'Let me see.' Snatching the *PLEASE HELP ME* note, Connie studied the unsteady, upper case letters. 'You can't really tell,' she decided as she showed it to Hooper.

'My gut tells me yes, it's her writing and she wrote it in secret and stuffed it into the lining of the tie,' I said. 'And you can see by the name tape that it's definitely her tie, which she was wearing when she vanished.'

Hooper studied the note. 'She was scared shitless when she wrote this,' he commented. 'The handwriting shakes and wobbles all over the place. But in one way we should be relieved – at least she did write it.'

'Meaning what?' Jack asked.

'Meaning, obviously she's still alive,' Hooper explained patiently. 'And, when you think about it, this guy does need to keep Galina alive as long as possible so he can carry on playing cat and mouse with Alyssa. Once Galina's dead, it's game over.'

My stomach flip-flopped, my heart thudded.

'Hey, Hooper, no need to pull your punches,' Connie muttered under her breath.

'I'm just saying . . .'

'We know and we agree,' I butted in.

Across the soundproofed room, Carlo the music maestro took up his baton and tapped it against his lectern. Eugenie and Marco picked up their scores.

'We'd better go and play for him or we're all in the dog house.' Connie grabbed her violin and strode across the room. Her Jo'burg language is like that – quaint, a couple of generations out of date.

Hooper followed with his cello, then Luke with his double-bass and Will with his viola. The quartet took their place by the side of the singers.

Tap-tap-tap. Bruno settled them down and appealed for full concentration. His manner was fussy and irascible, like Hercule Poirot. Come to think of it, that's not a bad comparison. Bruno is short and stout, dapper and methodical. Every time he conducts, he follows the bars, quavers and semi-quavers like a detective picking up clues. The musicians followed him, playing the quiet, slow prelude to the most famous aria from Verdi's *Aida*.

194

Egyptian slave girl Aida is waiting for Ramades, her lover. Eugenie is Aida; Marco is Ramades.

Eugenie opened her mouth and the beautiful words poured out.

> '*Ah, si tu vieni a recarni, o crudel*
> *L'ultimo addio.*'
> Ah! If you come to give me, so cruel,
> Your last goodbye.

'No, no!' Bruno *rat-a-tat-tatted* his baton against the lectern. 'More feeling, more passion, Eugenie. *L'ultimo addio* – last goodbye! Aida knows she will lose him. She is sad beyond words.'

Marco stayed in the background as Eugenie began again. The string quartet kept perfect pace and rhythm. Bruno conducted with theatrical intensity, head to one side, both arms raised.

Jealousy, exile and betrayal – that's the theme of Aida. Songbird Eugenie closed her eyes and sang as if she had an old soul in her seventeen-year-old body, a soul that had experienced all there was to know about love and loss.

> '*O patria mia, non ti vedro mai piu!*'
> Oh my homeland, I will never see you again!

'Yes,' Bruno said with quiet satisfaction at the end, after each of his students had sung their parts. He didn't praise or critique, but simply put down his baton and turned to the page where Aida and Ramades die together in a darkened tomb.

'I never knew Marco could sing like that,' I confessed to Hooper when the lesson had finished.

Six of us left the music room together, leaving Eugenie and Marco to take notes from Bruno. We were headed for dinner, me with Galina's school tie and the two Post-it notes stuffed in my jacket pocket.

'I expect there's a lot about Marco that we don't know,' Hooper suggested.

'Like what?'

'Like where he went to school before he came to St Jude's, how big is his allowance, plus why he hates his dad.'

'Does he?'

'That's my theory. Why else would he make a big show of saying no to following in his father's giant footballing footsteps then play anyway?'

Hooper braved the sub-zero gusts of wind, surging ahead of me across the car park then turning left round the front of the main building, his cello case in hand. I stopped to consider then ran to catch up with him at the main entrance. 'You think Marco's rejecting the whole football-hero lifestyle?'

He nodded. 'I know zilch about the game but even I realize that he's already good enough to play at professional level – you saw that for yourself.'

'In the five-a-side match – yes, you're right. I remember that he did say he hates the game. Is that the same thing as hating your dad, though?'

'Please yourself.' Hooper shrugged. 'I just thought it would be worth looking at. I'll do it for you if you like.'

'Cool. Yeah, go ahead.' Ever since the hearts text and the jealous-rival flare-up with Jack, I'd pretty much kept my distance from Italian lover boy so Hooper's offer to do a little investigating on my behalf was welcome. 'I don't think there's much there, though,' I warned.

Zara and the girls had my back and eager, introverted, brilliant Hooper had taken up the Marco trail. Both things felt good as I waited for Jack in the entrance to the dining room.

'This'll only take a couple of minutes,' he'd promised when he spotted Shirley Welford talking to Justine by the self-service counter. 'I need to change the time of our next tutorial.'

And this was a chance for me to contact Ripley about the tie and the messages, I decided. I took out my phone and found my list of contacts, but before I could make the call Will came up from behind and snatched the phone from my hand.

'Will, what are you playing at? Give me that!' I protested.

' "Give me that!" ' he mimicked, holding it out of reach. 'Who were you planning to call – your friend, Inspector Ripley? Yeah, I'm right – it was her.'

'What's it to you, Will?' Here was another person who

was not my flavour of the month – ever since the scuffle had broken out in the boys' dorm and Hooper had hared off to fetch Molly.

'Alyssa Stephens thinks that Alex Driffield is innocent –' Will sneers as he breaks off from his card game – 'holy shit! Now she's got her super-sleuth claws in me!'

Jack takes a swing at Will, punches him in the stomach and Will bends over double. Luke and Marco are the ones who drag them apart.

Hooper sprints off while Zara insists that we hear Will's version of events. 'Come on, Will, we're listening.'

'So, I knew Scarlett,' Will admits. He's furious with me for dragging his relationship with Scarlett into the open and still has one hand across his stomach to protect himself from another attack. 'But what am I going to do – go around telling everyone I was her ex and she dumped me for some other kid she met on holiday?'

And Will was suddenly suspect number one.

Ripley came knocking and interviewed him for two hours. But I still needed to be sure in my own mind – was Will a crazy psychopath?

'Will, give me back my phone,' I insisted.

'Like you and Hooper gave me *my* phone back? Or, excuse me, let me rephrase that: like you and Hooper did after you'd stolen it from me?'

'We didn't steal it!' I reminded him in a tone of injured innocence. 'You dropped it and Hooper handed it back to you.'

28th December, Scarlett to Will:
Really need to see you
Answer my texts
Where r u? We need to talk.

Those were the incriminating messages, word for word.

'The problem with you is that you keep missing what's under your nose.'

My stalker is in a constant state of disappointment with me. He keeps raising the stakes, taking major risks to return Galina's tie and leave me more messages. And I'm still not getting it.

Will is here right now, in my face, under my nose. He is challenging me. Is it him – is he my stalker?

'You read my texts,' he accused, waving my phone in front of my face then rapidly raising it above his head. 'You dropped me in deep shit.'

There was no point denying it. 'No deeper than the shit you dropped yourself in. You shouldn't have kept those pictures on your phone.'

'I didn't see why not.'

'Because she asked you not to. You kept them because you thought you could twist the knife by using some old photos against her. That's nasty, Will.'

He laughed then flung my phone at me. I stuck out a hand to catch it.

'You have no effing idea,' he mocked. 'The way you see it, Scarlett was Goody Two Shoes and I was – God knows – anyway, I'm worse than the dog muck you scrape off the sole of your shoe.'

'Unless you can tell me a different story and I decide to believe you – yeah.'

'I can, but you won't.'

'Try me.'

'OK, Alyssa, listen to this. With Scarlett Hartley, what you saw was not what you got. Sure, she looked fantastic, every guy's dream girl. But underneath she was a mess.'

Here it comes, I thought, the classic move to blacken the name of a dead girl who obviously can't answer back.

'I mean it,' Will insisted. 'Anyone going out with Scarlett had to turn into a cross between a shrink and her father, who by the way left home when she was seven years old. It messed her up permanently, so much so that when I started going out with her she came across as the most needy person I ever met.'

'That's not what Ursula told me,' I said stoutly. 'She said Scarlett was really upbeat. She came top in everything. That doesn't sound to me like a girl with serious issues.'

'Bright but flaky. The two things can definitely go together in one stunning, sexy package.' He said this with a meaningful stare.

'OK, I know you want to stick the two of us in the same boat.' Just like my insane stalker guy did, actually. My flesh crept and I raised my shoulders to try and stop myself shivering.

'You want an example? Take the night of the party,' he went on. 'Scarlett's made an effort and she's looking amazing but on the inside she's falling apart because Alex isn't there. She tells Jayden that Alex should've told his dad to sod off and come with her instead. She's had too much to drink so her guard's down and she lets Jayden know that someone's been stalking her, and now she's paranoid. Alex knows she can't stand to be alone. She says he's let her down big time – loud enough for everyone in the room to hear.'

'So what did you do? Did you try to calm her down?'

Will came right back at me. 'You're kidding me. I've spent my whole time since last summer trying to stay out of Scarlett's way. So was I honestly going to step in and mop up the messy pieces just because she'd had a fight with Alex?'

'Jesus, Will, is there a heart locked away behind all this macho bullshit?'

'What are you talking about?'

'The girl you once went out with, who at some time you must have really liked, is dead. Now all you do is trample her name in the mud.'

'No. I'm telling you the truth, setting the record straight like I did with Ripley. Sure, Scarlett was beautiful and mega bright, with that photographic memory thing.'

'Eidetic,' I corrected pedantically. At least get the correct terminology, please. 'It means you can pass exams, no problem, but otherwise it's not all it's cracked up to be.'

Will shrugged. 'You're right – Scarlett didn't appreciate having it. When we were together, she said she wished she could flick a switch and turn it off.'

This time I managed not to hitch my shoulders up

around my ears and instead took a deep breath, trying to dispel the familiar fear that Scarlett and I had led parallel lives and that at this rate, unless I pieced the clues together and solved the mystery, I too could soon end up face down in the canal.

'Are you OK, Alyssa?' Jack said as he rejoined me and Will. I saw that he was tensed up, ready to strike out in my defence.

'Yes, I'm cool,' I said wearily. 'Will was telling me about the real Scarlett – the one behind the smiley face we all saw in the paper.'

'Truth time – Alyssa thinks I killed her,' Will scoffed, refusing to move aside.

I stared at him for a long time. No, he wasn't devious enough, not unless this was a double bluff. But then Will was impatient and didn't pay enough attention to detail to carry that off. He had a brilliant mind, though. I went round in circles until finally I nailed it in one short phrase – he was angry but not crazy.

'No,' I sighed. 'You're wrong, Will. I crossed you off my list days ago.'

I ate dinner with Jack, or rather I pushed my food around my plate. Then we walked down a long, low corridor in the ancient part of the school building to the old library where no one went. It was a book-lined room with an Adams-style fireplace and leather chairs, low oak tables with magazines and periodicals, and leather-bound volumes on the shelves that gave off a fusty smell, which was somehow comforting.

'So – not Will?' Jack sighed, putting his feet up on one of the low tables.

I sat opposite him, curling my feet under me and tapping the arms of my chair. 'Not unless he's putting in an Oscar-winning performance to fool us.'

'OK.' Leaning back in his chair, Jack looked at me through half-closed eyes. Neither of us said anything for a long time.

Happy with the silence, I did my favourite thing of breathing him in. I thought how much I loved him without needing to say it, felt my heart loosen and lighten, my whole body relax.

'Why are you smiling?' he asked eventually.

I love you. I can't believe it – is it possible that I've been lucky enough to find the person I want to be with forever? Do you know that you make me feel light and airy, feathery and free? If I tell you, will you run a mile?

I didn't say any of this – just thought it as I gazed at him.

'Tell me,' he urged.

If I tell you that your eyes are the colour of clear honey and I know and love every centimetre of your face – those straight, dark brows; high, smooth forehead; and strong, perfect jaw (not too square, not too jutting, not too anything) – will you think less of me or more?

Jack sat in the glow from a table lamp, watching me watching him.

'You're not going to say it,' he guessed at last.

We were in the moment, smiling, loving. I shook my head.

I love you, he mouthed. Aloud – 'I love you.'

'I love you too.' And my heart was totally his.

'Narcissistic Personality Disorder,' Zara read.

It was Monday morning and we both had a study period. I came across her in the technology centre, busy looking up information on a website. Luke and Connie were there as well, but too loved-up to notice Zara and me sitting in a side bay overlooking the stand of bare beech trees set against an iron-grey sky.

'An individual who suffers from NPD is excessively preoccupied with issues of personal adequacy, power, prestige and vanity. He or she may need admiration and lack empathy. They have an unwarranted sense of self-importance.'

'Why are you showing me this?' I asked.

'I've been thinking. This guy we're after for Scarlett and Galina – he's mentally ill, right?'

'Most likely, yes. And he's on a power trip with me, for sure.'

'He lacks empathy, plus he needs you to say, "Wow, how clever you are to keep ahead of the game!" '

'Again, yes. It gives him a buzz – he enjoys it.'

'*I love you when you're angry, Alyssa. Catch me if you can.*'

Zara seemed pleased with herself for honing in on something that might give us a way forward. 'Historically, people with NPD have been megalomaniacs. Think Napoleon, Hitler, Catherine the Great.'

I nodded and we read on together. Statistically NPD

occurs on average in one per cent of the population, which doesn't sound a lot, but be aware – one in every hundred people you're about to meet is a potential power-hungry monster. Anyway, the sufferer takes advantage of others to achieve goals and fantasises about having great success and power. They're often extremely intelligent.

'Is this fitting the profile of anyone we know?' Zara wondered.

'Are you kidding? It fits *everyone* we know here at St Jude's!'

Let's face it – the outside world sees us as a bunch of arrogant, up-our-own-arses know-it-alls. We live in a hothouse of academic success. Forget Bryony's rhubarb metaphor – in fact, we're Narcissus personified. He, by the way, is the kid in the Greek myth who knelt by a lake and for the first time saw his own reflection. And what does he do? He only goes and falls in love with himself. Then he wanders off across country and loses his reflection. The poor, deluded sap searches for the reflection but never finds it again. He eventually dies of a broken heart.

'Now the really bad thing about NPDs,' budding neuro-scientist Zara pointed out with all the conviction of the recent convert, 'is that the underlying psychology is pathological.'

'Translation – this means it's a neurological pattern inside the brain that's outside the sufferer's control?'

'Exactly – it's involuntary. If this person is criticized, they may display anger-management issues and often turn violent.'

'But look – it says they can disguise the anger by feigning modesty as a disguise. That makes it really tricky to spot.'

'Yeah, but they also have hypo-manic moods that they can't disguise and if you push the right buttons the fake modesty blows apart and the psycho comes roaring out.'

'Useful tip for whenever I finally come face to face with the guy,' I muttered, feeling a shiver of fear run down my neck and spine.

'*The condition may be partly genetic.*' Zara read ahead and gave me a summary. 'Plus, the sufferer has over-indulgent parents, maybe, who hand out unrealistic praise on a daily basis. On the other hand, there could be severe emotional abuse as a child. Or a combination of both. Hey look – there was a guy called Blackwell, jailed in 2005 for killing his parents. Really bright kid, nicknamed "Brains". Used his dad's credit cards and beat his mum and dad to death with a claw hammer when they challenged him on the credit-card issue, then used the cards to take his girlfriend to New York for the weekend to stay at the Plaza Hotel. Spent thirty grand. Came back to collect his A-level results – straight A*s in all of them. Police eventually found the parents' bodies; he denied everything. Charge was reduced to manslaughter through diminished responsibility. Classic case study for NPD, apparently.'

Facing a gruesome death was not what I would have chosen to be focusing on in my free period, I told Zara. I had a translation to do for Justine, an essay to begin for Bryony.

'But it could be really useful in getting inside your guy's

head,' she insisted. 'All the stuff about taking advantage of others and seeking power – that really fits with what's going on here. And the fact that it's not always obvious – it doesn't have to be an in-your-face, show-off guy like some people I could name in this school. Marco, for instance.'

'Actually, there's probably more to Marco than his blingy car. But funny you should mention him – Hooper's interested in finding out more.'

'Well, let him go ahead. I'm just getting my own head round the fact it might not be someone that obvious.' Zara frowned at the screen, ignoring Luke and Connie as they strolled across and peered over our shoulders.

'NPD?' Luke read. 'Sounds like a title for a cop series. Oh sorry, no – that was *NYPD*!'

'Lame, Luke,' I sighed. 'So unless you have something useful to say . . .'

'. . . Which you don't,' Zara pointed out.

'I know – you want me to butt out.'

'Come on, let's go,' BWS told him, grabbing his hand and heading for the door.

Time to spoon-feed the guy some lunch, with Eton mess for dessert.

The clock was ticking; the hours were passing. I was waiting for my friend Ripley to touch base with me about Galina's tie.

It turned out she was busy on the Monday afternoon and sent Sergeant Owen instead.

He tutted when I presented him with the latest vital

pieces of evidence, took a pen out of his breast pocket and stuck it through the noose of the tie. 'You didn't have a sealable plastic bag available?'

'Not at the time, no.'

I'd been working in my room when he knocked at the door and brought in the sour, stale smell of tobacco smoke. Don't get the wrong impression – we weren't alone. Molly had shown him up to the girls' dorm and stayed while Jimmy and I exchanged information.

'Your fingerprints will be all over this. It's bound to affect what forensics can do with it.'

I swallowed hard then gave him a muttered sorry-I-didn't-think apology.

'Likewise with the Post-it notes,' he commented when I handed them to him.

'PLEASE HELP ME'.

'You keep missing what's under your nose.'

'I love you when you're angry, Alyssa.'

'Killing You Softly'

'Catch me if you can.'

They pile in thick and fast. He's creeping me out, breathing the same air, reading my mind.

Sergeant Owen put the contaminated evidence in separate bags and sealed them. He did everything deftly and quickly, but with a bored air, as if he'd sealed too many bags, collected too much evidence and wished to God he'd taken early retirement and hightailed it off to one of the Costas to sit under a sun umbrella. 'Any more contact from your stalker since you found these?' he asked.

'Not so far.' Though these days I didn't turn a corner or walk down one of these narrow corridors without expecting him to jump out, armed and dangerous, from behind the arras. Shadowing me, leaving me red clues and killing me softly, setting me challenges that I couldn't live up to.

'Looks like it's gone quiet, then,' Jimmy said.

Until the next time. I took a deep breath and flicked a glance in Molly's direction. Help!

She stepped right in, but didn't take us in the direction in which I wanted to go. 'The school principal and I have discussed the level of security we have in place here at St Jude's,' she began. 'We have security cameras covering most of the school grounds and some CCTV coverage of the inside of the building, but it's not comprehensive. There are no cameras in the dormitories for instance, or in the individual classrooms.'

'No armed guards protecting the students with semi-automatics,' Owen commented drily. That was his main quality, I realized – dryness. Dry, wrinkled skin; dry sense of humour; dry and matter-of-fact investigation of even the most gruesome murder. A wizened, wheezy jockey in faded, tobacco-stained racing silks sprung to mind and the image stuck.

Molly chose not to react to his tasteless wisecrack. 'Obviously we're worried about Alyssa's safety, but we'd like to know your opinion on security at St Jude's.'

'You mean – how much danger is she really in?' Patting his pocket as if checking to see if he had his cigarettes with him, Sergeant Owen shrugged. 'Are you asking me if you should be on the safe side and send her home?'

'No way!' I protested. I'd been here before over Lily and Paige, when Saint Sam had muscled in and ordered Aunt Olivia to take me out of school. Back then I'd overcome my fears, resisted and won the battle, but it might not work a second time. With police backing him, Sam could easily persuade my aunt that taking me out of harm's way was the best thing to do. 'I mean – no, I'm staying here,' I said as calmly as I could, though talk of danger made my heart race.

'You heard the girl,' Owen told Molly.

'So my next question, in the light of Galina's abduction—' Molly began.

'If she has been abducted,' Owen interrupted.

'*What?* So you're saying she staged the video shots of her lying tied up on the back seat of a car?' was where I came in again – this time, less calmly.

'It's not unheard of.'

'Why would you even think that?'

'One – Galina clearly wasn't happy here and faking her own kidnap would be a way of making a dramatic exit. Two, she could follow this up with a fake ransom demand from ridiculously wealthy daddy, payment of which would fund her through a couple of high-roller seasons in sunny South Africa, California, wherever.'

Now he was pissing me off big time. 'Except there's been no ransom demand. And she wasn't just pretending to be scared in the video and in the note I just showed you – her shaky handwriting shows she was actually terrified.'

210

'No demand for money,' he agreed with a quick snap and crackle of his finger joints. 'Not yet.'

I kept at the dried-up little detective sergeant like Bolt gnawing on a bone. 'And what about Anatoly Radkin – wasn't he planning to offer a reward for information? Did he do what he said he would?'

'Yes, he went ahead and did that but to date no one has come forward. Anyway, I hear he's got a lot of other things on his mind.'

Oligarch things like buying oil pipelines and fracking for shale gas, I guessed.

Jimmy the Jockey didn't enlighten us.

'So back to my original question,' Molly insisted. 'Can you recommend any practical way in which we could offer Alyssa more protection? Could you allocate her a liaison officer, for example?'

'That's not my call.' Jimmy picked up the bags containing evidence and got ready to leave. 'You want me to put it to the boss?'

'Or else Dr Webb will.' Molly opened the door for him. 'Perhaps that's the best way forward, Sergeant Owen – let me put it to my boss to put to your boss.'

chapter ten

Hours rolled into days and nothing happened, except that Hooper read through the Italian gossip mags online and found that early last summer Marco's dad, Paolo Conti, had publicly rowed with his only son after said son went awol with a very expensive boat that he had moored in the harbour in Monaco. *Footballing Family in Major Bust Up over Boat* – that sort of thing. And I didn't get my liaison officer for the same Catch 22 reason as before – nasty notes and dead birds don't constitute a crime and until a crime had been committed I couldn't get police protection, blah blah.

Oh, and it turned out I was wrong about Anatoly being busy extracting gas from the earth's crust. Actually, he was divorcing Salomea. Hooper picked this up on Twitter – a 'friend of a friend' of Salomea Radkin tweeted how he'd discovered she was having an affair with his missing daughter's bodyguard so he'd thrown her out of the Knightsbridge mansion. Salomea was traumatized, devastated, humiliated, heartbroken, etcetera.

Jack snuck into my room late on Tuesday night and I felt safe. That was one small period of calm on a stormy sea. Gentle eddies lapped around the bed as we lay arm in arm, looking out at the stars.

But Wednesday came and no one had moved a step closer towards finding Galina.

A calm before the storm, but when the storm did hit the waves rose and crashed down, rose and crashed, until they engulfed me.

'Where's Jack?' Hooper asked me at midday on Wednesday. I'd just come out of the pool next door to the sports centre after a thirty-length attempt at clearing my head and keeping fit, and was heading for the changing room.

'He cycled into the Bottoms to post a letter. Why?'

'Nothing. I just wanted to talk to him about possibly tracing that video – geeky techie stuff.'

'Anyway, I'm sorry. Like I said, Jack went to the village.'

Hooper behaved as if he wanted to stay and chat, whereas I clearly wanted to grab a towel and get changed.

'Are you sure about that?' he asked.

'Yeah – why?'

'Because I thought I saw him when I caught the bus back from town. Unless you tell me he's got a double, Jack was definitely outside Greenlea Shopping Centre. It looked like he was waiting to meet someone.'

'So he changed his mind.' Nothing about my conversation with Hooper was ringing alarm bells so I smiled and said goodbye.

Reluctantly he stood to one side, giving me his slow, shy smile.

'See you at lunch,' I said.

Lunch came and went. I chatted with Eugenie about

Sammy Beckett ('He's so o o o cute when you get to know him!') and her latest singing lesson with Bruno ('I hate that man – he's totally anal!') and with Charlie about Marco. She was still smitten. ('He's got what they call a Roman nose – you know, long and straight. Don't you think he looks like Michelangelo's statue of David outside the Uffizi Gallery? Oh, and he has eyes that melt you every time he looks at you!')

Puh-lease, I thought as I ate my couscous and roasted vegetables.

So where was Jack? I began to look at my watch and wonder.

'Where's Jack?' Shirley Welford echoed my thoughts at two thirty as I came out of my French conversation lesson with Justine. I'd been trying to decide whether or not to cycle into Ainslee to see if I could track him down. He wasn't answering his phone or responding to my texts.

'I have no idea,' I told Jack's maths teacher.

'We were meant to have a tutorial at two. We'd changed the time once already.'

'I know. I'm getting worried about him,' I told her.

But not too worried, not yet. After all, this didn't fit the pattern of recent scary events. Jack wasn't the gorgeous daughter of a Russian billionaire, for a start. And he might be the brainiest person I know, but he didn't have total recall like Scarlett and me. As I set off to cycle into town, I ran through the possibilities – Jack's phone had broken or was out of battery. He'd forgotten about the rearranged tutorial with Shirley and had taken it into his head to ride

214

on to Ainslee to collect some new tennis shoes he'd ordered through the sports shop in Greenlea Shopping Centre.

But no – Jack wouldn't forget his tutorial. That would be totally out of character. So maybe there *was* something wrong. I pedalled hard along the lane into the Bottoms, rode quickly down Main Street, waving at Tom who was defrosting his car windscreen in his drive, then speeding on along the long, straight road running parallel to Hereward Ridge towards Ainslee. When I came to the first set of lights on the outskirts of town, I checked my watch again. Three fifteen. All being well, I should make it to Greenlea by half past.

I would've done if some lowlife driver hadn't ignored the cycle lane and cut right across me in order to park on double yellows outside a tatty betting shop. I braked and narrowly missed crashing into the back of him as I put both feet on the ground and toppled awkwardly into the kerb. The car was a big old black Merc, carelessly abandoned kerbside by a driver who swung open his door and left it hanging as he dashed in to place his bet. I didn't think it was anyone I recognized, though it was hard to tell because he was wearing a black hoodie and I only saw the side and back views.

I clocked the reg, thought about following the guy into the shop for a quick confrontation then decided against it. Finding Jack was more important so I picked myself up, dusted myself down and cycled on towards the shopping centre.

No Bikes. No Skateboards. No Smoking. No Spitting.

I invented the last one, but there were still a lot of rules displayed on overhead notices at the main entrance to Greenlea. I parked my bike in a secure rack and walked up the gradual slope into the centre, past the old department store on the right. I turned the corner and walked on past Monsoon towards SportTec beyond.

'Hi,' I said to the young guy at the cash desk just inside the entrance to the sports shop. 'Have you sold a pair of Nike tennis shoes, size eleven to a tall, good-looking guy?'

'Today?' asked the kid in the black Ralph Lauren polo shirt.

'Yeah – around lunchtime.'

'No,' came the grunted reply. There was no apology, no flicker of interest from the salesperson.

Irritated, I walked across the shop, between a rail of North Face jackets and a rack of hiking boots and came to a second sales point where I asked the same question.

'Size eleven, tall guy, really fit?' the girl at the desk echoed. 'Actually, yeah, I have. They were on order. I texted a message to say they'd arrived and the customer called in here about half an hour later to collect them.'

'What time was that exactly?'

'Let me think.' The girl wrinkled her nose. She was fair-haired, pretty and petite, with a gymnast's slim build. The energy and concentration she put into trying to answer my query was in direct contrast to the Ralph Lauren kid. 'It would be after twelve but before twelve thirty because twelve thirty is when I went on my lunch break. And it was after twelve because my manager finished work then and it was definitely after he left.'

'OK, OK.' I stopped her before she had chance to pinpoint the exact second that Jack had collected the shoes. 'Did you happen to notice where he went after he left the shop?'

'Actually yes,' she said enthusiastically. 'I mean, this guy was about my age and he was drop-dead gorgeous. Sorry,' she blushed. 'I didn't say that last bit – my manager would kill me.'

'So?' I said brusquely, judging the poor kid harshly for ogling my guy, my Jack.

'So – what?'

I cleared my throat to give me time to get over my small spike of jealousy. 'So please could you tell me where he went from here?'

'OK, so he stopped in the entrance to answer his phone and talk to someone called Jayden.'

'Jayden? You're sure?'

'Yeah, I was at the sales point by the exit at the time, where Josh is right now, so I heard everything. Your guy's face went all serious and he listened for ages then he said he'd meet Jayden at half twelve by the main entrance to the shopping centre. You see, I was right about the time . . .'

'Thanks,' I said, hurrying away. 'Really, thanks for remembering all that – it's a big help. Thanks . . .'

Success! I'd got over the fact that a stranger had a crush on my boyfriend and had pinpointed Jayden as my next point of contact.

So I pulled out my phone, but there was no signal until I came out of the shopping centre, then I quickly called

Jack's number (still not answering) and then Jayden's.

'What do you want?' he grunted when I told him who it was.

I plunged straight in. 'Do you happen to know where Jack is?'

'No, why should I?'

'Did you meet him earlier?'

'Maybe. Why?'

'Jayden, why does talking to you always have to be like getting blood from a stone? Just tell me – did you meet Jack, what was it about and where did he go afterwards?'

'We met, we talked about a stolen car, he left.'

'Where are you now?'

'At home.'

'OK, meet me in the Squinting Cat in twenty minutes.'

Dusk was drawing in as I cycled into the Bottoms, so I was glad of my high-viz jacket, which I'd slung on over my uniform before I left St Jude's. It was cold, damp and foggy – the worst kind of winter day, the sort that gets into your bones and cuts down visibility to under twenty metres.

Would Jayden be waiting for me inside the cafe or was he going to be a no-show? I couldn't tell from the outside because of the condensation trickling down the original Georgian window.

Ding-a-ling – the bell tinkled as I opened the door.

'Hey,' Jayden said from a quiet corner. He sat with a mug of hot chocolate topped with pink and white marshmallows – very un-Jaydenlike, but then he was always one to surprise me.

'What's this about a stolen car?' I sat down breathlessly. This was what I'd been turning over in my mind on my cycle ride back to the village. 'You're not suggesting Jack's involved?'

'Chill, Alyssa. The cops haven't arrested your boyfriend, at least not as far as I know.'

'So just tell me – why did you two meet up? I already figured out it wasn't something trivial like fixing the next five-a-side match because Jack wouldn't have missed his tutorial for that. And what does a stolen car have to do with anything?'

At last Jayden got down to specifics. 'Black Merc, zero-three model, nicked from Alex's dad's workshop last night.'

'Registration number YJK03PSL?' I already knew the answer would be yes.

'Jesus Christ, so now you're psychic,' he muttered.

'No. The guy who stole the car was the same guy who cut me up and blocked the cycle lane when I rode into town looking for Jack. And no – I didn't get a chance to take a close look so I can't say I recognized him. But it's the same car, isn't it?'

'Yeah. Guy breaks in through a door facing on to the yard at the back of the workshop, *jemmies* it open. Door not connected to an alarm system so guy heads for office, takes the Merc key off a hook, puts key in ignition, gets it in gear and points the car at the front window and drives straight through it. Glass everywhere. Neighbour opposite dials nine-nine-nine – too late to stop the guy driving off towards town.'

'Carry on,' I urged when Jayden stopped to stare suspiciously at a customer who stood up ready to leave. 'I don't see the connection with Jack.'

'There wasn't one at first. Cops come to JD's to take details, Alex's dad feels sick about losing a customer's car so he cooperates. Cops don't seem hopeful about solving the crime; they leave. Then Alex finds a note stuck on the notice board.'

'A lime-green Post-it note?' I was remembering the note on my locker door and inside Galina's tie.

'No, for once you're wrong.' Jayden said. 'This was written on the back of a JD invoice form. So Alex comes to me with the note because he doesn't know what else to do. It's covered in scrawly writing, starting with "FAO Jack Cavendish". Alex asks me, what do we do? Do we hand it over to Jack? He tells me he's had it up to here with the cops lately so he doesn't want to be the one making decisions.'

'Jayden,' I interrupted, 'for God's sake, tell me what the note said!'

He unzipped the top pocket of his leather biker jacket and pulled out a note. 'Here, read it for yourself.'

FAO Jack Cavendish, in handwriting so untidy I could hardly read it. Hey, Jack. It's me. Alyssa's just not getting it, is she?

Oh God! Oh God! I'm in my tiny boat on a big ocean and a wave swells on the horizon. It rises and rolls towards me.

I told her things would get worse if she didn't find answers to the clues I'm leaving scattered around the place, but she didn't listen, did she? So now I'm talking to you, Jack. I'm asking you to consider the following traffic-safety information: if I drive a car and hit you at thirty miles per hour, you bounce off my bonnet and collect a few broken bones. Forty miles per hour — serious head injuries. Fifty — you're dead. Interesting statistic.

'What else could we do, me and Alex?' Jayden asked. 'A psycho wrote that note so we definitely had to show it to Jack. I said I'd do it.'

My boat rocked and rolled as the giant black wave rose and broke. I pushed the note back across the table with a trembling hand. 'What happened after Jack read it? Why didn't he call or text me? Where the hell has he gone?'

'Jack's first reaction?' Jayden recalled. 'He swore and got on his bike. Rode off, changed his mind and cycled back towards me, says "Don't tell Alyssa." '

'Then what?'

'He said he'd tell you himself, but obviously he didn't.'

'How many hours ago is this? Three and a half – four? Let's figure this out – he sets off to tell me about the message, but he never makes it. Plus, suddenly his phone's out of action. Jayden, I'm scared!'

He nodded as he watched me stand up then collapse weakly back on to the chair. 'You want me to help you look for him?'

'Yes – no! It'll be quicker for me to go on my bike.'

'How do you know which way to head?'

The wave roars in my ears; it towers over my head; I feel icy spray on my face and hands. Within seconds the wave will hit me and my boat will splinter into matchstick fragments.

'Back to town,' I told Jayden. 'Whatever happened to Jack, I think it was soon after he split from you in Ainslee.'

It started to rain heavily. Cold drops fell on my bare head, soaked through my school skirt and spattered loudly against my high viz jacket. The road into town was soon shiny under the orange street lamps and the rain gathered in oily puddles in the gutters.

I gathered every ounce of strength and pedalled like a crazy person, ignoring lights and mounting pavements, weaving in and out of the rush-hour traffic.

OK, in amongst all this panic I had to think: My psycho stalker always leaves clues – I just have to pick up the latest in the series to track Jack down. He breaks into JD's and steals a car, writes a note obliquely threatening Jack with God knows what kind of car crash. Psycho guy is always telling me to look right under my nose, to follow the most obvious thought. The next unarguable thing I know is that he uses the car to cut me up on my way into town. The location is significant – it has to be. I have to head back to the betting shop, get off my bike and investigate.

I arrived outside Betmate and threw down my bike. A guy in scuffed and stained construction-worker boots came out, head down, heavy jacket zipped up to his chin. There was a loose flagstone on the pavement, which tilted when he stepped on it. Muddy rainwater gushed up from under it and splashed my legs.

I looked up at the neon-lit Betmate sign. To the right of the betting shop was a fast-food place, to the left a dark side road with temporary orange traffic cones across it. I peered past the cones and saw no sign of road repairs. My heart lurched. Hold steady, keep going, I told myself as the tsunami roared in my ears.

I squeezed between the cones and walked down the side street. There were blank brick walls to either side. A broken down-pipe sent rainwater gushing on to the narrow pavement.

A bike lay beside a row of overflowing wheelie bins, its buckled back wheel jutting out on to the road, its front wheel jammed between two of the bins. I stepped over it then heard a sound from beyond the bins – something between a sigh and a moan.

There was Jack, propped up against the filthy wall next to the broken down-pipe, his head hanging, chest heaving, as he struggled to breathe. I fell on to my knees, scared to move him, praying, praying, praying, that I'd found him in time.

Blood trickled from a gash on his forehead. His eyes didn't seem to focus.

'Jack,' I whispered. 'It's me – Alyssa.'

He opened his mouth and groaned.

'Listen to me – don't move! I'll call an ambulance. You're

going to be OK. Stay where you are.'

I had to keep on begging him not to try to get up because, even if he wasn't seeing me clearly, he was hearing my voice and leaning forward from the wall, putting his hands flat on the pavement and bracing himself to try to stand.

'Don't!' I pleaded. I put my hands over his and trapped them.

Water from the down-pipe gushed and splashed on to Jack's smashed mobile phone.

'I need an ambulance!' I pulled out my phone, dialled 999 and gasped out the words in response to the calm voice at the other end. I gave a location, pleaded with the woman to be quick while she asked me was Jack breathing? Was he conscious? Then she continued to talk me methodically through the situation as if it weren't the worst thing that had ever happened in my life – finding Jack injured on the pavement, blood running down his face, struggling to breathe.

'Try to keep him awake. The ambulance is on its way. It should be with you in five minutes. How is he doing? Is he still conscious? Good. I'm staying on the line – I won't leave you. Stick with it. You're doing a great job.'

These people are saints, I swear.

Five minutes felt like five hours. Then I heard the sirens and saw blue lights flashing, heard the cones blocking the street being dragged clear before the ambulance got through to Jack and me.

Two paramedics jumped out. The guy eased my fingers om Jack's hand, giving space for the woman to work.

She bent over him. I heard him groan.

'OK,' she told her partner. 'His airway is clear and he's conscious, but he's not responding to questions. Let's get him out of here.'

And they did – they lifted Jack on to a stretcher and carried him into the ambulance. I followed. They let me drive with them to the hospital, siren blaring, lights flashing. Jack lay surrounded by monitors, his face pale and bloody, unable to grasp my hand as he drifted in and out of consciousness.

'What's this?' the female paramedic wondered as she carefully removed Jack's helmet and a piece of paper fluttered out.

The message was in the same scrawly handwriting – almost illegible because the paper was soaked by rain and blood.

Oh dear, Alyssa – I'm so sorry! You're still not paying attention so there was no way around it – I had to hit him at 40 mph exactly. Good job he was wearing a helmet.

The nurses worked hard to persuade me to leave Jack with them in the high-dependency unit at the Queen Elizabeth.

'You did your bit, now there's nothing more you can do. Go home and rest,' the sister in charge advised.

These nurses were firmer and calmer and harder to argue with than you would ever believe – I guess it's part of the professional persona. I was desperate to stay overnight, but they clearly wanted me to leave so they could get on with their jobs.

'What did the chest X-rays show?' I whispered.

Machines beeped. Jack had a dressing on the head wound. His eyes were closed.

'Two broken ribs. And the doctors say the left lung is punctured. This tube is to drain fluid from the lung.'

'What about his head? What did the CT scan show?'

'Too early to say.' The sister was more defensive as she made an entry on the chart at the bottom of Jack's bed. 'And, to be honest, we can't tell you any more until after we've spoken to the parents.'

'Come on, it's time to go.' Molly stepped in to prise me away from the bedside. She'd driven over from St Jude's as soon as the hospital had informed Dr Webb about the accident. His job was to speak to Mr and Mrs Cavendish while Molly came to collect me.

'I have to go now,' I whispered in Jack's ear.

His eyelids flickered open and he tried to smile – a shadow of his usual brilliant one.

'I'll be back first thing tomorrow.'

His eyes closed.

'Come on, Alyssa. Let's go,' Molly insisted. She led me by the elbow out of the unit. The door swung closed. Through the small glass panel I caught a glimpse of Jack lying immobile in the bed closest to the nurses' station.

mind leaps back to a previous visit to the Q.E.

ing in intensive care when Jack and I arrive.

ear soft shoes, which squeak as they walk.

*'Three broken ribs, one punctured lung, broken collarbone . . .
X rays and brain scan . . . possible aneurysm . . . skull fractures,
small splinters of bone lodged in the frontal cortex . . .'* The
words slip out between doors leading to the ICU.

Jack grips my hand.

*'I should've pulled her clear of the horse,' I moan. 'But I was
scared so all I did was yell for her to get out of the way. She didn't
listen.'*

'She'll be OK,' he insists. 'They know what they're doing.'

But Paige wasn't OK. She didn't pull through.

And now it was Jack's turn and the feelings were even
worse – a mixture of strength-sapping guilt and fear as
sharp as a blade twisting in my gut.

Molly was silent as we walked down the corridor to the
lift, still silent as she paid the parking fee and we went out
into the foul rain and wind. It was only when we were
driving home that she spoke again.

'How are you doing?' she asked. 'OK, no need to answer
that. I can see you're struggling.'

'It's my fault,' I said.

I was drowning, dragged down by the current, tossed
about like a rag doll.

She braked at a set of lights. 'That's nonsense.'

'No, it's true. All this is happening because I'm not
getting it.'

'No. It's happening because there's a psycho on the
loose and it's the job of the police to find him, not you.'
The wipers swished, the lights changed to green.

'It's still my fault,' I said again.

'Alyssa, what are you doing!' It wasn't a question from Connie at seven thirty next morning – it was pure disbelief.

I was sitting in Marco's car, waiting for him to run and fetch his credit card to buy petrol when Connie jogged out of the woods towards me at the end of her pre-breakfast run.

'I'm getting a lift to the hospital.' My fear hadn't receded overnight. In fact, I'd spent the whole time, second after tortuous second, drowning in my tsunami of panic and guilt.

'With Marco?'

'He offered. I said yes.'

'Marco offered? But Jack wouldn't be happy. In fact, he'd hate it that you're getting a ride with Marco of all people.'

'Jesus,' I sighed. 'What's it matter who takes me to the hospital, as long as I get there?'

'I can drive you. Or Hooper.'

I spotted Marco emerging from the archway leading to the dorms. 'Too late –he's here now.'

Connie stood back. 'OK, Alyssa – tell Jack hi,' she muttered as Marco slid into the driving seat. Then she stood a long time watching him reverse out of his parking space and, with a crunch of gravel, swing the car round.

'You OK?' he asked above the purr of the engine and the swish of the tyres through the puddles on the drive. It had stopped raining at last and clouds were clearing from the dawn sky.

'You're the tenth person to ask me that this morning.'

'OK, stupid question,' he agreed.

If I'd imagined he would leave me in peace to worry about Jack for the rest of the journey into town, I'd have been dead wrong.

'So how long have you and Jack been together?' he asked as soon as we left the school grounds.

I forced myself to respond to his small talk. 'I guess that depends on what you mean by "together". He invited me to a party at the beginning of last term, but it didn't really take off until much later.'

There you are – this was all it took for me to drift off on another eidetic episode, back to the time when the police had dragged the lake.

I'm standing on the shore of the lake where Lily drowned.

'Don't stand too close to the edge,' I hear Jack warn.

I don't look round. I know his voice, feel his presence.

'Alyssa, step back,' he says as he takes my hand.

I pull away.

He waits for me to be ready to talk. 'I saw you walk down this way.'

I stare at the water, dark and deep.

'I'm sorry,' he says.

'What for?'

'Being a loser. Not knowing how to act.'

'When?'

'All of the times I'm around you. I've been a total tosser.'

'No.' Yes, actually. I remember how it was – exchanging cool and distant 'heys' with Jack after Tom's party, even though we'd shared the high point of the kiss as we climbed a wall back into

229

the school grounds. But then that stupid hiatus had been partly my fault too. I'd been shy, scared, too proud to show how I felt. And then 'Lily' had happened.

Now we talk through the misunderstandings, we step back from the water's edge. Jack tells me all about his earlier relationship with Lily and how they'd drifted apart. He shows me the email she sent him before she disappeared.

'Sorry to dump this on you, Jack,' she tells him before she signs off. 'And tell Paige and Alyssa hey and sorry to them too. We had fun sometimes, didn't we, girls?'

I cry. The sobs wash over me. Jack holds me and hugs me and we don't need to say another word.

And now I sat in Marco's sports car, cushioned by the cream upholstery, sobbing again, without Jack to hold me.

I suppose it's because he's Italian that he didn't back off from this display of emotion like most guys would.

'How crazy is that?' he demanded. 'Why did Jack wait so long?'

'He went to California for tennis coaching. Things just got in the way,' I sniffled.

'I wouldn't have let that happen. Sorry, Alyssa – no way!'

'But you're not Jack.'

'Yeah, he's lucky I wasn't around to step into his shoes.'

'Marco, please.'

'I'm just saying.' Talking and driving, swishing through Chartsey Bottom in his look-at-me car, telling himself that no girl on this earth could resist his charms.

'Anyway, you weren't around.'

'And now you cry over him because he had an accident

and got hurt, but don't worry, you don't have to be alone.' With confidence undented and undentable like the immaculate, shiny bodywork of his silver-grey car, he drove me to the Q.E.

At least Marco had the decency to wait in the cafe area while I went up to the high-dependency unit. Or else he had something else to do because a quick glance over my shoulder told me that he'd taken out his phone and was talking animatedly, oblivious that three nurses standing in the queue for Kit-Kats and coffee were openly admiring his Latin looks.

I shut Marco out of my mind as the lift door closed. When I stepped out again on the first floor, I walked right into Jack's mum and dad.

'Alyssa?' Julia Cavendish was the first to speak.

'Yes.' I instantly recognized the tall woman in smart black trousers and boxy, asymmetrical jacket even though I'd only caught a glimpse of her at the end of last term when she'd arrived to pick Jack up for the Christmas holiday. She owns an art gallery off Piccadilly, so her style is slightly quirky and very expensive.

Jack's stockbroker dad introduced himself and shook my hand. 'Giles Cavendish.' He gave no sign that his son lay on a hospital bed with broken ribs, a punctured lung and possible head injuries.

'Don't worry – he's doing OK,' Julia assured me. 'He slept well. There's no internal bleeding and no serious head injury. A touch of concussion – that's all.'

231

I let out a long sigh. As the breath emerged from between my lips and I inhaled again, it felt like an iron band round my chest had loosened.

'Will you come down with us for coffee?' Jack's mum asked.

I shook my head.

'No, of course you want to see Jack. I understand.' She smiled, touched me lightly on the arm and stepped into the lift. 'He wants to see you too.'

'Don't tire him out,' Giles Cavendish warned as the lift door slid closed.

'See – I'm going to be fine,' Jack said.

I held back from the bed in case my arm snagged on one of the tubes or wires. 'You don't look fine.'

'I am. The ribs will heal. I'll be back to normal before you know it.'

Drawing up a chair, I felt tears well up and sniffed to hold them back.

'Don't cry.'

'I'm not. How's your head?'

'Sore.'

My hand crept forward over the white sheet until our fingers interlaced. 'After you talked to Jayden, what happened?'

Jack shifted position and winced.

'It's OK, you don't need to talk about it if you don't want.'

'No – I do. OK, so Jayden showed me the note on the

back of the invoice and all I could think about was getting back to school to make sure nothing bad happened to you. I took the quickest route out of town, but by the time I reached the Chartsey Road I realized I was being trailed by the black Merc.'

'Did you try to lose him?'

'That was my plan – as soon as I hit the country lanes I was intending to go off-road along the bridle tracks where I knew the Merc couldn't follow me. Only, I never got that far. Before I knew it he was overtaking me and pushing me on to the pavement, blocking me from getting back on to the road. I had to swing left down the alleyway next to Betmate.'

'And he followed you again?'

'Yeah – big car, narrow cul de sac. There was only one way it could end.'

I pictured the chase down the dark, wet side street, heard the roar of the Merc engine, could almost smell the petrol fumes Jack would have inhaled as it drew nearer.

'Jack, I'm so sorry . . .'

He shook his head but even this small movement was painful. 'You can say anything you like to me except sorry. This is not down to you.'

'But it is. Whatever anyone says, this wouldn't be happening if I could just work out what's staring me in the face.'

For a while Jack closed his eyes and was silent. His grip on my hand tightened. When he opened his eyes again, his gaze was intense. 'I'd do anything for you – you know that.'

I nodded.

'So now you have to do one small thing for me. I know – we don't usually put pressure on each other, that's not how we work, but this is important.'

His hand was round mine, holding tight; his brown eyes looked deep into mine.

'What is it? What do you want me to do?'

'Don't *do* anything. Just make me a promise.'

I nodded slowly.

'Don't go anywhere alone. You hear what I'm saying? Always keep someone with you, tell a member of staff what you plan to do, where you'll be, every minute of every day.'

I sighed and nodded again.

'Because I'm stuck here in this lousy bed, Alyssa, and there's a killer out there, and it's driving me crazy that he's stalking you and making all these threats, kidnapping Galina and crashing into me. So promise you won't do anything to push his buttons until I get out of this hospital!'

'OK, cool,' I murmured. 'I won't go out by myself. I'll stay safe.'

Jack seemed satisfied but he still kept hold of my hand. 'Because I can't lose you, Alyssa. Not now, not ever.'

'Me neither.' I could still recall the wave breaking over me, the helplessness and the empty, rag-doll despair. 'Just get better,' I whispered. 'That's all I ask.'

chapter eleven

'Where are you going?' Connie demanded.

Ever since I'd got back from the hospital earlier in the day, I'd been focused on keeping my promise to Jack. I'd followed my timetable and gone with Hooper to a special English tutorial then I'd met up with the girls for lunch, which is when I'd updated Connie, Eugenie, Charlie and Zara on the latest events.

'We won't let you out of our sight,' had been Zara's fast-as-lightning response.

I can't tell you how good that had made me feel. I'd hugged her and nodded, hugged her again.

Connie had agreed. 'OK, Alyssa, from now on you can't even take a pee without telling us.'

This was how come they'd shadowed me throughout the afternoon, during a French lesson with Justine then afterwards during a free period in the technology centre. And it was why Connie challenged me now as we turned off our computers, ready to go for dinner.

'Come on, Alyssa – where are you going?'

'Actually, I *am* going for a pee,' I replied with an embarrassed grin.

'Don't be too long – I promised I'd hook up with Marco at six thirty,' Charlie grumbled, while Eugenie grabbed her jacket from the back of her chair and reminded the others not to let me out of their sight.

'So, Eugenie, where are you sloping off to?' Sergeant Major Connie wanted to know. She boxed Eugenie in behind her computer station.

'Out.' Eugenie zipped up in a hurry. 'OK, if you must know, I arranged to meet Sammy in the Bottoms. There – happy now?'

Connie nodded and slowly stepped aside. I watched Eugenie give her a shove in her hurry to leave and I felt a small stab of anxiety.

Please be careful! I thought as our red-haired diva dashed out into the darkness and I headed for the cloakroom with Zara hot on my heels.

In the privacy of the grey cubicle I told myself to get a grip. It wasn't as if every student at St Jude's was in danger. My stalker wouldn't be interested in harming Eugenie, only the people really close to me. So get a grip and think, Alyssa – above all, activate that eidetic memory and isolate the one tiny clue that will give you the answers you need. Think, remember – win this surreal game of cat and mouse!

'OK?' Zara asked when I emerged.

I rinsed my hands under the tap then stuck them under the drier. 'Relax. Nothing's going to happen to me while I'm in the loo.'

'So, I've been thinking,' she said as we rejoined Connie and Charlie then set off together towards the refectory.

'Whoo, Zara's been thinking!' Charlie mocked. 'Watch out, Einstein – you have serious competition.'

Connie clamped her hand round Charlie's mouth. 'Listen and learn,' she advised our super-confident American friend.

'So – narcissistic personality disorder.' Totally unruffled, Zara launched into her pet theory. 'It means a person can't empathize with his or her victims. Empathy is what stops most of us from doing cruel stuff to other people – we imagine how it would feel to be whacked off our bike by a big old Merc or tied up and gagged then thrown into the back of a car.'

'Bashed on the head then chucked into the canal,' Connie added for good measure, though it wasn't necessary to remind us.

'Exactly. Which is the reason why sane people don't do these things.' Satisfied that she'd got her message through, Zara fell silent.

The wind cut through me as we went outside. I hunched my shoulders and braced the wintry conditions.

Zara again: 'The second thing I've been focusing on is the power aspect. It's not enough for NPD people just to do bad stuff, they need to show off about it – that would be the reason behind the notes our screwed-up psycho leaves for Alyssa, the song lyrics, the fake photos, the video . . .'

'That's definitely him being an arrogant shit,' I agreed. 'It's his "catch me if you can" signature.'

'Which could also be his weak point,' Zara explained earnestly. She's going to be a top forensic psychologist, I swear. She'll be awesome in court, giving evidence against terrorists and serial killers. 'You see, this guy can't bear to be overlooked. If you do ignore him, he's going to get very angry.'

'Wait, wait,' Connie cut in. 'You're saying Alyssa's best tactic right now is not to respond in any way to these challenges he's been setting? How does that work exactly?'

Zara explained. 'The more you ignore him, the angrier he gets. And an angry person makes mistakes – we know that for sure.'

'Which, when you think about it, Alyssa, fits in exactly with your promise that you wouldn't do anything to try to catch the guy before Jack gets out of hospital.' Charlie had the good grace to acknowledge what Zara was getting at. She held the door to the refectory while we went in out of the cold.

Connie was the one who laid it on the line for me one more time. 'So do nothing. Step well back. Watch the fireworks from a safe distance – whoosh!'

This is the way I got through one of the hardest days of my life – with a little help from my friends. I made it to midnight, when I found myself alone in my room and wide awake.

'Hey, can't you sleep?' Connie stuck her head round my door. 'Sorry, I saw the light was on.'

'No, don't apologize. I was rewatching the video of Galina.'

Sleepless and tormented, unable to switch off. Sifting through the clues that my stalker had left, laid like crumbs that made a trail through the forest for Hansel and Gretel to find their way back home.

'Can I come in?'

I nodded. 'Go through it with me. Tell me what you see.'

Dressed in tennis shoes and summer PJs that revealed goose bumps and a thin band of star tattoos round her tanned upper arm, Connie sat down on one of the spare beds. I angled my laptop screen so she could see the footage of Galina in uniform walking eagerly down the drive. 'All OK, nothing bad happening yet,' Connie commented.

Cut to close up of Galina. She's smiling in anticipation; her eyes sparkle.

'Bastard!' Connie muttered, knowing what was coming next.

Cut. My pulse raced at the sequence showing Galina's silent scream. Open mouth, terrified eyes. Cut. The eight-second video jerked towards its terrifying end. We saw Galina lying in a foetal position on the back seat of a car. The duct tape over her mouth was silver. Her hands were tied with thin cable, which cut into her wrists. I was staring at the screen, paying attention to a particular detail for the first time.

'What is it?' Connie asked.

I'd gasped. The video had ended.

'Alyssa, what are you thinking?'

'Did you see the upholstery?' I whispered. I could smell the cream leather, feel its recent, soft, seductive contact with my own skin. 'Don't you recognize it?'

'No. Come on, tell!'

'That's the back seat of Marco's car,' I told her. One hundred per cent certain, no doubt in my mind – the final sequence of the video showed Galina tied up in Marco Conti's Aston Martin.

Action girl Connie immediately forgot her own good advice. Stand back, do nothing – it went clean out of the window the second I identified the cream leather car seat.

'Oh my God!' she cried, jumping up from the bed. 'It's him all along – it's Marco!'

I swallowed hard to push down the rising fear inside my chest. 'It's his car,' I said, trying to stay rational. At last I'd found a crumb on the Hansel and Gretel trail that the forest birds hadn't pecked at. I had something new to work on.

'If it's his car, then it's got to be him doing all this crazy stuff! Come on, Alyssa, I don't care what time it is – we have to call the cops.'

'It's his car, but that doesn't necessarily mean he's guilty. Say, for instance, the kidnapper used the car to shoot the video but doesn't actually own it. In fact, it could be a trick – yet another way to mislead us.'

'Jesus, Alyssa – for once in your life will you stop analysing. Pick up the phone, dial nine-nine-nine!'

'Wait. Give me time to work it out. Marco didn't arrive until the start of term, remember. And Scarlett was murdered early on New Year's Day, before Marco got here.'

Still hung up on the evidence from the video, Connie flung open the door and strode down the corridor towards the portrait of Lady Anne. Hearing a disturbance, Zara opened her door and stepped out of her room to join us.

'What's going on?' she wanted to know.

'It's Marco. He's our guy, but Alyssa won't call the cops.'

'I'm not saying I won't,' I argued. Lights were going on all along the girls' corridor. Charlie was the next to open her door and join the group. 'I'm saying wait, let me be sure of what we've worked out. Yes, it's Marco's car in the video, but no it doesn't have to mean he kidnapped Galina. For a start, he hasn't been around long enough to link up with what happened to Scarlett.'

'Why are we talking about Marco? Will someone please tell me what's going on?' Charlie pleaded.

'Stand back, give the girl some space.' Zara's voice was cool and calm; she was in forensic mode. 'Connie, cool it. I agree with Alyssa – we need to know exactly what we're accusing Marco of before we do anything. And, by the way, it's the middle of the night so it would be a good idea to keep the noise down.'

Too late – Eugenie appeared in her PJs, grumbling about the racket.

'So the timing's wrong for Marco to have been involved in Scarlett's murder, and anyway there's no way he even knew her. She lives in Ainslee. He's in Monaco . . .' I stopped so suddenly that I almost bit my tongue off. I was immediately into an action replay of a conversation between me and Ursula outside the gates of Upwood House.

'Anyway, Scarlett?' I'm asking Ursula what she knows about the dead girl.

'Yeah. Really clever but not geeky. Everyone liked her, especially the boys. Alex practically stalked her for a whole term

*before he found the balls to ask her out. Then, within a week –
look what happened.'*

*'What did happen?' It's freezing cold. I'm talking to scary
Ursula. She's asking me to find out who killed her mate.*

*'You're the super-sleuth, you tell me.' Typical answer from
the girl who got chucked out of Ainslee Comp for going into
school with a pocketful of drugs.*

I tell her I don't know much, only what I read in the Metro
and what Tom told me.

*'You actually knew her. What was she like? Was there an
old boyfriend who got jealous when she chucked him and started
going out with Alex? Where'd she been on New Year's Eve? Was
she at a party? Who with? Did she try to walk home alone?'*

*Ursula looks at me through narrowed eyes and lets the
questions stack up.*

'I'm not standing around waiting for Alyssa to make up
her mind,' Connie said angrily, and she darted into the
room she shared with Zara. 'If she won't call the cops, I
will!'

*Ursula answers an important question. 'Scarlett didn't go out
with many guys. There were a couple in our year at school and
there was one with a foreign name, he lives in Italy.'*

It felt like someone had punched me in the sternum,
knocking the air out of my lungs.

*'A foreign name. She met him on holiday last summer, but he
lives in Italy so I guess he doesn't count.'*

I repeated the words to myself, finally letting the light
go on in my brain by saying the one word that mattered –
Marco. Marco. Marco!

'Connie's right,' I gasped. 'Call nine-nine-nine. I have to speak to Ripley.'

'The inspector's on her way,' Connie reported after she'd made the call.

Too stunned to move, we sat on the floor in our pyjamas under Lady Anne's portrait, shivering in the cold. Charlie had stopped asking questions, thrown a jacket over her PJs, stuffed her feet into a pair of Uggs and sprinted to the staff quarters to inform whoever was on duty.

'Ripley said to stay where we are,' Connie went on. 'Especially don't go anywhere near Marco's room.'

'That figures,' Zara said uneasily.

And I thought of Brains, the notorious NPD kid who had killed both his parents. He was stealing money from their credit cards and had taken a hammer to them when they began to suspect. I thought of Zara's warning about this type of psychopath who seems meek and mild until the monster is unleashed.

'We'll wait right here,' I told the others.

'Where's Charlie? She's taking forever,' Eugenie noticed. She crept to the bottom of the stairs and looked out into the dark courtyard. 'Marco's light is on,' she reported back. 'And so is Hooper's. Uh-oh, someone's turned the boys' stair light on – OK, don't worry, it's only Hooper.'

'What's with the "only Hooper"?' he wanted to know as he pushed past Eugenie and took the stairs up to our dorm two at a time. 'Why are you all out here? Alyssa, what the hell's going on?'

'Nothing. Well, something – but we can't tell you.' Connie took charge as usual. I guess that she was afraid that he might lose it and run back to alert the guys in the dorm, which was the last thing we needed. 'Honestly, Hooper, you don't want to know.'

He gave me a disappointed, hangdog look.

I shook my head and mouthed that I was sorry.

Eugenie backed Connie. 'Don't anybody tell him.'

'Tell me what exactly?' he demanded. Surrounded by girls, the wall of silence drove him crazy. 'Alyssa!'

'OK, everyone chill – let Hooper and me have a talk.' Separating myself from the group, I led him down the corridor towards my room where we sat side by side on my bed. 'We've got a situation,' I told him, hoping to make him understand. 'It's sensitive.'

'It must be something really big for that lot to gang up on me.'

'It is, believe me.'

'So they're saying I can't be trusted, is that it?' Hooper gestured through the open door towards the rest of the girls.

'Yes, but don't take it personally.'

'How else can I take it?' he argued. 'Don't they know about all the work we've done together, you and me?'

'Probably not. Anyway, I'm sorry.'

Frowning, he got up to open the window then gazed out into the darkness.

'Truly, I'm sorry,' I sighed, glancing at my watch and desperately hoping that Ripley would get here.

'It's about Marco,' Hooper predicted, still with his back turned.

'No,' I replied, but not quickly enough.

'See – you hesitated. That's a dead giveaway. This "situation" involves Marco, and don't lie.'

'God, Hooper . . .'

He turned angrily. 'You're cutting me out, Alyssa. I don't understand why.'

'OK, OK. But if I tell you, you have to stay here with us until the police get here.'

'OK – deal.' Watching me like a hawk, he waited for me to go on.

'You won't do anything stupid – promise?'

'I agreed, didn't I? You tell me what's going on. I listen. I hang around until the cops get here.'

'OK, two things. First, Connie and I replayed the kidnap video and it was Marco's car.'

Hooper considered the new fact. He didn't say anything, just gave a quick, short expulsion of breath.

'Two, it turns out that Marco probably knew Scarlett. They met when she was in Italy.'

'Holiday romance,' he muttered, then laughed. 'Jesus, Alyssa!'

'I know. I've been so slow to remember the details I could cry. So this is why Connie called the cops. And that's who we're waiting for now – Inspector Ripley and her guys.'

'Thanks,' Hooper said. 'Now I get it. And you're right – it's big.'

I never knew Marco could sing like that,' I confess to Hooper as we leave the music room with the aria from *Aida* ringing in my ears.

'I expect there's a lot about Marco that we don't know,' Hooper suggests.

'Like what?'

'Like where he went to school before he came to St Jude's, how big is his allowance, plus why he hates his dad.'

Hooper's carrying his cello, walking ahead through the car park, thinking far faster than me.

Does Marco hate his dad? If he does, is it important? Yes, he hates football, but is that the same thing?

Hooper shrugs. 'Please yourself. I just thought it would be worth looking at. I'll do it for you if you like.'

I welcome the offer. I don't think there's much in it though.

'You suspected Marco all along, didn't you?' I whispered.

'That he killed Scarlett and kidnapped Galina? I was working on the premise, yeah, but I didn't want to come out and say it until I was certain.'

Hooper's laid-back answer made me feel even guiltier than before. 'I'm sorry I tried to shut you out – it was the others . . .'

'The Black Widow.'

'Connie, yeah. Shhh!' My gang of girls stood guard at the end of the corridor and I didn't want them to overhear. I thought of Hooper beavering away, checking Marco's personal history. 'How far had you got?'

The frown had gone, his head was up and he was pacing round the small room. 'OK, I found out that Marco travelled around Europe after the fight with his dad – you know, when he stole the boat and went for a joyride. He didn't stay in any one place for more than a week. First Paris, then back to Monaco, but his dad kicked him out of the apartment again and he had to stay with a friend. Then he headed to Rome to see his grandparents and he was in the gossip mags – pictures of him dating a Brazilian millionaire's daughter, etcetera.' Hooper listed Marco's movements on his fingers, methodical and precise. His energy was up now that he was back in the loop.

'Hooper, sit down,' I pleaded. 'You're making me dizzy.'

He ignored me and went on pacing. 'Rome was early August then he went to Tuscany to his uncle's house.'

'Tuscany is probably where he met Scarlett.'

'Quick flings with a tourist or two then on to Greece, to Crete for a couple of weeks sailing round the island in a luxury yacht and then that was the end of Marco's summer holidays. After that, we get London and a language school in Kensington. He did a course for a whole term, got invited to a couple of film premieres while he was there and lots of parties. Still no contact with his dad.'

'Wow, Hooper, this is genius!'

He stopped pacing and beamed at me. 'Christmas, Marco was still in London even though the language course was finished. So, anyway, it was harder to keep track of him between the end of last term and the beginning of this.'

I nodded. 'It means it's at least possible that he got in touch with Scarlett again, maybe even arranged to meet her here in the Cotswolds.'

'But she wouldn't tell Alex about that,' Hooper said.

'We're relying on guesswork now, but at least that puts Marco in the right place at the right time.'

'Yeah, Hooper – thanks. This is going to be so useful.'

'That's OK.'

'You spent a lot of time on this.'

'Yeah, but it was an interesting challenge.'

'Only you would say that,' I laughed. 'But then you're a born storyteller and sometimes life turns out stranger than fiction.'

'So maybe I'll quit writing novels and be a journalist instead.'

We were winding down, still waiting for Ripley to arrive. 'What do you say we tell the others what you just told me?' I suggested.

We left my room and went down the corridor, but before we reached the top of the stairs Connie broke away from the others and rushed to meet us. 'It's weird – Charlie hasn't come back yet,' she said with a worried frown.

'Where did she go?' Hooper asked.

'To find a member of staff. I don't know what happened – they should have shown up by now.'

'Unless she couldn't find anyone in the staff quarters and she had to run down the drive to Saint Sam's house.'

'Or else the member of staff on duty told her stay over there and not come back in case Marco saw them.'

Connie, Hooper and I tried to work out what might have happened to Charlie.

'Wait,' Hooper said, suddenly remembering. 'When I opened my door to come over here, I just missed a couple of people running downstairs ahead of me. I heard them, but I didn't see them.'

'For Christ's sake!' Connie groaned. 'Why didn't you tell us?'

'I didn't know it was important.'

Charlie and Marco. We were so stupid. 'She went up and warned him.' I spoke quietly with a sinking heart.

'If she did, she's a stupid airhead.' Connie strode ahead to raise the alarm. 'Eugenie, Zara – guess what. Charlie turned traitor. She went and told Marco the cops were on their way!'

'We *think*!' I stressed the second word. 'We don't know for sure.'

From the landing window we strained to see out across the courtyard.

'His light's still on,' Zara reported.

'But Hooper heard footsteps,' Connie said. 'God knows what Charlie was thinking.'

'She wasn't,' Zara muttered. 'Charlie is totally fixated on Marco. She'd do anything to keep him out of trouble.'

That was it – we weren't waiting any longer for the cops to show up.

The girls went out in pairs – me and Connie, Eugenie and Zara – while Hooper set off in his own direction to find the runaways.

'I'll let Justine know what's happening,' he promised as we went our separate ways. 'She's the member of staff on duty tonight.'

'OK, but be careful,' I told him. I didn't have time for any more, since Connie was ahead of me, running through the darkness towards the car park where we found Marco's car safely parked.

Connie peered in through the window then tried the door handle. The Aston Martin was locked, as you'd expect.

'So they left on foot,' I decided. Seemingly the car had been too obvious a choice and the police could easily have tracked it down.

I pictured Charlie and Marco running down the stairs from the boys' dorm, across the quad and straight out on to the lawn leading down to the lake. They probably had a flashlight with them, but there would have been no time to pick up anything else. 'We need Justine to get here quick, and we need a torch,' I said.

'Duh-dah!' Connie slipped her hand in her pocket and held up a mini flashlight attached to her key ring. It gave a narrow, bright beam of light.

'Let's try the lake first then the footpath through the woods. We'll be OK with this flashlight and it's the quickest way out of here on to the Chartsey road.'

We ran together into the darkness, hearing the frost-covered grass crunch underfoot until we came to the edge of the lake. 'Charlie's an idiot!' Connie said through gritted teeth. She shone the beam along the tall reed bed. A hidden creature rustled through the spiky undergrowth and slid with a hollow plop into the black water. 'Didn't she listen to a word Zara said?'

'Yes, but she didn't believe it could be Marco. She still doesn't.'

'And now look,' Connie groaned. 'They could be anywhere. He could lose it with her, do anything to her . . . She could be at the bottom of the lake – anywhere!'

With a shuddering intake of breath, I turned away from the water. 'No. Let's suppose – let's *hope* that Charlie is useful to him. He wants to keep her with him for the time being. Look – two sets of footprints!' Grabbing Connie's torch, I directed the light back up the slope to pick out a curved trail across the frost-covered lawn. I tracked it down and round the far side of the lake – definitely two sets of prints heading towards the trees.

Connie reacted swiftly. She set off ahead of me again, steering wide of the reeds and taking up the trail at the edge of the woods. By this time we were roughly five hundred metres from the school buildings. We could hear nothing except our own breathing and see nothing in the dark shadows ahead.

'What do we do? Do we follow them?' I asked.

'We try,' Connie decided. 'Come on – they can't be more than ten minutes ahead of us. They're aiming to get out on to the road – we can take a short cut away from the path.'

A short cut? Jesus, did Connie have a clear idea of how we would do this? Did she know how dark it would be once we stepped out of the faint moonlight into the shadows?

'Come on, Alyssa!' Snatching her torch back, she ignored the narrow pathway and plunged off to her right, stumbling over tree roots and dropping down into an unseen ditch.

She swore and clambered back out.

'Your hand,' I pointed out as the beam of light flashed across her upper body.

The right one was grazed and bleeding.

Connie swore again.

'Let's keep to the path.'

'No, we have to reach the road before Marco and Charlie. This is the quickest route.'

'But only if we don't lose our way in the trees,' I argued.

'I'm going to try it.' Losing patience, Connie plunged on through the darkness, her weak beam of light picking out low branches and tangles of thorns and dead wood that lay in her path.

No way, I thought in the heat of the moment. I'll stick to the track – that way at least I'll stay in one piece.

So I split from Connie and followed the path, every now and again picking up recent scuff marks in amongst the rotting leaves, then an actual footprint in a patch of unfrozen mud – the size and shape of an Ugg boot. I looked up and to my right in the direction Connie had taken. Should I call out and tell her what I'd spotted? Was she still within hearing distance?

Before I could make up my mind, I sensed a movement in the shadows to the side of the path. I froze and waited. Had I imagined it?

No – there was a pale shape close to the ground, moving away from the track deep into the trees. Maybe a deer or a fox creeping between some dark bushes. Something living, at least.

I followed it to make sure, stepping stealthily, trying not to snap twigs underfoot.

The shape stopped moving, seemed to be listening – too big for a fox and too pale. Not swift or agile enough for a deer.

I stopped when it stopped, held my breath, waited.

It crept on, seemingly without purpose, bending back on itself towards the track again. It went slowly on all-fours, head hanging, back arched. Then it collapsed flat on the ground and let out a groan.

I ran towards it, fell down on my knees and spoke. 'Charlie – it's me, Alyssa. Can you hear me?'

She groaned again. There was blood on her cheek and rips in her jacket where thorns had caught.

'What happened, Charlie? Where's Marco?'

Struggling on to her knees, she let her hair fall across her face. 'I fell and hurt my ankle. I told him to go ahead without me.'

I pushed her blood-streaked hair back and made her look at me. 'He left you here?'

'I told him to go. I knew the cops would get him if he stayed to help me.'

'The ankle – is it broken?'

'I don't know. I can't put any weight on it so I had to crawl.'

OK, she'd betrayed us, but she was suffering for it. 'Oh, Charlie,' I murmured.

Angrily she shoved me away. 'These aren't tears – I'm not crying,' she protested. 'I'm not sorry I helped Marco to get away either, if that's what you're thinking. I'm actually glad!'

For Christ's sake, the deluded girl had just aided and abetted a dangerous psycho and she wasn't apologizing. My pity for her vanished and a big part of me now wanted to leave her there to find her own way home while I picked up Marco's trail again.

'What was the plan?' I asked. 'How far did you think you'd get?'

'There was no plan. After I warned Marco the cops were on their way, we just ran. And, no, he didn't force me to go with him – it was my idea, I wanted to.'

'So I'll help you get back home,' I said wearily. I slung Charlie's arm round my shoulder and hauled her upright, pointing us in what I hoped was the direction of the school. Then I took a deep breath and yelled out Connie's name.'

'Over here!' came a distant shout.

'I found Charlie. She can't walk.'

'Keep talking.' Connie's voice grew stronger. 'I'll follow the sound of your voice.'

'It looks like she broke her ankle, or maybe it's just a bad sprain. Either way, I can't leave her here.' I heard more noises as Connie drew near – her feet trampling through undergrowth until at last I saw the beam of light wobbling towards us. 'What do you want to do – come with us or go on?'

'Do you even have to ask?' she muttered, directing the light at Charlie's tear-stained face. She didn't say anything, but her anger filled the silence and I knew that at this point she was deaf to common sense.

'I'm not sorry that I helped Marco!' Charlie repeated, more defiant than ever.

'There's no point asking her any questions because she doesn't have the answers,' I told Connie. 'She didn't even know where they were headed – they just took off together.'

'Then he dumped her. Charming.'

'Come or go?' I repeated.

'Go,' she said sharply. And that was it – I warned Connie to be careful then Charlie and I staggered back towards St Jude's while Connie headed deeper into the woods.

chapter twelve

It seemed to take forever. Charlie leaned heavily on me, groaning and hopping all the way. It turned out she was a person with a low pain threshold.

'I'm never going to make it,' she complained as we emerged from under the trees on to the lawn. 'My ankle hurts like hell.'

'No way can I carry you,' I warned, looking beyond the lake to the lights of St Jude's where the people I could rely on – Eugenie, Hooper, Zara and the rest – were waiting for the police.

'Then leave me here and get help,' she pleaded. 'Go, Alyssa – find a couple of guys. Will and Luke – they're strong.'

'OK, but don't move,' I agreed. 'Don't double back and try to catch up with Marco.'

'How could I even if I wanted to?' she whimpered. She wasn't sorry, she wasn't grateful or gracious and she definitely didn't care that a killer was on the loose.

I gave up on her and left her sitting on the cold ground, propped against a tree trunk. If I sprinted, I could cover the ground in under three minutes, tell the guys to come and fetch Charlie then find out from Hooper, Eugenie and Zara the latest on the cops and their failure to show.

Where's Ripley? I asked myself as I ran. Why am I not hearing sirens, seeing flashing blue lights?

I was glancing over my shoulder, not looking where I was going when I crashed into Hooper at the edge of the car park. I almost knocked him off his feet.

He reeled back against the nearest parked car – Marco's Aston Martin as it happened.

'Sorry!' I gasped. 'Hooper, listen to me – I found Charlie in the woods. She hurt her ankle. We need to send a couple of guys to fetch her back – Will and Luke maybe.'

'Or I could.' He sounded offended that I hadn't included him.

'Yeah, course – you find either of the others. Grab a torch. Charlie will be waiting for you on the edge of the wood, close to the footpath leading down to the road.'

Nodding eagerly, Hooper set off round the front of the main school building towards the quad. His running style was so jerky and uncoordinated that even now it made me smile. I hadn't had time to ask him whether or not he'd alerted Justine and if Saint Sam or Molly Wilson had any idea what was taking place in their school grounds. Maybe that was what I should do next – run down the drive to the principal's house. Or then again no – I should get back on Marco's trail instead of leaving it all to Connie.

Yes, that was my decision – to go back right away and discover how Connie was doing.

I ground gravel under the ball of my foot as I spun round, but I hadn't even got into my stride when the passenger door of the Aston Martin flew open and slammed into me.

The impact of the heavy, swinging door sent me staggering against the side of the car under one of the orange lights that stayed on all through the night. I bent double, disorientated and struggling to breathe. Then I felt a strong hand round my wrist, and found myself dragged towards the car and yanked inside. Marco leaned across me and slammed the door.

Fear jolted through my whole body like an electric shock. Marco must have changed his plan after he'd abandoned Charlie in the wood. He'd obviously back-tracked, gone up to his room to collect the car keys, got back to the car and sat inside in time to watch me sprint up the hill and talk to Hooper. He'd ducked out of sight until I was alone again, then he'd flung the door open to stop me in my tracks.

Now he sat next to me, staring straight ahead.

In plain sight. Taunting and mocking, telling me he loved me when I was angry, saying how disappointed he was that I missed what was there, right under my nose.

Who rattled at my window in the middle of the night? Marco.

Who put the fake photos on Facebook?

Marco.

Who killed Cock Robin?

'A metaphor, a warning,' Eugenie suggests. 'Dead bird sings no more. It represents the fall of something beautiful, the ending of a brief life. Soaring in the sky one moment then dead and cold the next.'

Marco killed the robin and left it on my windowsill.

He stared ahead. I grabbed the handle and tried to open the door. It was locked.

'I', said the Sparrow

'With my bow and arrow, I killed Cock Robin.'

Come on, Alyssa – they said you were smart! Why so slow to pick up the clues? Bad things are happening under your nose. It's up to you to work them out, which I'm sure you can do if you're as good as they say. The killer is in plain sight. Catch me if you can, memory girl. Love and kisses . . .

Marco sat beside me, turning the car's ignition.

Four red hearts in a text message from an unknown number, which turned out to be Marco's.

Red, like the other carefully laid clues, like the red of Scarlett's name. How could I have ignored it? Had I not been paying attention, for Christ's sake? No, I'd been knocked sideways by Jack's jealous reaction and spent all my energy convincing him that I wasn't the least bit interested in Marco. Prime example of dramatic irony, as Bryony would doubtless have pointed out.

Killing me softly.

Red, red, red, the connection between all the clues – the hearts, the handwritten messages, the lipstick.

Red is the colour of anger. A red mist is said to form before a killer's eyes, he points the gun and shoots, raises the knife and stabs. Lady Macbeth has so much blood on her hands she can never wash them clean.

It's also the colour of romance.

Roses are red, my love,
Violets are blue,
Sugar is sweet my love,
But not as sweet as you.

Killing you softly.

I groaned as Marco started the engine. I tried the handle again though I knew it was hopeless.

The car shot forward, spitting gravel. Headlights raked across the lawn as he swung towards the drive.

'Stop,' I pleaded.

He put his foot on the accelerator.

'Marco, this is futile. The cops are on their way.'

We gathered speed past Saint Sam's house, out through the gates on to the road, swinging left away from Chartsey along a winding lane that would eventually meet up with the main road into Oxford. There were no street lamps, no road markings, only high bare hedges to either side.

'Talk to me, Marco. Say something.'

He unleashed a torrent of foul, unrepeatable insults, took us up to seventy on an icy road that snaked viciously up and downhill.

I groped for the seat belt and tried to strap myself in, but a sudden sharp bend made me lurch against him, sending us swerving across the road. He steadied the wheel and pulled us back on course, drove on like the maniac that he was.

'OK, you win!' I gasped. 'If that's what all this is about, I admit it – you were too good for me.'

He kept his foot down, didn't even glance sideways at me. All I saw was his beautiful, fixed profile, which could have been sculpted in marble for all the emotion it conveyed.

But something that Zara had explained about the narcissist's craving for admiration made me keep on with the flattery. 'Much too clever. I was so slow in comparison, and I guess Scarlett was too. You must feel really good about beating us both.'

We came to a crossroads and without braking Marco shot straight across.

'Marco, I'm sorry I disappointed you. I did my best but you were too good.'

'I'm laughing so hard my gut aches. Honey, how wrong can you be?' he gloats in his fake Texan drawl.

He'd enjoyed every moment.

'Catch me if you can.'

He'd posted a video of Galina's kidnap on Twitter.

'This is going to get worse.'

The locker door swings open, Galina's tie hangs from it. 'PLEASE HELP ME,' Galina writes.

But I'd failed. I hadn't helped her. I'd suspected Alex, Mikhail, Sergei, Will, even Sammy Beckett, but not Marco, or at least not for long. Because I'd taken him at face value – a privileged, self-satisfied player who skimmed over the surface of life, who was too busy partying, travelling around Europe and appearing in gossip mags to be taken seriously.

I didn't for a moment imagine that Marco could have been the driver of the old black Merc.

'If I drive a car and hit you at thirty miles per hour, you

bounce off my bonnet and collect a few broken bones. Forty miles per hour – serious head injuries. Fifty – you're dead.'

I find Jack, my Jack, down a dark side street, amongst the garbage. He's semi-conscious and bleeding from the forehead. I beg him not to move. Water gushes from a broken down-pipe, I'm drowning in a tsunami of fear. I call 999.

'Try to keep him awake. The ambulance is on its way. It should be with you in five minutes. How is he doing? Is he still conscious? Good. I'm staying on the line – I won't leave you. Stick with it. You're doing a great job.'

I wasn't. I was failing, floundering drowning.

Five minutes feel like five hours. Then I hear the sirens and see blue lights flashing.

I heard sirens. Blue lights flashed above the tops of the hedges. Marco pushed his speed up to eighty. We came to a roundabout, converging with two police patrol cars racing towards us from opposite directions.

Swearing, gripping the wheel, Marco drove his car straight over the hump-backed roundabout. I shot out of my seat and struck my head on the roof, slumped back in the seat and tried to grasp hold of the door handle. He chose the only clear exit, but we'd only travelled a few hundred metres down a new side road before there were more blue lights and sirens ahead of us. Marco took a final bend then found a white police Range Rover blocking our way. He braked hard. Tyres squealed as we swerved, shimmied and careered into the ditch. Air bags inflated and the engine cut out. Marco's door was jammed. Mine was the only one that would open.

Ripley leaned in and gently helped me out.

'Stupid bitch!' Marco yelled as he struggled in vain to free himself.

'You – you're unspeakable!' I shot back at him as dry, angry sobs erupted from deep in my chest. 'You revolt me – you know that?'

He shook his head as Ripley freed me from the wreck.

Her two uniformed guys were less careful with Marco. They hauled him across the central gear control and out of the car. I'm not saying they didn't follow police restraint procedures. What I am saying is that when I last looked, before Ripley drove me away in her car, Marco was lying face down on the road, arms pinned behind his back, not going anywhere.

'So, my advice is the same as it was last time we spoke,' my buddy the inspector told me. 'You need to go home.'

It was like throwing a bucket of cold water in my face. I stared at her in disbelief. 'You know I don't want to do that.'

'You may not want to, Alyssa, but that's because you're too close to the situation to see things clearly. My job right now is to take a long, cool look and advise you on how best to keep you safe.'

We were back at school, where there was an unprecedented amount of activity going on, given that it was 2 a.m.

Saint Sam was up and about, dressed in his grey principal suit. Molly was there too – equally immaculate.

263

She'd corralled my friends inside the technology centre – Eugenie, Zara, Connie, Will, Luke and Hooper. Charlie wasn't there because she'd joined Jack in the Queen Elizabeth for treatment to her ankle, according to Zara. I'd told her the latest about Marco – currently held in a police cell in Ainslee, waiting to be interviewed by Sergeant Owen and Inspector Ripley, as soon as Ripley was through giving me advice.

'It's a free country. You can't make me leave,' I pointed out.

'That's perfectly true.'

'Besides, it's not logical. Why would I leave now that you've arrested Marco and the whole thing is almost over?'

'To let events settle down, give yourself breathing space.'

'What if I want to stick around and visit Jack in the Q.E.?'

'Jack's not in danger. He'll survive a couple of days without visits from you. And don't worry – we'll keep you informed about Galina.'

'You'll let me know as soon as Marco tells you where she is?'

'The minute we find her – yes. I've got your mobile number so I'll keep in touch.'

'And where would you like me to go if I agree to leave?'

'To your aunt in Richmond?' Very cool and formal. In fact, excessively so, given the buddy–cop relationship I thought we had.

'She's not at home. She's in Brussels on business.'

'Don't you have other family members you could stay with?'

'No. My parents died when I was three. I'm an only child. Aunt Olivia never had kids. The family tree of living relatives stops right there.'

'Close friends?' Ripley was dogged – you know, nose to the ground, bloodhound style – sniffing out solutions.

'They're all here at St Jude's.' Milling around the computer decks in the depths of night, deep in the latest Marco shock-news. It came to me with a small shock of realization – Zara for all her flirty, girlie stuff, Connie for all her strident confidence and intense, geeky Hooper – I counted them as my closest friends.

Ripley frowned. 'So go home to Richmond and stay inside the house for a day or two. When will your aunt be back?' She'll be home for the weekend, won't she?'

'Probably.' Reduced to a sullen, one-word response in the face of Ripley's stonewalling, I began to think my way round the back of her advice.

Why did she want me to leave? Was it really to keep me safe? And if it was, why not station an official, uniformed version of the Sergei–Mikhail heavy brigade at the entrance to St Jude's to keep out unwelcome stalkers? Anyway, no – my psycho-stalker was in a police cell, remember.

My ex-buddy took a couple of paces down the central aisle of the big glass and steel building then she paced back, arms folded, looking me directly in the eye. 'They put a new guy in charge of the case,' she told me quietly. 'Chief Inspector Todd. He'll be here by lunchtime.'

Oh, she wants me out of the way so that I don't complicate things for her! Todd might decide she's been letting me off on too long a leash, doing too much investigating of my own. I stared back at her.

'You see what I'm getting at?'

Yes, she wanted to set up a clean sheet with her new boss. I nodded.

'Excellent. I thought you would.'

I gave a good impression of backing down. 'OK, so you've got Marco and sooner or later he's going to tell you where Galina is. Then you'll go get her – that's the main thing.'

'Agreed. We'll interview Marco as soon as we get him back to the station.'

'So I'll take a train to Richmond.' I'll let you think I'm out of your hair. 'And you'll keep me in the loop?'

'For sure,' Ripley said, without meaning it.

What did she think – that she was fobbing off a four-year-old with an empty promise? Maybe that was how she saw me, as a kid way out of my depth who hadn't done anything except get in the way of police investigations – starting with the visit to the canal with Jayden and Bolt, where I'd been in danger of compromising vital forensic evidence, right through to tonight's car chase – in the way again as police patrol cars closed in on Marco.

'OK,' I told her, turning to walk down the central aisle of the technology centre, out into the black night.

Marco Conti had made a fool of me.

He'd killed Scarlett Hartley and thrown her body into the canal. He'd snuffed out the light in her lively grey eyes. Then he'd started on me, kidnapping Galina and using her as a form of collateral damage in the war against my eidetic memory.

All along he'd stalked me and tricked me, played the game and almost won.

Slowly, methodically packing a change of clothes into a backpack as the first streaks of grey light appeared in the January sky – jeans and black T-shirt, clean socks and knickers, toothbrush and toothpastc – I shuddered as I thought of the moment when I'd recognized Marco's Aston Martin in the kidnap video and his intricate network of games and challenges had unravelled.

Ripley could at least have said thanks for that, I thought as I zipped up the bag. It was me who did it – I recognized the car.

I projected ahead to the police interview with Marco. It would be in a small, windowless room with puke-yellow walls. There would be a table – two grey plastic chairs on one side for Marco and his duty solicitor, two chairs opposite. Sergeant Owen would be at one of them, gnawing away at Marco's lies. Inspector Ripley on the remaining chair would wait until, at a psychologically appropriate point, she would put pressure on him to reveal Galina's whereabouts. Chief Inspector Todd would stand behind one of those one-way glass partitions (What are they called? I wondered), clocking each of Marco's answers, reading his body language, waiting for him to crack and confess everything.

Would Marco crack?

I put on my jacket, pulled back my hair and twisted it

into a clip at the nape of my neck, took one last look around Room twenty-seven.

No, I didn't think he would. His beautiful, chiselled face would give nothing away. He would keep on loving himself, nurturing his psychotic narcissism, refusing to admit defeat.

The interview would terminate. Papa Paolo would be informed of his son's predicament and straight away forget recent family differences. He would hire the most expensive legal team to construct a clever defence. Meanwhile, no one would discover where Marco had hidden Galina.

I took a quick look in the mirror. Don't quit now, I told myself.

Then I walked out of the room, along the panelled corridor, past Lady Anne Moore in her stiff lace ruff and pearls, down the stone steps, and silent as Lady Anne's ghost I crossed the quad before anyone else stirred.

Don't quit now.

Knock-knock on Jayden's door in Upper Chartsey at 7.45 a.m. I heard Bolt hurtle down the hallway, sharp claws on stripped pine floorboards, then saw his blunt snout appear through the letter-box flap. Jayden's kid brother, Brad, eventually opened the door in his T-shirt and striped boxers.

'I'm looking for Jayden,' I explained.

Bolt gnawed at my Uggs; Brad swore colourfully.

In time, Jayden emerged fully dressed from his bedroom and stomped downstairs. 'What the . . . ?'

'I know – it's a lousy time to visit.' I'd already started to apologize when Jayden elbowed Brad out of the way and stepped out on to the garden path. Bolt tried to squeeze through but – *bang* – Jayden slammed the door behind him.

'What's it about?'

'They arrested Marco Conti.'

Jayden's eyelids flickered and frown lines appeared on his forehead. He didn't say a word.

'I remembered it was his car in the kidnap video.'

'Conti kidnapped Galina?'

'It was his car,' I said again. 'He found out from Charlie Hudson that the police were after him.'

'So he took off?'

I nodded and filled in a few more details about the chase and about Ripley not wanting me to stick around. 'No way will Marco tell them where Galina is,' I predicted.

By this time we'd been on our way down the hill into the Bottoms, me, Jayden and Bolt – the old team. 'If he even knows,' Jayden added.

'Of course he knows! Wait, what are you saying?'

'I'm not saying anything. I'm thinking.'

'Anyway, I need somewhere to stay without people knowing. Ursula has a flat – right? – but I don't know exactly where. Do you . . . I mean, will she . . . ?'

'Let's find out,' he'd muttered, which is how come I found myself knocking on a tatty blue door above the organic veg shop in Chartsey Bottom.

*

'You want to stay here, with me?' an incredulous Ursula echoed. 'Are you serious?'

'Be nice,' Jayden advised. 'Let her sleep on your sofa.'

'You know I don't have a sofa.' Ursula looked as if she was ready to leave for work – she had her jacket on and was holding one non-weather-resistant boot. The other lay on the living-room floor behind her, next to a pile of laundry.

'She can sleep on your floor, then.'

'I won't get in your way,' I promised. 'I'll be visiting Jack in hospital later today. I just need somewhere to kip.'

'You told her where I lived!' Ursula's voice rose an octave as she challenged Jayden.

'Yeah. They arrested Conti.'

'For Scarlett?'

'And Galina Radkin – yeah.'

'Shit,' Ursula said through gritted teeth. 'That can't be right.'

'I know – that's what I thought at first,' I said. 'But there's a link none of us knew about, which is that Scarlett could have met him in Italy last summer – he's the Italian guy you told me about – remember?'

'Jesus!' Stooping to zip on her boot, Ursula's face was red when she stood up again. 'OK, there could be a connection, but I still say no, it's not right.'

Her gut reaction unnerved me and made my stomach twist, but I stuck with the logic of what I knew. 'The police think it's him. They're trying to get a confession.'

Ursula reached for her other boot. 'I take it you're not just hanging around to visit your guy? If I know

270

you, you'll carry on looking for Galina.'

I took a deep breath then nodded.

'So stay,' she decided. 'There's a spare key on the table. I have to go. I'm late for work.'

I'd only spoken briefly to Julia Cavendish on my first visit to the Q.E. She was by Jack's bed again, without his dad this time, and as soon as she saw me at the door to the ward she went in search of another chair.

'You can never find anywhere to sit in these places,' she complained. 'They tell you not to sit on the beds, Matron's orders, but then they don't provide an alternative – what's that about?'

Jack raised his eyebrows. 'Write to them,' he suggested. 'Complain about a serious chair shortage in the NHS. See where that gets you.'

'Jack, you have to give me permission to moan about something while my only son is lying here with broken ribs and a punctured lung. What else is a mother to do?'

'Bring me grapes? Tell me what's going on in the real world?'

'You ate all the grapes. The real world hasn't changed too much in the two days you've been in here,' she argued. 'Your father is back brokering stock in New York, my gallery is still selling ridiculously overpriced paintings, it's January and the weather is lousy – what more can I say?'

And what can I say about Jack's mother? That at first glance she didn't seem to have a maternal bone in her beautiful, sleek, fashionable body that everyone on the ward – both staff and patients – was staring at her either in envy or admiration, or both. That, if you looked beneath the surface, she was in fact horribly frightened for Jack and trying to cover it up with light banter.

'Jack tells me you were the person who called the ambulance,' Julia said to me when we were both settled on either side of Jack's bed. He'd reached for my hand and held it.

I nodded. 'Jack was cycling back to St Jude's, trying to warn me that something bad was about to happen, but the car ran him down before he had the chance.'

'So anyway the police say that they got the person who did it – the driver of the Mercedes,' Julia said quickly. 'We can all relax now.'

Jack's grip tightened – a sign for me to agree.

'Yes, thank heavens,' I said, and wondered how long it would be before Jack's mother gave us some time alone.

It turned out she was a mind reader. 'I'll leave you two together,' she went on, standing up suddenly and smoothing the front of her dress. 'I'll go down to the cafe for the worst cup of coffee in the world, no doubt.'

I gave her a grateful smile.

Julia came round to my side of the bed. 'Thank you, Alyssa,' she said quietly and seriously. Then she switched back. 'The worst coffee and even worse tea. Plus, I'll get lost in these endless corridors or be run down by a porter's trolley, and I won't have enough cash for the parking-machine token when I eventually come to leave. Hospitals – don't you just love them!'

And she was gone, her cloud of Chanel fighting and losing to the antiseptic smell of the ward, the click of her heels growing fainter.

Jack sighed and I cupped my free hand over our clasped ones. For a long time we just looked into each other's eyes.

'Ouch,' he said as he tried to lean forward to kiss me.

'Stay where you are!' I cried. I leaned forward instead. We kissed gently on the lips.

'So they've got Marco,' he said afterwards. 'Tell me exactly what happened.'

'Exactly?' For a few seconds I debated editing events, wondering whether to give a sanitized version, minus the chase through the oak wood in the dead of night and especially taking care to omit Marco's death-wish dash along the country lanes.

'Don't leave anything out,' he warned. More mind reading – it must run in the family.

'OK. But promise not to be mad.'

'You went against what we agreed?'

'A bit, but not on purpose.'

'You were meant to stay clear of trouble – you swore.'

'Jack, please!'

'No, Alyssa. You did – you promised me. Because I was chained to this stupid bed, you said you wouldn't risk going anywhere alone.'

'And I meant it. But then I remembered . . .'

'What?'

'The video – part of it was filmed in the back of Marco's car. We called the police and Charlie went to fetch Molly, but when they didn't come back, we realized what Charlie had done.'

'She warned Marco?' Jack guessed.

'Yes, but I still didn't split from the others – I went out with Connie to look for Marco and Charlie. We found Charlie in the woods, but she was injured and I had to go back to school for help. Marco was still on the run. He hid in his car. I wasn't expecting him to jump out . . .'

Jack closed his eyes and shook his head. 'And I was stuck here,' he groaned.

'It's OK – I survived. I'm still in one piece and Marco's in a police cell.' Should I go on? Should I tell Jack about me resisting Ripley's advice and holing up in Ursula's flat above Five-a-Day?

'They want to keep me here over the weekend then discharge me on Monday. But even then I'll have to go slow because it'll take six weeks for the ribs to heal properly.'

'It's OK, it's all over.' Except for Galina and the ticking clock, which meant that every hour that passed her situation grew worse. I pictured her in a small, dark room down a back street in Ainslee without food or water. Or worse – held prisoner out in the countryside, hidden away in an unoccupied cottage or barn. Then I tried not to picture it because it was too horrible.

Again Jack echoed my thoughts. 'But now Galina's in an even worse situation than before.'

'Yes. From what Zara tells me about Marco's psychotic disorder, he's not about to give the police the information they need – he won't break; he'll just keep on playing the game.'

'And you're dead set on finding Galina yourself?'

'I can't lie to you – so, yes. But honestly, Jack, it's not dangerous any more, not with Marco safely locked up. I just need time and patience to figure it out, to go back in my mind to the very beginning and pick up clues to where he's hidden her.'

He thought for a long time, all the while softly stroking my wrist. 'I can't stop you, can I?'

'No. And you wouldn't want to.'

'I love you,' he sighed, stroking my skin with the pad of his thumb. 'Remember that.'

That afternoon, just before dusk, Jayden came with me to search the grounds of the ruined abbey. It was an obvious place to start – too obvious, probably – but then Marco didn't know the Chartsey area very well and perhaps he would choose a landmark like the abbey to hide his victim. After all, there were the cloisters and outlying buildings, still intact, where visitors seldom went at this time of year.

We tramped down from the road through about three centimetres of snow – enough to give a wondrous white covering to the fields and mounds of fallen stone that had once formed graceful gothic arches, enough too for us to see that we were the first people there since the snow began to fall.

'Baa-aa!' Jayden said to a lone, black-faced sheep shivering under a spindly hawthorn tree.

'Baa!' the sheep said back.

Bolt chased it down to the river then circled back to join us. We checked the row of gloomy cloisters then went on across a graveyard to a Victorian lodge at the back entrance to the abbey estate. We rattled the rusty iron handle on the front door, found that it was locked then went round to the back and peered through panes of filthy glass. The lodge looked empty and undisturbed.

'It doesn't feel like Galina's here,' I told Jayden.

'We need more than a feeling,' he argued.

So we called out for her as we searched a barn with only half a roof and found more sheep, and after that a ruined cottage with roof timbers exposed to the elements, without windows and doors. The snow kept on falling. If Galina was here, the poor girl would probably be dead from hypothermia before morning.

We left the abbey and trudged on up the hillside and along the bridle path towards Upwood House. We met Ursula after work and got her to let us into the parts of the estate that the public weren't allowed to see – the old stables, a store for farm machinery, even a disused greenhouse in the walled garden. We found nothing – not a single clue that Marco had even considered the National Trust property as a hiding place for Galina.

It was almost four o'clock. We were running out of daylight and fresh ideas at about the same time.

'Let's try again tomorrow,' Ursula suggested. 'It's my day off. I can spend all morning and afternoon helping you look.'

'Unless we take a bus into Ainslee and keep going,' I suggested weakly, even though it seemed a needle-in-a-haystack situation, searching randomly for a missing girl.

'Not me,' Jayden decided. 'I'm out of here.' And off he lurched with Bolt to heel in the direction of Upper Chartsey.

'They'll stop the buses because of the snow,' Ursula reminded me. 'You'd be stranded in town.'

'OK, let's leave it till tomorrow.' I hated to give in, but I had to admit it made sense to go back to Ursula's.

'And hope that the cops have more luck than us,' she added. 'You never know, Marco might do a deal with them – tell them where Galina is in return for a lesser charge. They do that sometimes.'

'Who do?'

'Crims on cop dramas – it's called plea bargaining.'

We followed Jayden into the village, stopped at his gate for Ursula to arrange to meet him in the Smith's Arms in half an hour, then walked on to Chartsey Bottom.

'I've got a sleeping bag you can use,' Ursula told me once we were back in her flat. 'Feel free to watch a DVD. Here's the remote.' Chucking it in my direction, she disappeared into her bedroom, re-emerging after ten minutes with her hair taken down from its dark-rooted, blonde ponytail and frouffed up in every direction like an untidy haystack. She'd lashed on the mascara and slicked candy-pink lip gloss over her lips. Transformation – ta-dah! 'Fish fingers in the freezer,' she said as she left. 'Baked beans in the cupboard. See you!'

I went through Ursula's stack of DVDs – *Lion King*, *Pirates of the Caribbean, Harry Potter* – relics of a more innocent childhood than I'd expected – and chose Johnny Depp. I was only half watching it, noticing how skinny Keira Knightley was, when a message came on to my phone.

Unknown number.

Hah, gotcha! I read.

Who was this? What was happening? My mouth went dry and my heart practically jumped out through my ribs.

Sent you another video. Check it out, why don't you?

Oh God, oh no! My fingers fumbled as I opened the app and played the short, jerky footage.

I saw a dark room with rows of rusty tools hanging from racks on the wall – dozens of spanners of various sizes, three hammers, another row of spanners and wrenches. Cut. Open on red graffiti dribbling down a rough, whitewashed wall.

PLEASE HELP ME!

Cut. Open again on a close-up of a girl's face, duct tape across her mouth, eyes terrified, a damp lock of dark hair across her cheek. A voiceover of Galina breathlessly croaking the words to the children's rhyme.

'All the birds of the air fell a-sighing and a-sobbing . . .'

Cut. Open on a longer view of her sitting with hands tied behind her back on a wooden bench under the *PLEASE HELP ME!* message.

Red, like blood, trickling down the wall. *PLEASE HELP ME!* Red, red, red.

A man's voice talking. 'Hey, Alyssa, you never really thought it was Marco, did you? Well, you were right – it wasn't. I give you twenty-four hours to get the right guy. Twenty-four hours – OK?'

chapter thirteen

I ran down the back stairs of Five-a-Day out into the snow, unable to make sense of what I'd just seen.

'Twenty-four hours – OK?'

That was the phrase that echoed inside my head. Light-hearted in tone, as if it was a bet he was making with me – inconsequential, disconnected from the terror I'd seen on Galina's face.

So where was I planning to go at six on a January evening, in the middle of a snow storm?

As I say, I was so mixed up inside my head that I didn't even think to call Ripley and it must have been instinct that took me to the house where Raisa had been staying.

I only knew one thing without any shadow of doubt and it was that unless I found Galina she'd be dead this time tomorrow.

'PLEASE HELP ME!' in red letters dribbling down the rough, unplastered wall. I had a day to make the difference between Galina living or dying.

My phone beeped to tell me I had a new message. Unknown number. My head told me to prepare for more shocks to my system.

Hey, Alyssa, did you see the new video? Filming isn't

as easy as it looks, but it's cool, isn't it?

I resisted the urge to drop the phone, to fling it over a garden wall and never open another flesh-creeping message.

Beep. He was back with another gloating message – a voicemail this time – firing his sharp, deranged arrows from the safe distance of a stolen phone.

'I see you right now, Alyssa – no, don't worry, not for real. In my mind's eye I imagine you panicking, your lovely red hair flying loose, skin pale and pure as snow. Did you ever see a headless chicken running around? I did. It's hilarious actually. You chop off its head and it leaves the bloody thing – beak, beady eyes, tiny bird brain – lying there in the dirt, but its body keeps on running. Then suddenly it drops down dead. That's you, Alyssa. Bye for now. Cluck, cluck.'

Oh Jesus! Oh God! I slid and skidded on the snowy footpath until I reached Raisa's door. I had no idea if she would still be there or what she would be able to do to help – but, as I said, I was desperate.

It wasn't Raisa who answered the door but off-duty Mikhail. I could tell he wasn't working because he was minus the *Men in Black* suit, dressed instead in navy blue sweatshirt and jeans, with bare feet and three days' worth of stubble on his chin. Despite some bruising on his forehead and cheek, plus a cut under his right eye, he looked relaxed and totally at home.

He stared at me as if he was trying to remember who I was then Raisa came up from behind, pushed him to one side in spite of his bulk and dragged me into the cottage. She brushed snow from my shoulders. 'You have news?' she begged. 'You have found my Galina?'

I shook my head and her round face puckered with despair. 'You have to help me!' I told them.

Mikhail clicked into professional mode and while Raisa led me into the living room he ventured outside barefoot to check that I was alone.

'What's he doing here?' I hissed. The last I'd heard he'd been taken out of the check-in queue for a flight to Moscow by members of Anatoly Radkin's private army.

'He came back to be with me.' Raisa was defensive, refusing to meet my gaze.

'Does Mr Radkin know?'

She shook her head and looked up from under hooded lids. 'You won't tell?'

'No.' Something clicked in my head as I took in her evasive response, a slow adding up of two and two to make four. 'You and Mikhail . . . ?'

She switched from defensive to defiant, chin up. 'We are married for ten years.'

'Oh, I didn't . . . !' I just hadn't realized. It had never crossed my mind until now, and why should it?

'That's why he is here. They hurt him and punish him for letting Galina vanish. He loses his job but he is still my husband and I am still his wife.'

'What about Sergei? I bet he got more than a black eye.' Not for failing to protect Galina, but for moving in on Salomea behind Anatoly's back. He was dead in a ditch probably, or entombed in the concrete foundations of a major building development near Heathrow.

Raisa shrugged. 'For Sergei I don't care.'

'No – me neither.' We agreed on that. By this time Mikhail had stopped scouting around outside and had come back into the house. 'So you'll both help me to find Galina?' I wanted to know.

'How?' he asked. 'It is not so easy. Anatoly Radkin, he has ten men working on this. He offers money, a big reward.'

'But nothing happens,' Raisa sighed.

In out of the snow, I was starting to breathe more normally, getting over my latest panic but feeling exhausted and wrung out as the fear subsided. I took my phone from my pocket and laid it gingerly on Raisa's table, ready to show them the recent Vine video.

'Take a look at this,' I offered. 'And, Raisa, I warn you – you'll be shocked.'

Mikhail and Raisa watched the tiny screen, saw the rows of tools in the dirty workshop, the red letters on the wall. Raisa put her hand to her mouth as Galina appeared, gagged by silver duct tape, eyes staring in terror, and we heard the sound of her recorded voice attempting to sing the words to the first verse of 'Cock Robin'. Mikhail clenched his fists.

'Listen. He's giving me twenty-four hours to find her,' I warned. 'That's before six o'clock tomorrow night.'

There was the final image of Galina sitting on a rough wooden bench and then the voiceover. It was too much for Raisa, who collapsed sobbing on to a chair.

I spoke to Mikhail instead. 'You see what he's doing?

He's giving me my final test – one last chance to prove that I'm as clever as he is.'

Mikhail looked helplessly from me to his wife, who, between sobs, translated what I'd said.

'The ultimate challenge,' I whispered.

I can't stop Psycho Man. I'm not good enough. Galina will die.

I thought it but I didn't confess any of this to Raisa and Mikhail.

He's winning. He's in control.

Mikhail picked up my phone and reran the video. A new message arrived in the middle of it. He quickly handed the phone back to me.

It was a message from Jack, not my psycho.

Call me soon as you can.

I called with fingers that fumbled. I had to tap and re-tap until the call went through. 'Hi. Jack, are you OK? What's happened? There's nothing wrong, is there?' I plunged in and he talked over me. Our voices drowned each other out.

'Alyssa, wait. I need you to listen – it's important.'

I stopped mid sentence. 'OK. What?'

'I've just had a visit from Hooper.'

Ah – hospital-visitor Hooper who always does the right thing. 'OK, good. I'm listening.'

'It's just something he dropped into the conversation – it started me thinking.'

'What's he been saying now?' I sighed. I didn't have time for this – I really didn't.

'A few things actually.' Jack spoke slowly, hesitating between words and repeating things as if negotiating his way cautiously through each sentence. 'It was about Marco. You know, we were talking, Hooper and me, and I was saying I was glad the nightmare was over, really over at last, and all we needed now was for the cops to force Marco to say where he's been hiding Galina. Anyway at this point I figured there was something Hooper wasn't telling me. He was shuffling his feet, clearing his throat, you know how he does.'

'Did you find out what was bugging him?'

'Yeah, finally. He told me he didn't think they'd got the right guy.'

I let out a short groan then drew in a deep breath. Thanks for that, Hooper. Now Jack would be worried out of his mind about me again. 'He's changed his tune,' I muttered, 'given that Hooper was the one who spent all that time and energy digging dirt on Marco.' I needed time to get my head round this new situation before I was ready to face reality and tell Jack about the latest poison dropped into my ear: *'Hey, Alyssa. You never really thought it was Marco, did you?'*

Twenty-four hours to find out the truth and counting down, minute by minute.

PLEASE HELP ME!

Jack used the long pause to carry on explaining. 'No, listen. We both know Hooper's smart. He has a sixth sense about these things. I said to him, if Marco's not guilty, why did he take off in his car with Alyssa the way he did? An innocent guy doesn't run.'

285

'And?'

'Hooper already had an answer for that. According to him, Marco was in Monaco at the same time as Galina last summer – you know how good he is on researching dates and stuff. So the way he sees it is that Marco went joy-riding in his Dad's speedboat – remember?'

'I do,' I sighed. I was finding it hard to focus, desperately wondering how to break the news to Jack that Hooper's hunch was right and our psycho had been busy filming me again.

'Well, Hooper did some more digging into news reports etcetera and it turns out that Marco's dad's boat was the same model, same colour as the boat involved in the accident with Galina and her two mates – where one died, OK? And the dates were close. So Hooper's new theory is that Marco kept his dad's boat for a day or two, during which he accidentally killed the kid in the boating incident, but the Conti family covered it up and the Monaco police never prosecuted.

'And Hooper thinks that's why Marco went on the run when Charlie warned him the cops were after him over here in England?'

'It would make sense if you think about it.'

'Which we didn't,' I admitted. 'Because we were far too busy thinking about other stuff.'

'Anyway, Alyssa, do you see what I'm saying to you now?'

I pictured him lying in pain beneath the blue cover of his hospital bed, his face pale under the stark overhead reading light, turning over the information, tormented by the new possibility that Psycho Man was still free but he, Jack, was unable to do anything about it.

'I'm trying to warn you just in case Hooper turns out to be right – *if* they got the wrong guy . . .'

'. . . Then I'm still in danger,' I interrupted. 'And actually he is – he's right.'

'What are you saying – that the psycho's still out there?'

'Still sending me messages. Still filming Galina,' I admitted, though telling the truth was like pulling teeth.

'Oh Jesus, Alyssa!'

'I know. But I'm safe. I'm staying in the village with Ursula. No one knows where I am except her and Jayden.'

And Raisa and Mikhail. And probably the owner of Five-a-Day and half the curtain-twitching, nosey neighbours in Chartsey Bottom.

'Try not to worry,' I told Jack. 'Keep your phone switched on. I'll call you as often as I can.'

He ignored me and spoke over me again. 'Don't move. Don't go outside. Don't do anything. I'm going to call the cops.'

'What do we do?' During my conversation with Jack, Mikhail had put his arm round Raisa's shoulder and she'd wiped her eyes. She turned to me, asking me the question with a desperate edge to her voice.

I put up my hands, palms towards her. Don't ask me. I don't know. I am scared beyond belief.

'Alyssa, you know my Galina,' she went on. 'She told

me – you talk to her about everything. You are her best friend.'

I shared a room with her for a short time – I knew very little about her actually. This was something else I didn't say out loud. If I really was Galina's best friend, what a lonely life she must have led up till now.

'I want to help. I've been in contact with the police and we're all trying to find the answer,' I insisted.

'You two talk about boys.'

'No.'

Raisa didn't believe me. 'Girls talk. She tells you who she likes, who likes her.'

'Honestly, she didn't.'

'One of these boys – they take her now and keep her in prison, make this bad film of her with her hands tied.'

I had to give it to Raisa straight and make her understand. 'She didn't have a boyfriend at St Jude's. She was a new girl. She didn't have time to start a relationship or at least, if she did, she chose not to tell me much about it. Anyway, she'd stayed in her room – our room – after she cut her lip. She was too embarrassed to go out.' It was time for me to glance at Mikhail to study his reaction.

He looked away and muttered something to Raisa in Russian.

'Mikhail only does his job,' she translated. 'Galina runs away into the village. He must follow.'

'And punch her in the face?'

She shook her head. 'Galina, my poor baby, she falls to the ground. She is in trouble with her father for running

288

away many times before. She makes up this story.'

'Leave me!' Galina yells at Mikhail, who's in hot pursuit. 'I tell my father what you do!'

I remembered how Galina fled across the street into the churchyard.

Beautiful girl runs away from thick set man in suit and tie. Jack, Marco and I – we can't stand by and let this happen.

Jack and Marco tackle Mikhail. I follow Galina into the church porch. She's sobbing on a stone bench, hiding her face in her hands.

I ease her hands down, see a deep cut on her bottom lip and a trickle of blood. It's not an accident, she says. It's Mikhail – he punched her in the face. He tried to kidnap her. 'I am scared but I escape,' she says. 'I run to village. I am very, very scared.'

Jack and Marco pin Mikhail to the pavement.

'What do I do?' Galina whimpers. 'Who will believe me?'

'Me,' I decided. 'I believe you, Galina.'

But I'd been the only one. Salomea hadn't backed her when she took her call. The police hadn't either – they'd questioned Mikhail and released him without charge.

'What sort of trouble would she have been in with her father?' I asked now.

'Big trouble,' Raisa said. 'He warned her, if you run away again, I will take away money, bag business – everything. You will stay home, not go shopping, not see friends.'

'So she lied about you?' I asked Mikhail, who nodded.

'It is hard for Mikhail. Like me, he has been with Galina since she was small girl. He sees her sad life. He cares about her.'

Really? This guy with the muscles and stubble had a heart that could care?

Doubt must have shadowed my face because Mikhail stepped forward to speak for himself and prove it. 'I show you. I put on shoes, jacket. Right now we look for Galina.'

I still didn't know whether I believed him but his deep voice and animal energy swept me along and took me with him out of the house on to the dark street, with Raisa trailing behind, zipping up her jacket and hurrying to catch up.

'Which boys does Galina know?' she asked, taking up her old train of thought. 'Say names. We visit their houses now, ask questions.'

'She knows Marco, but obviously it's not him,' I replied. We came out of Raisa's cul de sac on to a short stretch of hill leading down to Main Street. 'I guess she knows Luke, but he's with Connie so he's off limits for Galina, and Jack, my Jack – ditto off limits, plus Hooper and Will from St Jude's. She might have bumped into a few of the Ainslee Comp crowd, either here in the village, or back at St Jude's when the Comp kids came to play football. People like Tom Walsingham and Alex Driffield.' I was running through the list as fast as I could, wondering where the hell we were going, unable to get out of my head the gory image of headless chickens running around like crazy before they dropped.

'Wait!' I cried.

Mikhail stopped outside the boarded-up front window of JD Workshop.

I see a dark room with rusty tools hanging from racks on the wall – dozens of spanners of various sizes, three hammers, another row of spanners and wrenches. Cut. Open on red graffiti dribbling down a rough, whitewashed wall. 'PLEASE HELP ME!'

I slammed the flat of my hand against the boarded window.

'All the birds of the air fell a-sighing and a-sobbing . . .' Cut. Galina sits on a rough wooden bench with her hands tied behind her back.

I slammed the board a second time then leaned against it. 'She's somewhere around here,' I predicted in a whisper.

Mikhail and Raisa stared uncertainly at me.

'We were looking at a workshop on the video. Galina's kidnapper stole the Merc from JD's which means he knows the layout of the building. There's a yard round the back with small workshops. I think maybe he chose one of those to hide Galina.'

Raisa rapidly interpreted and before we could consider what to do Mikhail was running through the archway at the side of the small car showroom into a stone-flagged yard. We followed. A movement-sensitive light flashed on as we entered the courtyard. And there we were, looking at six units, three of which were run down and unused. The rest were padlocked, with shabby signs over the door. 'Harrison Plumbing Supplies', 'Dean Mackay, Electrician' – and on down the row.

Mikhail chose the nearest unit. The sign above read 'Chartsey Lawn Mower Repairs'. He shoulder-charged the wooden door and after three attempts broke the flimsy lock and smashed the door off its hinges. Raisa covered her eyes, unable to look. I joined Mikhail to peer inside a workshop no more than five metres square. We saw big mowers, small mowers, electric and petrol, in various states of reassembly. There were no hidden corners, no Galina.

Mikhail swore and moved on to break into the next premises. My previous confidence began to waver. What if I was wrong?

The second door gave way at Mikhail's first attempt – it was one of the disused units, empty except for dust, cobwebs, a stack of empty plastic sacks in one corner and rusty oil cans strewn across the floor.

Mikhail breathed heavily. He ran at the third door, secured only by a small padlock, which broke under the force of his shoulder charge. Dean Mackay, Electrician would not be pleased.

Empty again except for cable, switches and sockets neatly stacked on shelves, three metal ladders and, unexpectedlly, two brand new kids' bikes propped against a wall. Recent presents from Santa Claus perhaps, stored here by Daddy Dean until the weather improved.

I was getting distracted, feeling my hopes of finding Galina fade. But then I heard a new noise – different to our hollow footsteps, Mikhail's heavy breathing and the sound of wooden doors splintering. It was an urgent tapping sound, coming from another disused unit, right at the far end of the row. I ran through wet, slushy snow, heard the sound again – a frantic tapping, growing louder. 'Mikhail, over here!'

He slithered through the slush and came to a halt beside me, nodded once when he heard the tapping then immediately charged at the door.

Raisa stood under the light in the stone archway, hands balled into fists, which she kept pressed against her mouth. I swear she'd stopped breathing as Mikhail made his final charge.

The door shattered and fell inward. I smelt dampness and decay, waited for my eyes to grow used to the gloom.

The workshop was a mess. There was a piece of heavy machinery stacked against the right-hand wall, its innards spilling out across the floor – springs, cogs, steel rods. Dirty rags, perished hoses, coils of rope hung from the wall opposite. I took it all in as I stepped inside. Then finally I made out the writing on the far wall. Big red letters, daubed and dribbling down the rough whitewashed surface, a wooden bench underneath.

PLEASE HELP ME!

And finally, *finally*, I turned round to see Galina extricate herself from the broken planks of wood that had once been the door. She hadn't stepped back in time, had slipped as it splintered and toppled on to her. Her hands were tied, her mouth taped.

I ran to her, gave her my hand to help her up, gently unpeeled the tape from her mouth.

She gulped in air, sobbed, fell against me.

Raisa rushed in, crying and wailing. Mikhail cut through

the cable that tied Galina's wrists with a knife he drew from his back pocket.

'You're safe,' I whispered into her ear.

Galina rested her head against my shoulder and sobbed like a five-year-old wrenched out of deep sleep by a terrible nightmare. Raisa took off her jacket and wrapped it round Galina's shoulders. We led her slowly into the yard.

'I think I am dying!' she gasped. 'In that filthy place. I am dead. No one will find me.'

'No – you're alive.' I pushed her tangled hair back from her face. 'Take deep breaths. No one's going to hurt you now.'

A fresh terror seized her and she reached out for Raisa. 'He will come back – I know he will!'

Raisa's arms went round her. 'No, *lyublmaya mou*, he will not.' She hugged her as she always had, since she was a child small enough to sit on her lap. 'I will not let him.'

'Who's "he"?' I urged. 'Who did this to you, Galina?'

She hid her face against Raisa and shook her head.

Answer me! I pleaded silently. End this misery. 'Come on, tell us who he is. Don't be afraid.'

'I don't know his name.'

'But you must. You left school to come into the village and meet him. You said you'd tell me when you got back.'

'But that was not him,' Galina said through her tears.

'Who was that then?'

'That was Luke. He likes me but he is going out with Connie. He is scared she will find out. He will find a time to tell her later.'

'OK, I get that. Meanwhile you have to keep it a secret. So you go out to meet Luke but it's not him who kidnapped you?'

'No, I tell you this already!'

'Hush, *lyublmaya.*' Raisa squeezed her and rocked her from side to side.

Wracked by sobs, still shaking, Galina allowed Raisa to lead her out of the yard on to Main Street.

'If it wasn't Luke, who was it?' I wouldn't let this go, even though Mikhail had taken out his phone to call the police, and events were moving rapidly on.

'At first I think it's Luke waiting for me in the trees behind the church. It is who I expect. I smile, I walk towards him. He is filming me, his hands hide his face. I smile again.'

'Then?' I prompted as Galina paused, frowned and shook her head.

Then he lets one hand go away from face and he wears black scarf like this, covering face up to eyes. And he wears sunglasses at night time and grey hat over forehead. He takes something from his pocket, something you use to fix a car.'

'A spanner?'

'Yes. Still he films. And he puts the spanner up like this and I think he will hit me.' Once more she broke down and hid her face at the memory.

'OK,' I said gently. 'I understand.'

I understood but I was devastated. There was no identification. Even when Ripley and her team arrived, there would be no way forward. They would slow things down with police procedures, going at snail's pace with criss-crossing slimy trails that led nowhere.

Meanwhile the psycho was still on the loose.

Ripley! She wasn't supposed to know I was here and when she found out I was she'd want to send me to Richmond as planned. Mikhail had finished his 999 conversation, and put the phone back in his pocket. I knew I only had a few minutes before the sirens blared down Main Street.

'When the police get here, don't mention me,' I told Raisa hurriedly. 'Please!'

'But you save my Galina's life,' she protested.

'Leave me out of it for now. I have a reason.'

She nodded, too taken up with comforting her darling girl to question me.

'I'll see you later,' I promised Galina. 'Raisa will take care of you.'

She looked up and for a moment gave me a glimpse of the old, unbroken Galina. 'My father thinks he will take me from St Jude's, but I don't let him,' she vowed. 'I make much money with my bags, pay school fees!'

'You betcha.' I grinned, glad to see a flash of the old spirit. 'You take care, Galina, and I'll see you very soon.'

I snuck off then, down the street and round the back of Five-a-Day, up the stairs to Ursula's flat. I fumbled in my pocket for the key then I was in through the door, turning on the light, gasping in horror.

Ursula's room was wrecked. Her glass coffee table was shattered into lethal fragments, her TV flung against the radiator, DVDs everywhere. Cups and plates lay smashed on the kitchenette floor.

And the message. It was scrawled in lipstick (red, of course) across the mirror in the tiny bedroom.

CONGRATS, MY LOVELY ALYSSA! YOU FINALLY WORKED IT OUT. NOW THIS TURNS INTO A REAL CONTEST – YOU AND ME, RIGHT DOWN TO THE WIRE!

chapter fourteen

In a total panic I called Jack. A polite female voice told me he was unable to take my call. I left a voicemail message as requested.

'Hey, Jack. Galina's safe. Call me.'

Then I did my best to pick up the pieces of glass scattered around Ursula's floor, wrapped them in newspaper and decided to wait until morning until I took them down to the wheelie bin in the yard.

I kept checking my phone – no message from Jack. Maybe the hospital told patients to switch off their phones after a certain time – I didn't know.

I closed Ursula's blind, peeping through the slats to see that the snow had stopped falling and there was a clear night sky – half moon, millions of stars.

At nine o'clock I had a phone call from Zara. 'Well done, you!' she told me. 'You found her.'

'Yeah. Is she OK?'

'She's at the Q.E. They're dealing with some cuts and bruises – nothing serious, but they want to keep her in overnight. Raisa's with her.'

Hooper took Zara's phone and spoke to me. 'Ripley's there, waiting to interview her. By the way, why didn't you stick around?'

'I'm not supposed to be here, remember. Anyway, I've only solved half the problem. There's still the small matter of nailing the guy who did it.'

There was a pause then it was Zara again. 'I've been thinking about that. Me and Hooper – we were talking before I called you. We both think it really is time to hand the case over to Ripley's team.'

'Not this old story,' I sighed. 'Zara, you can stop right there.'

'No. Let them do forensic tests – they're bound to find our psycho's fingerprints in the workshop or a strand of his hair on Galina's clothes. They'll find a way to identify him.'

'They haven't up till now,' I reminded her. 'Forensics worked for ages at the scene of Scarlett's murder. They didn't come up with anything, so far as we know.'

Hooper again. 'You need to put yourself first for a change, Alyssa. Forget the super-sleuth stuff. Your safety is more important.'

'This *is* my safety,' I argued. 'Hooper, he's threatened me again, saying it's going right down to the wire this time.'

'Wow, that's bad – honestly, Alyssa, it's really bad.' He paused then went on, 'So where are you? What will you do?'

'I'm staying with Ursula in the Bottoms. He already found that out and trashed the place. That's where I am now.'

Zara again, as I paced the floor and lifted the blind to peer out. 'So is there anything we can do?' she offered.

'Just don't tell Ripley where I am – OK?'

'OK.' She sounded reluctant and uneasy.

'And try to get hold of Jack for me. I've tried his phone, but it went on to voicemail.'

'Hmm, OK. We could go to the hospital, except it's after visiting hours so they probably wouldn't let us in. Anyway, what do you want us to say if and when we do get hold of him?'

'I don't know. Just keep an eye on him for me, will you? The last thing he said to me was that he was going to call the cops about it not being Marco.'

'Well, they know that now even if they didn't before.'

'Exactly. So what you have to do is make sure Jack doesn't do anything stupid.'

'Like what?' Zara asked.

'Like try to sneak out of the hospital to find me.'

'Whoa, that would be stupid,' she agreed. 'Broken ribs and all.'

'But it's the kind of thing Jack would do if he thinks I'm still in trouble. So talk to him, would you? Tell him everything's cool. If not tonight, then first thing tomorrow.'

'Gotcha,' Zara said.

'What about you? What will you do?' Hooper wanted to know.

'I don't know. I haven't worked it out yet.' I frowned as I let go of the blind and turned to look at the chaos inside the room. 'Probably tidy up more mess here before Ursula gets back.'

Hooper laughed. 'Typical Alyssa,' he said. 'Your life is on the line and all you can think about is housework.'

'I'll go over things in my mind as I restore order, the way I always do,' I promised. 'Something will come to me.'

'Like what?'

'The tiny missing link. The one vital thing I've overlooked that'll allow me to identify the guy. If I think long and hard enough, I'll remember.'

I put Ursula's TV back in place and found that it still worked, so that was one good thing. I re-stacked the DVDs. When she texted me to tell me she was staying over at Jayden's, I texted back OK.

Midnight came and went, with an old suspense/horror movie called *Don't Look Now* on the telly, which was a bad thing because it totally freaked me out, but I couldn't make myself stop watching images of a tiny missing kid in a red hooded coat running down the labyrinthine back streets of Venice. Sod's law – the coat would have to be red, wouldn't it? Shiny red plastic with a hood.

The movie ended and I went back to the window to peer through the blind on to a back yard piled with plastic crates and empty cardboard boxes sagging under the weight of recent snowfall. There was more cloud in the sky now, obscuring the moon.

What had I missed? What wasn't I seeing?

It was twelve thirty and the light bulb in Ursula's living room died. The TV went off as if a gremlin had grabbed the remote.

No gremlins, I told myself firmly. Ursula's electricity must be controlled by a fuse box, which has just thrown a major wobbler. All I have to do is find the bloody thing in pitch darkness!

I fumbled under the sink, checked the storage cupboard between the living room and the bedroom and decided that the fuse box must be in the hallway at the bottom of the stairs.

But before I could find out if I was right, up came a message on my phone. Heart skips several beats as I identify sender – Hooper. Relief. It's a short message.

I'm always here for you, Alyssa. Remember that.

He signs off with a single emoticon heart.

I made a mental note to thank him next time I saw him – 'Thank you, Hooper, but what's with the heart?' Keep it light when you talk to him, try not to offend him, but as always keep the boundaries very clear.

What's with the heart? I was standing in the dark at the exit to Ursula's flat.

Four red hearts from Marco that turned out not to be from Marco.

My stalker kills me softly, tells me he loves me when I'm angry.

And I'm back to the start of term, having breakfast with Hooper.

'We don't do Christmas at my house,' he tells me through a mouthful of honey-roasted ham.

It's the first time I see him after I get back to St Jude's. We're talking unenthusiastically about our lacklustre vacations.

'My mother's a pagan and my dad's a mean bastard.'

'Hah!' Hooper amuses me – he always does. I tell him I wish we had normal parents, or any parents at all in my case. I also tell him that Jack is stuck in Denver and can't get back to school until Tuesday.

'How will you go on living without him?'

'I have no clue.'

'Maybe I could stand in for him for seventy-two hours,' Hooper offers with a hopeful look.

I laugh again. He's cool – we joke along and say all kinds of stupid things.

'No?' he asks.

I shake my head. He's amazing but not my type. Jack is. End of.

Now I had a red heart from Hooper on my phone. No electricity, someone watching my every move, restricting every breath. I stood paralysed by the door.

'My mother's a pagan and my dad's a mean bastard.'

'. . . Come on, Alyssa – they said you were smart! Why so slow to pick up the clues?'

'. . . Why is this guy sending you love and kisses, Alyssa?' Jack asks.

'. . . The killer is in plain sight.'

No electricity. Total darkness closed in on me, forcing me to remember more details.

An email message from cockrobin@gmail.com. The killer tells me he is doing all he can to point me in the right direction.

He cares about me; he wants to warn me. Killing me softly.

Flashes of light penetrated my consciousness. I was

finally remembering, stringing it all together like precious, glowing pearls in the depths of a dark ocean.

Hooper asks me over breakfast – why so bleary eyed?

'*Am I? Sorry.*'

'*It's not because you regret these pics by any chance?*' *He turns his iPad towards me and gives me time to study an image of a girl in a tiny red bikini, posing provocatively by the edge of a swimming pool. It takes me a while to realize that the girl is a Photoshopped image of me.*

It was Hooper who came up with the theory that the pictures could be revenge porn. Hooper had been the one to run off and drag Molly into the row with Will about my missing laptop, Hooper again who set me on Will's trail, who told Jack that it was Marco who sent me the row of red hearts and suggested to me that Marco was right in the middle of the frame. I wasn't making it up – it had been Hooper at the centre of the action all down the line, every centimetre of the way.

Think about it. Remember. Trace it back. And forward.

A red heart now. '*I'm always here for you, Alyssa. Remember that.*'

Always here. Always looking over my shoulder, being my friend, offering to stand in for Jack, sending me a heart.

Shock blasted through me like a hurricane. I crouched against the wall at the head of the stairs, stubbornly refusing to examine my whirling memories, but finding that one blast followed another in a relentless storm.

I'm in the calm before the storm when I run into Hooper in the sports centre.

'Where's Jack?' Hooper asks me on the day Jack gets run down.

I'm in my bikini, heading for the changing room. 'He cycled into the Bottoms to post a letter. Why?'

Hooper wants to stay and chat. I want to get changed. I'm wrapping my towel around myself, feeling embarrassed. Is Hooper looking at me in a different way to usual, or am I being super-sensitive? Yeah, it's me – imagining a frisson that isn't there.

'Are you sure about that?' he asks.

'Yeah – why?'

'Because I thought I saw him before when I caught the bus back from town. Unless you tell me he's got a double, Jack was definitely outside Greenlea Shopping Centre. It looked like he was waiting to meet someone.'

'So he changed his mind.' I'm not alarmed. I smile and say goodbye.

Hooper was in Ainslee the day the guy in the Merc ran Jack down! He was everywhere, over everything all the time – the puppet master pulling the strings.

But I'm not his puppet – I'm a good mate. We became friends because we're both outside the mainstream movers and shakers at St Jude's – people like Luke, Zara, Connie and the rest. Hooper wants to help me; he always has my back.

We're in the girls' dorm, waiting for Charlie to fetch Molly so we can tell her our suspicions about Marco. A light goes on in the boys' dorm. Someone comes down into the courtyard.

'Don't worry, it's only Hooper,' Eugenie reports.

'What's with the "only Hooper"?' he asks. 'Alyssa, what the hell's going on?'

'Nothing.' Connie takes charge. 'Honestly, Hooper, you don't want to know.'

He gives me a disappointed, hangdog look.

I feel sorry for him. I lead him away from the gaggle of girls. He accuses me of not trusting him, after all the work we've done together, him and me.

'Don't take it personally,' I say.

'How else can I take it?'

Out of loyalty I eventually have to tell him that I've recognized the interior of Marco's car in the video.

He expels a quick, short burst of breath.

I captured Hooper's face, freeze-framed in my eidetic memory.

He doesn't say anything and he doesn't look shocked. It's more an expression of contempt – a kind of 'pah!'.

He's arrogant and trying not to show it. He actually finds it funny.

For Christ's sake, Hooper is the enemy and didn't I just speak to him on the phone and tell him what I planned to do next? He'd laughed at me again. He'd made me tell him that I was alone.

He's the enemy taking it right to the wire.

He's here now! I crouched at the top of Ursula's stairs, blown to smithereens by the terrible truth.

No, he can't be here. He was just at St Jude's with Zara. So how long will it take him to get from school to the village so that he can ratchet up the terror? Will he drive or come

306

on foot through the woods? He'll drive, I decided. No way will Hooper choose the hard, slow way.

There were noises down in the yard. The door at the foot of the stairs opened and then someone shone a torch up towards the landing.

'Ursula?' a woman's voice queried.

'Not here.'

'Who's that?' She came up the stairs. The torch beam wobbled against the wall.

'I'm a friend of Ursula's.'

The woman found me crouched against the wall. 'What time did the lights go out?'

'Not sure. I was looking for the fuse box.'

'The fuses aren't the problem,' she explained, shining the light on my face. 'A neighbour called me to say the electricity along the whole of Main Street is out. Snow the other side of Banbury brought down cables. It won't be fixed till morning so I drove over to check things were OK here and to give Ursula these, just in case.' She handed me two spare torches.

I stood up from my crouching position and took them.

'Are you OK?' Ursula's landlady asked. She was middle-aged, Cotswolds-smart in Barbour jacket and Hunter wellies.

'Fine, thanks.'

'Were you scared of the dark?'

'No. Yes. But I'll be fine now, thanks.'

She nodded then turned to go. 'You're sure you're OK?' she said over her shoulder.

'Sure.'

'And you're a friend of Ursula's, a visitor?'

'Yes.' I was willing her to get the hell out of there. She nodded then turned, and I waited to hear her footsteps retreat across the yard, followed by the opening and shutting of a car door, an engine starting.

I'd lost time. Hooper could have left school and be almost here by now. And I wasn't going to sit here and wait for him to arrive – no way!

Thank you, Ursula's landlady, for the torch and the dose of cold reality. My head was back together and I was thinking straight again.

OK, so if Hooper thought I would sit like a hare caught in car headlights, I'd prove him wrong. I'd be out of here, torch in hand, before he had time to drive across.

In seconds I was down the stairs, following in the landlady's footsteps through the snow, out on deadly dark Main Street, cutting quickly through the churchyard into the woods beyond. Through the trees I caught sight of a car driving down the street and stopping outside Five-a-Day.

Too late, Hooper – I'm gone!

I hurried under moon and stars through the oak trees until I came to a frozen stream with a stone footbridge. Then more trees and hard going through the slow-to-melt white drifts, torch beam too faint to predict obstacles ahead, slipping and sliding, tripping over roots as I met the bridle path leading to St Jude's. Then it was easier, smoother, quicker. I saw where the trees ended and the school lawns began. Able to pick up my pace even more, I skirted the lake and headed up the slope towards the dark, stately buildings

308

where centuries of wind and weather were etched into the walls and the ageless moon glinted in the leaded windows.

Too late again, Hooper. I'm heading for the boys' dorm. I'm sneaking in behind your back, creeping along the corridor to your room where I'll find evidence that you killed Scarlett and kidnapped Galina. This is it – you won't be able to stop me.

My torch was off so as not to attract attention. I climbed the worn stone steps until I reached the long, low corridor and felt my way along.

Generations of landed gentry in lace collars and cravats followed me, staring silently from their gilt frames. The uneven floorboards creaked.

'Bloody hell, Alyssa!' The door to Hooper's room suddenly opened and Will stood there, almost naked.

Shit! I'd overlooked Will. I should've thought through the consequences of taking Hooper's roommate by surprise. What now? 'Shh!' I said. 'No need to wake everyone.'

'Who are you looking for?' Will challenged, pumped-up body blocking the doorway. He made it clear that no way was he suddenly going to start trusting me, not after what I'd put him through with the cops.

'Hooper – I'm looking for Hooper.'

'Not here. Anyway, Jesus, it's the middle of the night!'

'That's OK. I just want to pick up something that belongs to me,' I lied. 'It's in his bedside cabinet.'

'At two in the morning?'

'Yes. It won't take a minute.' I was on a wing and a

prayer, improvising as I went along. 'Are you going to let me in or not?'

Will shrugged and let me squeeze past him, only because he couldn't be arsed to argue. He watched me go ahead and rummage through Hooper's belongings.

First I opened the shallow cabinet drawer and found a hairbrush, a shaver, toothbrush and toothpaste, a box of tissues on top of a box of thin latex gloves – the sort surgeons wear – everything neatly arranged. There was a small mirror, a plug adaptor, black and red felt tips, a couple of computer memory sticks, which, in my haste and without thinking, I slipped into my pocket.

'I thought you said it wouldn't take long.' Will stayed by the door, impatient for me to leave.

'Yep, I just need to look in the cupboard.' Opening the cabinet door, I found more orderliness from Hooper (who does that remind you of?). There was a black scarf carefully folded, a grey knitted hat on top of a shoebox. I lifted the hat and scarf opened the lid of the box and found about a dozen mobile phones. 'Yeah!' I said, as casually as I could. 'Found what I was looking for!'

I slid the scarf, hat and box out of the cabinet, tucked them under my arm and headed for the door. 'Thanks,' I told Will.

So what does a guy want with twelve pay-as-you-go mobile phones if not to send anonymous threats?

They said you were smart, Alyssa . . .

. . . Hah, gotcha! Sent you another video. Check it out, why don't you?

310

And every creepy, weirdo message in between – all on anonymous phones, expendable and untraceable. Hooper had planned ahead and covered every angle in his obsessive, one-step-ahead-of-the-game, inimitable way.

I carried the items back along the corridor, down the stairs. OK, I had what I needed and was ready to head back to my room and finally call Ripley.

Across the courtyard and up the stairs to the girls' dorm, saying a silent hi to Lady Anne and her surprised Jacobean eyebrows then quietly along the corridor to the refuge of Room twenty-seven, stockpiling evidence to hand over to the police.

Check out the grey hat and black scarf to see if they match the ones worn by the guy caught on CCTV outside The Fleece, close to Ainslee Westgate station. Then check out these phones.

I opened my door.

The first thing I saw were fragments of the ceramic head taken from Jack's room, smashed and scattered across my pillow. Phrenology by L. N. Fowler. Intuitive, reasoning, reflective facules – destroyed by a heavy hammer abandoned amongst the broken pieces. The second thing was a red, scented candle flickering on my bedside cabinet. Third, a big heart lipsticked on to the mirror. Fourth, Hooper sitting quietly on Galina's bed.

chapter fifteen

'Good work, Alyssa,' Hooper said. 'I have to admit I was disappointed at first, when you were so slow to make sense of what was going on – especially the connection between the red clues and Scarlett's name – but you got there in the end.'

'What are you going to do?' I backed towards the door, but he was there before me, moving faster than I'd expected, knocking me to one side and blocking my way.

'That depends.' He saw his things tucked under my arm and wrenched them from me. The phones spilled out of the box. One by one, slowly and deliberately, he trod on them and ground them under his heel. 'Now give me yours,' he demanded.

Scared and shocked, I handed him my phone, which he put in his pocket. 'So what's the issue you'd most like to talk about now that you know the truth and you're starting to come to terms with things?' he asked. 'Is it the loss of trust? That's a big one for starters. You know – I was your "friend", you trusted me and I betrayed you, yaddah yaddah. That must really hurt.'

I refused to enter into discussion. Instead I stayed silent and studied him, noticing the way his Adam's apple slid up and down as he swallowed and smiled. And I remembered.

'What we'd both give for normal parents, hey?' I say to Hooper as Connie eats spoonfuls of Luke's Eton mess.

Flash forward. Zara reads to me about narcissistic personality disorder.

'"Sufferer may have over-indulgent parents who hand out unrealistic praise on a daily basis. On the other hand there could be severe emotional abuse as a child. Or a combination of both."'

Hooper's dad is a prize-winning novelist, his mother is a society photographer. That's all I knew and it wasn't enough to make sense of their son's psychosis. Think some more.

NPD has a neurological basis. If a sufferer is criticized, he displays anger-management issues. He can be hyper – push the right button and any fake modesty falls apart then the psycho comes roaring out.

'Useful tip for whenever I finally come face to face with the guy,' I tell Zara.

Here, now, staring at loyal, modest, sensitive Hooper, waiting for the maniac to pounce. Fear rose so high in my throat that I could hardly breathe.

'Are you not comfortable with this?' he asked me with a show of concern. 'We could stop talking if you'd prefer.'

'You talk, I'll listen,' I said. Flatter his narcissistic ego, don't move, play for time.

He took me up on it. 'I really do like you, Alyssa, so the friendship thing was genuine. I admire your type of intellect – the way you pay attention to detail and use logic to work things out. You do that more than most girls, and I'm sorry if that sounds sexist. It must be part of the

313

eidetic-memory syndrome because I noticed that was how Scarlett was too. Anyway, it sets you both apart from the mainstream, plus of course you're both very, very beautiful and sexy. And, actually, you know, that's where it went wrong between you and me – you being so far out of my league and you making sure I knew it.'

'I didn't . . .' I began.

'You did.'

'I could stand in for him for seventy-two hours,' Hooper offers with a hopeful look.

I laugh.

'No?' he asks.

I shake my head.

Hooper watched me as I recalled the incident in the refectory. 'You see – you did, you laughed in my face.'

They're excessively preoccupied with issues of personal adequacy, these people with NPD. They need admiration. I'd failed to boost Hooper's fatally flawed ego. And now we stood here at the door to my room and he was talking at me, lecturing me about how it had all been my fault.

'Call me over-sensitive if you like, Alyssa, but that conversation over dinner is what kick-started this. And of course I'd been through the whole thing with Scarlett before you. You want me to explain that in more detail? Come on – how come you're not responding?'

'I'm still listening.' Keep a grip, don't show fear.

'OK, so I'd stayed over in Ainslee after the end of last term, delaying the moment when I had to go home to those two pathetic excuses for parents. Honestly, if you

314

knew them, you'd immediately get what I mean. Anyway, I'd seen Scarlett around town but I didn't know her very well, only that Will Harrison mentioned she was top of her class, A* in everything, all that.'

Hawk-like, I watched his every move, waiting for I don't know what.

'That was a kind of challenge in itself,' he mused. 'She couldn't be that beautiful and that ridiculously clever, could she? Not cleverer than me, surely. So I was bored hanging out in town by myself and I decided to start testing it out, sending Scarlett poetry and lyrics from songs and waiting for her to respond. And you know what – she never did reply, probably just deleted them, so in the end that made me angry with her and that's when my messages started to get a little threatening, so she couldn't ignore them any more.

'I took pictures and Photoshopped them – you know the routine. I was dropping clues left, right and centre, making it more and more obvious for her. And it was funny – while I was away for Christmas, Alex found a really interesting picture of Scarlett on Facebook, much more explicit than the one I posted of you, by the way. He went totally ape-shit.'

Still I held back, using every ounce of willpower not to react, but with a hundred thoughts and feelings flickering through my brain, but mainly, Poor Scarlett, poor Alex.

'You asked me what I got for Christmas,' Hooper reminded me, pulling up the sleeve of his sweatshirt. 'Well, nothing this year, but up until I was eight years old my main present would be this.' He showed me a mass of healed scars on his forearm. 'Amongst his manifold faults, my father is one of those nicotine addicts who can't give up the smoking habit,' he explained. 'Sometimes, when I was a little kid, he didn't bother to use an ashtray to stub out his cigarettes.'

The old scars on the inside of Hooper's arm went from wrist to elbow. They made me shudder then recoil as he thrust the arm close to my face.

'If only people knew what goes on behind educated, middle-class doors,' he said. 'Ah well, obviously I still can't stand being *en famille* for very long, so this year, as always, I got out of there as fast as I could and came back to school early. Only I couldn't stay at St Jude's until term officially started so again I hung around in Ainslee, continuing to offer my little challenges to Scarlett, and finding out that her detective skills were well below A* standard, I'm afraid.'

Didn't she tell anyone what was happening? I wondered.

'Yes, good point,' my mind-reader psycho interjected. 'You're right, she did eventually confide in her parents – especially when her little grey cat, Mimi, was found strangled and dumped in her bed, Godfather style. A touch of melodrama never harms in a situation like this. The Hartleys actually reported that one to the police, but the on-duty desk sergeant handed it over to the local branch of the RSPCA, which was a major mistake in retrospect.'

Unwarranted self-importance. Severe egocentrism. Preoccupied with fantasies of power and intelligence. These were the textbook terms for NPD and now I was living that nightmare, watching the frown lines on Hooper's thin face, the pauses for reflection and, worst of all, the chilling smiles.

'The trouble is, even the best-laid plans can go wrong,' he went on. 'Like for instance the CCTV cameras outside The Fleece. I hadn't reckoned on them. But luckily it turned out OK, since they only captured my back view and there wasn't a cat in hell's chance of identification – oops, cat metaphor probably inappropriate here, given one dead moggy recently slipped between the sheets.'

'Hooper!' I said weakly.

'You're right – bad taste. But funny.' There was another long pause while he pulled my phone out of his pocket. 'No new messages,' he reported as he took his time to slip it back in. 'Actually, in case you're wondering, The Fleece incident was very significant. True, you can't see my face on the footage, but I'm asking Scarlett if she'd like a lift home from the party, all very nice and polite. She says no, she'd rather walk. I say, "Why's that?" She pushes her hair back from her soft-as-a-petal face and says she doesn't accept lifts from people she doesn't know, as if there's something amusing about that, and she struts off. You know how kids from Ainslee Comp can be about St Jude's kids – not very nice at all. It stems from inverted snobbery if you ask me.'

'Is that it?' I gasped. Hooper offers his victim a lift and picks up an implied insult. It's enough to push his NPD button and turn him into a killer.

Like now, like my three-word challenge – 'Is that it?' spoken with disbelief.

This is what sent him suddenly crazy.

He lunged at me without warning, pressed me back against the door and shoved his elbow into my throat so hard that I gagged. I fought back, bringing my knee up to his crotch so that he released the pressure on my throat and I fell forward on to my knees. He used the few seconds that it took me to get back on my feet to run to the bed and grab the hammer. He raised it and came back at me. I crouched forward and used both arms to cover my head.

Hooper smashed the hammer wide of my head into the oak door panel. Smiling, he then tapped it lightly against the splintered wood – once, twice, three times. 'Not here,' he decided with a final tap that pinned a lock of my hair to the door.

I jerked my head sideways then tried to tug my hair free.

'No, definitely not here. Come on, let's go.'

'Where?' I pleaded with tears smarting in my eyes. 'Hooper, where are we going?'

'Ah, that would be telling.' Shoving me against the door and stooping to pick up the black scarf, he quickly wrapped it round my neck and pulled it tight.

Then, as I struggled to stop him from throttling me, he opened the door and tugged me backwards down the corridor. 'Hush!' he warned, finger to his lips, trying not to giggle, as if we were naughty children out of bed in the middle of the night and trying not to wake our parents.

He dragged me down the stairs and out into the silent quad, talking normally again now that we weren't in danger of being overheard. 'I thought we might revisit some of our old haunts. You know, the grounds, the lake, the woods – a walk down Memory Lane.' He seemed delighted by the idea. 'One last chance for you to use your eidetic talents.'

Down the sloping, snow-covered lawn to the lake where the tall reeds rustled and rattled in the wind, to the spot where police divers had recovered Lily Earle's body in early December.

I watch with Paige from the window of Room 27. The water is black and freezing. Lily has been submerged in her watery tomb for four whole days. Her dark hair streams back from her face. She wears her black leather jacket and one shoe is missing.

'Remember that?' Hooper asked. 'Silly question – of course you do.' And he pulled the scarf tight to drag me away from the lake, the ruffled surface of which reflected a fragmented moon. 'If we had time, I'd take you up to the stable block to give you a chance to remember Paige.

The tack room door flies open. A figure in a grey hoodie flies out, a hoodie with an Adidas logo and triple stripes down the arms. He has a knife in his left hand. He takes hold of a wheelie bin and thrusts it straight at Mistral. The horse rears, Paige yells, hooves crash down and pin her against the stable wall. He rears again, lands on top of her.

There's silence. No blood, but Paige doesn't move. Her eyes are closed and though they take her to hospital and put her into intensive care she never opens them again.

'But we really don't have time,' Hooper decided. 'It won't be long before Will starts looking for me. You woke him up, didn't you? I'm not safely tucked up in my bed and eventually even he's bound to wonder what's going on.'

The pressure on my throat made me tilt my head back and I lost my footing as Hooper dragged me to his Peugeot in the car park. I was still off balance and choking when he thrust me inside and locked the door.

He ran round the back of the car and sat behind the wheel. 'Comfy now?' he asked, starting the engine and reversing out of his parking space. 'It's OK, don't bother with your seat belt – to tell you the truth, there isn't much point.'

Amused, unflustered, he drove past Saint Sam's house where all was dark and quiet, between stone pillars and into the lane leading to the Bottoms. At the first junction, he slowed at a Give Way sign and I grabbed the door handle and tried to open the door.

'Thank goodness for child locks,' he commented as the door stayed shut.

I groaned and lurched forward as he shot out on to the main road. 'Don't worry, we won't be stopping in the village. We'll be heading straight into Ainslee.'

'Don't!' I begged as he picked up speed. 'Please, Hooper!'

'Sorry, Alyssa, I can't slow down, not when I'm in one of my hypo-manic moods. And yes, I recognize that's what this is. I have full understanding of my condition.'

'But you don't have to—'

'Don't have to what? Don't have to kill you the way I killed Scarlett and would definitely have killed Galina if you hadn't got in the way?'

'Yes, you've proved your point. You can stop now.'

He tutted and shook his head, drove on in silence until we reached the village.

'You won,' I insisted. 'You played the game better than me and you beat me.'

'What's this – is it flattery?' He grinned. 'Are you trying to win me over? Is that what Zara said would work with nut-jobs like me?'

'No. I mean it!'

'And of course it's true – I did win. But I'm writing your life story and I can't stop short of the satisfying ending, can I?'

The country lanes ended and we entered the town's quiet streets. 'Yes, you can,' I argued. 'The main thing is that you won – you're better than me, no contest.'

He shook his head. 'No, you don't understand – I found with Scarlett that I got an enormous buzz from the killing part. Besides, you still have to be tomorrow's headline: "*Second Body in Canal*".'

A fresh, powerful shockwave ran through my body and I tried again to open the door, shoving against it with my full weight. Still it stayed shut.

'I like the symmetry of that, don't you?'

Oh God, he meant it. He was fixated on an ending he'd planned from the start. He would throw me into Ainslee canal and the water would close over my head.

My phone rang inside his pocket. I tried to lean across and snatch it, but again he was too quick. He took it out and waited for the ring-tone to end. 'That was Jack,' he reported casually. 'Must be driving him crazy, not being able to get in touch.'

Jack, my Jack! I love you. I want you to know.

'What do you see in a guy like him?' Hooper seemed genuinely puzzled. 'It's got to be more than the six-pack, surely.'

Much, much more but not something that you would ever understand.

'To me he doesn't seem that special,' Hooper continued. 'He's too easy to read for a start. There are no twists and turns, no depth to his personality.'

I love him. He loves me. I will carry one certainty in life, right to my grave. It will be enough. But Jack, promise me you won't miss me forever – just for a while. Then live, be the best you can be. *Nihil sed optimus.*

'Here we are,' Hooper said chattily as he pulled up by Lock-keeper's Cottage.

I noted where we were – the steps down to the canal, high brick wall to one side, narrow towpath and the hump-backed bridge ahead. My mood had switched and I felt calm now, beyond shock or terror, completely out of Hooper's reach. Which didn't mean that I'd given in – no way.

He held my door open and I got out of the car. He had the hammer in one hand, the black scarf in the other. I met his gaze, searching for one small sign that the old, sane Hooper still existed somewhere in there amongst the tangled, twisted neurological mess that comprised his brain. He returned my look with an empty unfocused stare.

Then he turned me towards the steps and prodded me in the back with the head of the hammer. 'The Industrial Revolution introduced many amazing feats of engineering, but none more so than the network of canals that still criss-cross our nation – don't you think, Alyssa?' Prod-prod, down the steps, which smelt of damp and urine, on to the path littered with cans and black plastic bin bags emerging from the melting snow. 'Bunches of navvies working with picks and shovels – no mechanical diggers in the eighteenth century, of course.'

I was taking everything in – old snow trodden underfoot, yellow stains where dogs had peed against the wall, an upstairs light on in what I remembered was Sammy Beckett's house. I was no longer tuned in to Hooper's robotic chattiness.

'Of course, the last time I was here I used a spanner from Alex's dad's workshop and, though it spoils the symmetry slightly, I'm afraid on this occasion this hammer was all that came to hand. Plus the trusty old phone-charger cable,' he added, withdrawing one from his pocket.

We were down the steps on the towpath, our footfall deadened by the slushy snow. I deliberately didn't look down to my right at the black, oily surface of the water. Instead I looked up at the moon.

Jack, ignore what I said earlier. Don't forget me. Always keep a little place in your heart for me.

'Ready?' Hooper asked, raising the hammer.

No, this is not how it ends! I dodged as he brought the hammer down hard. It hit the wall and I sprinted towards the bridge. But the path was slippery and my feet went from under me. Hooper quickly caught up and bent down to hook the scarf around my neck and pull me to him. Then suddenly he stopped. He looked over at the bridge.

I followed his gaze. Jack was crossing the canal, eyes fixed on Hooper. He was ten metres away, appearing out of nowhere, out of the black silence.

Hooper saw him and panicked. He shoved me to the ground, face down, then knelt on the small of my back. I saw out of the corner of my eye that the hammer was raised over my skull once more.

Jack broke into a run. Hooper smashed the hammer down but I scrambled clear. Jack reached us and swiped him with the back of his hand, sending him sprawling. More figures sprinted towards us out of the darkness – Zara, Connie and Will. But it was Jack who snatched at Hooper's jacket when he tried to crawl away, Jack who stopped him and turned him over then sat astride his chest and punched him in the face, mad with anger until Will yelled for him to stop or else he would kill Hooper. Will grabbed Jack's raised fist, which threw him off balance and gave Hooper the split second he needed to wriggle free.

Hooper crawled forward to the edge of the canal and peered at his own reflection in the dark water – a pale oval disc in a liquid mirror. He twisted round to look at me and all I could think of was Narcissus, in love with his own image, who got separated from his beautiful reflection and died of grief. He smiled at me then rolled sideways and toppled into the canal.

chapter sixteen

They wrap you in silver, heat-retaining plastic, the kind they give to runners at the end of a marathon. And they sit you down, tell you to take deep breaths.

'Breathe, Alyssa,' Ripley said as I sat propped against the canal steps with Jack beside me.

They were all there – police cars, ambulances, Will, Connie and Zara.

And don't worry about Hooper – they weren't going to have to dredge the canal.

He rolled over the edge. There was a splash. I held on to Jack's arm to stop him jumping in as well.

Hooper vanished under the water, which swirled with oily eddies.

Connie would have jumped in after him too. 'The shitty little bastard doesn't get away that easy!'

But Zara and Will held her back.

Anyway, Hooper came back up to the surface and struck out in an untidy crawl towards the bridge.

'Idiot,' Zara muttered. 'Not even worth getting wet for.'

Hooper struggled through the water, clumsily flailing his arms and slowly sinking. Well, you wouldn't expect him to be a good swimmer, would you?

'Are we going to let him drown?' Connie asked, as if it was a serious possibility.

Anyway, we heard the sirens and saw the blue flashing lights so none of us had to make a decision about fishing Hooper out. The cops did it for us.

'Deep breaths,' Ripley insisted after they'd hauled Hooper back on to dry land and driven him off in an ambulance. They handcuffed him and walked him up the steps. I didn't look at him as he passed by and he didn't look at me.

Personally, I'd done all the looking and talking with Hooper I ever wanted to do. Now the system – police interview, charges, remand, trial, sentence – could roll on around me.

Jack sat shivering inside his silver cape, knees hunched to his chest.

'He has two broken ribs and a perforated lung,' I told the paramedics.

'We know,' they said. 'He discharged himself. There was nothing the hospital could do.'

'He called to warn us what he was up to,' Zara explained. 'We tried to stop him.'

'But he was too worried about you to listen,' Connie added. 'So we said we'd come over to Ainslee to meet him. He said to check your room first, make sure you hadn't snuck back to school. That's when we found everything smashed up and in chaos – phones, that ceramic head from Jack's room, a candle, a lipstick heart . . .'

'Plus, by this time, Will had come across to the girls' dorm to tell us you'd paid him a visit, Alyssa, and that you were looking for Hooper.' Zara filled in more gaps. 'One minute Hooper was with me in my room, talking to you on the phone. Next thing, he's vanished and his car is missing from the car park.'

'We're saying to each other, what's this with Hooper? Why is Alyssa risking coming back to St Jude's and taking stuff from his cabinet?' Connie went on. 'None of it is making sense, but all we know is we have to get into town to meet Jack.'

'You swore you'd stay where you were,' I reminded him, reaching out to take his hand. 'He has a perforated lung,' I said again to whoever would listen.

A paramedic squatted down beside Jack and did routine medical stuff – pulse and blood pressure for a start. 'Careful, mate,' she murmured when he tried to stand up, and she made sure he didn't move until the stretcher arrived.

'Is that why you didn't answer my calls?' I asked. 'Because you knew I'd try to stop you leaving the hospital.'

'Anyway he did pick up my call, thank God,' Connie said. 'Zara called 999 to tell them what was happening, then the three of us met Jack outside the train station before the cops got there. Then at that point we were stuck. Where were you and Hooper? What should we do next?' She turned to Zara. 'Over to you, Dr Maxwell Stirling.'

'First I had to get over my shock,' Zara said.

Connie nodded. 'I mean – quiet, reliable Hooper, for God's sake. Who'd have thought it?'

Zara picked up her thread. 'I tried to get inside Hooper's mind. If I was right about his type of mental illness, I knew he was on a major power trip. He'd want every single thing to be under his control, like he'd scripted the scenario and was forcing you to play it out.'

'That's exactly right,' I murmured.

Hooper takes me down to the lake, down Memory Lane. The black reeds rustle and rattle in the wind. He forces me into his car.

'Thank heavens . . .' No, ' . . . Thank goodness for child locks,' he says as he drives me away from the school grounds.

'Don't!' I beg. 'Please, Hooper!'

I beg, I flatter. I hit the brick wall of his psychosis.

'I'm writing your life story and I can't stop short of the satisfying ending, can I?' He tells me I have to be tomorrow's headline. 'Second Body in Canal'.

'So in a way he made it too predictable,' Zara continued. 'For a start, he'd probably put a cord round your neck like he did with Scarlett.'

Jack held my hand more firmly. He mumbled to the paramedic that he was able to stand and walk to the ambulance without help.

Zara waited until Jack had listened to professional advice and settled back down beside me, then she picked up where she'd left off. 'I figured Hooper would use some sort of workshop tool.'

'A hammer.'

The grip tightened again. I whispered to Jack that I was OK.

'And he'd bring you to a familiar place to act out his final scene.'

'Then it was over to Jack.' Connie was determined to give Jack the final credit. 'He said two words – "the canal!" It was his idea for us to come here.'

Young bones heal quickly, though minds may take longer.

Jack was back in hospital for three more days then they let him out with a programme of physio and gradual rehab.

'No major exertion,' they warned. 'Give it time and you'll be back to normal fitness.'

Back to playing tennis, working his way up the international rankings. I grinned, but had to be careful how hard I hugged him.

I forgot about this once we were back at school and I overdid the embrace.

'Ouch!'

'Sorry.'

I was visiting in his room at night-time, breaking the rules. We were heading for the half-term break and everything was back to normal.

'Do your ribs still hurt?' I asked, tracing my fingertips across his chest.

'No. I got cramp in my leg, that's all.'

'Liar!'

'OK, yeah. They hurt a bit.'

'Is that better?' I murmured, leaning over to kiss him.

Still without Jack in their team in the first week after half term, St Jude's five-a-side football team lost three–nil to

Ainslee Comp. Alex scored the first goal, followed by two from Jayden.

Ursula was Jayden's biggest fan. Dropping her über-cool image, she cheered every time he got the ball, jumped up from her seat in the mezzanine coffee bar each time the ball hit the back of the net.

'How are things?' I asked her after the match, while the teams were showering.

'Good. But you want to know something funny? Last Tuesday Ripley finally got around to asking me if I needed to speak to a victim support officer after Hooper wrecked my flat.'

'You said no but Hooper would need one if you and Jayden were let loose on him,' Connie quipped. She'd been cheering for the losing team, Luke especially.

We laughed. We'd already agreed to stop thinking too hard about Hooper and what he'd done.

'No,' Ursula grinned. 'I asked, what about my telly? I'm not insured so who pays for that?'

'But it wasn't broken,' I reminded her.

'So?' she challenged. 'The cops don't need to know that.'

'Oh, OK – no, yeah. I mean, I get it.'

We laughed again.

'I do deal,' Galina told Ursula.

Yes, our Russian heiress was still in school, forging her own way without family support like she said she would. Her lip was healed and she'd just signed a modelling contract with Storm – Cara Delevingne's agency – branching out from designer bags.

'What kind of deal?' Ursula wanted to know.

'I give you bag from new season collection. You sell online. Take this as thank you for helping Alyssa.' Then Galina turned to me. 'And, Alyssa – I show agent your picture.'

'You didn't!' I protested.

'No. Tomorrow, I show her.'

'Tomorrow I *will* show her,' Zara corrected.

'Tomorrow I will show her. You *will* be model too.'

'You will be *a* model . . . Oh, I give up.'

'No,' I told Galina. 'I can't see me as a model.'

'We can!' my mates cried.

Zara, Ursula, Connie and Galina all tried to convince me that I would be fabulous, darling.

'You *are* fabulous.' Jack and I walked through St Jude's wood. Green shoots of early daffodils held out a promise of warmer days.

If two people can walk with more physical contact than we were managing, square centimetre for square centimetre, I'd like to see it.

Our arms were entwined round each other's waists, our hips and thighs touching, and we were perfectly in step.

'But can you see me in front of a camera, day in day out? I mean, come on!'

Jack stopped and turned to face me. 'That's the only thing about you that I don't get, Alyssa.'

'What? What did I say?'

'I don't get the false modesty. You've got the height, the

hair, the figure – any modelling agency would bite your hand off!'

'It's not false – it's genuine. I honestly don't have the confidence . . .'

'Exactly. I don't get it.'

'So now we're arguing about my confidence or lack of it. We've been here before, remember?'

Actually, come to think of it, during my first few weeks at St Jude's it had practically scuppered any chance I had with Jack.

'Don't,' Jack said.

'Don't what?'

'Don't start with the total recall.' He walked on and pulled me with him. The woods and the fields beyond were beautiful. The sky was blue. 'Live for the moment, Alyssa. Live now.'